No C
Intended

Books by Mollie Cox Bryan

The Cora Crafts Mystery series

DEATH AMONG THE DOILIES

NO CHARM INTENDED

The Cumberland Creek Mystery series

SCRAPBOOK OF SECRETS

SCRAPPED

SCRAPPY SUMMER E-Novella

DEATH OF AN IRISH DIVA

A CRAFTY CHRISTMAS

SCRAPPILY EVER AFTER E-Novella

SCRAPBOOK OF THE DEAD

No Charm Intended

Mollie Cox Bryan

KENSINGTON PUBLISHING CORP.
http://www.kensingtonbooks.com

KENSINGTON BOOKS are published by

Kensington Publishing Corp.
119 West 40th Street
New York, NY 10018

All Kensington Titles, Imprints, and Distributed Lines are available at special quantity discounts for bulk purchases for sales promotions, premiums, fund-raising, and educational or institutional use. Special book excerpts or customized printings can also be created to fit specific needs. For details, write or phone the office of the Kensington special sales manager: Kensington Publishing Corp., 119 West 40th Street, New York, NY 10018, attn: Special Sales Department, Phone: 1-800-221-2647.

Kensington and the K logo Reg. U.S. Pat & TM Off.

ISBN-13: 978-1-4967-0466-5
ISBN-10: 1-4967-0466-5
First Kensington Mass Market Edition: May 2017

eISBN-13: 978-1-4967-0467-2
eISBN-10: 1-4967-0467-3
First Kensington Electronic Edition: May 2017

10 9 8 7 6 5 4 3 2 1

Printed in the United States of America

For my grandfather, Paul Eugene Carpenter,
a man I knew for only eight years,
but whose influence and love
have stayed with me all of my life.

Acknowledgments

I'd like to thank my readers for coming along with me and my new Cora Crafts Mysteries. I love hearing from you and appreciate you more than I can express.

Special thanks go to my beta readers Amber Benson, Jennifer Feller, and Mary Sproles Martin. I don't know what I'd do without you giving your time so freely to look over early drafts.

I'd also like to thank writer Reece Hirsch for answering my questions about the Darknet. Thanks to the Museum of the Cherokee Indian in Cherokee, North Carolina, for inspiration and help in understanding the tradition and artistry of Cherokee basket making. If you ever have a chance to visit, take it. This is an amazing museum.

In addition, I'd like to thank my editor, Martin Biro, my publicist, Morgan Elwell, and the whole Kensington crew for the hard work they do every day. I'm so honored to be a part of the Kensington family.

A deep heartfelt appreciation goes out to my friends and family who have lifted and supported me during a particularly rough time in my personal life. I didn't know how I'd get through each day, let alone write the rest of this book. Your encouraging Facebook messages, e-mails, and cards worked a special magic. Thank you hardly seems enough.

As always, thanks to my husband and daughters for all of the encouragement over the years.

Yours,
Mollie

Chapter 1

I kidnapped her.

Cora blinked and reread the message. It had been sent early this morning. She hadn't checked her phone all day. Between looking over supplies for the next craft retreat, making certain Kildare House was spotless and ready for the arrival of her teachers and crafters, and writing her next blog post, checking her own messages had slipped through the cracks of a very hectic day.

No name was attached to the text.

Her heart raced as she clicked and scrolled and tried to find out who sent such a message to her.

Could this have been an errant text? A complete mistake? Or, had one of her previous clients tracked her down in her new home?

Switching states and getting new phone numbers sometimes just wasn't enough. She had been warned. But she tried to sort through the Rolodex in her mind of clients this could possibly be—and didn't come up with a thing. Did anybody ever mention kidnapping to her?

Not in so many words. But parents often took children from other parents—this she knew. Cora remembered one case where a grandmother stepped in and took her grandson. The mother hadn't realized it for a few days—she'd been on a heroin binge. It was best for the child to be removed from her care, but the grandmother still had faced kidnapping charges. You had to follow the letter of the law when you took a child from his or her home, even if it was a bad home.

Cora sighed and vowed to break out the thumb drives where she stored all her ex-clients as soon as she had a moment.

"Okay, calm down," she said out loud. Luna's ears twitched and she glanced at Cora as if to say, "Are you talking to me?" The cat blinked in disgust when she realized Cora wasn't speaking to her.

It was probably a wrong number. It probably was not an ex-client. It had been almost a year now that she held her post as a counselor at the Sunny Street Women's Shelter in Pittsburgh. Surely none of them would contact her at this point. Cora's life was now in Indigo Gap, North Carolina, in the craft retreat business. This was her new life.

Still, the text chilled her.

Kidnap?

Should she tell someone? The police?

And what would she say? "I've got this weird text message . . ." As if she hadn't already had a snootful of the local police.

No, she'd let it rest for now. It wasn't the first

strange text message she'd ever gotten. Besides, she had enough to do to prepare for the Spring Fling Retreat. Her teachers were already here. The retreaters were arriving tomorrow.

Cora glanced at her watch. She was already a little behind. She allowed herself one quick check in the mirror. Her 1970s blue minidress suited her more than she thought it would, and the white go-go boots were perfect. She smoothed her pink lipstick on her lips, ran a comb through her red curls, and she was ready for dinner with her guest teachers.

She opened her door and walked to the half flight of stairs to the third floor, where she almost bumped into Jane.

"What are you doing here?" Cora said.

"I have weird news." Jane's eyes were wide and she grabbed on to Cora's arm.

"What?" Cora said, thinking this retreat could not be any worse than the last one, where a teacher slept with her students and a murder happened right down the street. But the look in her best friend and business partner's eyes gave her pause.

"Remember Gracie?"

"Gracie who?" The name seemed familiar, but Cora wasn't making the connection.

"She babysat London a few times. She's her friend's nanny, remember?"

"Oh yes," Cora said. "We better get going. Can this wait?" she said, pulling away from Jane and walking down the hall.

"No," Jane said with urgency, grabbing her arm, stopping her. "You need to know this."

"What is it? Spill it. C'mon, woman," she said.

"She's missing," Jane said.

"Missing?" Cora's heart skipped a beat. "What do you mean?"

"She was supposed to babysit London tonight, so I called Jillie's mom because she never showed up," she said. "She's gone."

"Do you mean she took off?"

"Jillie's mom is calling the police. She says she's not been there all day. Her stuff is still there. Her car is still there. Everything. So I either have to bring London with us tonight or stay at home."

"I don't think London will be a problem—just bring her along," Cora said after a moment. The child was the most well-behaved child Cora had ever known—a bit precocious, but manageable.

Cora stopped in her tracks, remembering the strange text. It wouldn't have anything to do with the missing girl, would it? She didn't even really know her. Why would someone send her a text?

"What's wrong?" Jane said.

"I just remembered this weird text I've gotten," Cora said.

"Hey, Cora. Hey, Jane. You about ready? We're starving!" Ruby said as she walked up the stairs toward them. Sitting in the foyer just below them was a group of crafting teachers. Cora took in the foyer of Kildare House, a large, old-fashioned room. The Victorians knew how to welcome guests, especially rich Victorians.

Cora smiled. "We're here. Everybody ready?"

London was also sitting in the foyer and peeked up as they came toward her. She hopped up out of the chair and ran to Cora, who scooped her up in her arms. Jane's daughter had seen way too much change in her short life and yet seemed to have kept it together. Cora was in awe of her.

"Are you ready to eat?" Cora said.

"Yep," London replied, sliding out of Cora's arms. "I'm in the mood for pizza."

"You're always in the mood for pizza," Jane said.

"No pizza tonight," Cora said as she walked toward the door, the group following close behind her. When she opened the door, she gasped—Officer Glass was standing there, about ready to ring the doorbell. They'd gotten to know him very well during the last craft retreat, when he was investigating a local murder.

"Can I help you?" Cora asked. "We were just leaving."

"Hello, ladies," he said. "Cora, can we speak for a moment?"

"Is this important? As I said, we're leaving for dinner. We have reservations," she replied.

"It's about a text message," he said with a lowered voice.

"What? How did—"

"There were several sent today and the digital forensics team sent me over here to discuss it with you," he said.

Jane sighed. "Good Lord, what have you gotten yourself into?" she whispered.

"Nothing!"

"It's getting late," Jane said.

Cora took in the group. They were a famished,

weary lot. "Why don't you all go ahead. I'll meet you there." Despite her own hunger pangs, she supposed it was the right thing to do—after all, she couldn't help wanting to help, even if it was the local police, who seemed to be always under her feet.

Chapter 2

As Cora watched the group leave, her heart sank. She thought this Wednesday evening dinner before the retreaters arrived was important to establishing ground rules and camaraderie among the teachers. How would it look if she didn't show up?

"What is it, Officer Glass?" she asked, hoping to cut to the chase.

"First, let me ask if you did indeed receive this text message," he said, holding up a phone with the same text she'd gotten earlier.

"Yes," she said. "I've gotten it. Actually, I just got it. I hadn't had a chance to check my messages earlier."

He slipped the phone back into his pocket.

"How did you know?" she asked.

"We've gotten about twelve reports about it, but there are more recipients than those who reported it," he stated.

"How did you know who the recipients are? I mean, I tried to see who sent it and—I don't know—there was nothing there," she said.

He eyed the area, making a big show of searching. Was he trying to impress her? What was he up to? They were still standing on the front porch and Cora's stomach was still empty.

"Can we go inside?" he asked.

She dreaded the thought. She and Officer Glass had coffee together once and she really thought the married man was coming on to her. He made her uncomfortable. Where was his partner? Didn't they always travel in twos?

"Okay," she said, "but I really have to get going."

"I know," he said. "This won't take long."

She decided to stand at the banister, hoping he would take the hint they would not be sitting down and getting comfortable. But he walked into the sitting area and sat on the red velvet couch, surrounded by her upscale craft décor.

She sighed. What could this be about? Why was he insisting on taking up her time over an obvious prank text message?

"We're investigating a possible kidnapping," he said.

She gasped. But what could this possibly have to do with her?

Glass fished around in his pockets and pulled out a rumpled piece of paper. "Do you know this young woman?"

Cora sat next to him. "Yes," she said. "She babysat London a few times." Cora scanned the photo of Gracie. It was just as Jane had feared: Gracie was missing. Maybe kidnapped. Cora's stomach tightened.

"How about this person?" he asked. He showed her a photo of a young man. Skinny, pimple-faced but handsome, the man had a cocky grin plastered on his face.

"Yes, I think this is her boyfriend, isn't it?" she said. He'd hung around Jane's a bit helping her with odd jobs and painting her kitchen. Seemed like a nice young man.

"We're not sure," he replied. "He claims he is."

They sat in silence a few beats.

"I don't understand why you're here. What does any of this have to do with me?" Cora asked.

"You received the same text message from the same source as this other group of people," he said.

"How do you know all this?"

"We're just forming this unbelievable cybercrimes unit. I don't really understand the technospeak," he explained. "Anyway, one person brought their phone in and the unit was able to get a group of names from that. They can also tell us the text came from the same source."

"Him?" she said, and pointed at the boyfriend.

"No," he responded. "I wish it were that easy."

"I do know that Gracie was supposed to babysit London tonight and she didn't show up. So Jane called and Gracie's employer said she was missing," she said, glancing at her phone to see the time. Late! She was very late.

"Is there anything else?" she said, standing, rubbing her hands across her skirt.

"Why would Gracie have your number?" the officer asked as he stood up.

"I have no idea. Unless it was to use as an emergency when she was sitting with London," Cora said, not wanting to be impolite, but at the same time her stomach growled loudly. How embarrassing.

"I'm sorry. I'm keeping you from dinner," he said. "Please just don't leave town. We may have more questions."

"I'm hosting a four-day retreat weekend. I'm not going anywhere," she assured him as she attempted to usher him out. As if she'd have anything to add to this investigation. She really didn't know the young woman and certainly didn't know her boyfriend.

"Good to know you'll be around," he said with a warmth and familiarity in his voice that made Cora cringe. Why couldn't he just be businesslike? Matter-of-fact? "Do you need a ride downtown? I'm heading back to the station."

"No," she said a little too quickly. "Thanks so much for asking me, but I really need to walk."

He glanced away, sheepish, then back at her. "Okay."

She watched as he opened the car door and gave a little wave as he drove away.

Cora grabbed her purse and made a run for downtown.

As she walked toward the diner, she thought about the oddness of her text message, then the even odder appearance of the police, showing up right away and asking her about it. It was scary how easily the police could trace people—even scarier when she thought about criminals being able to do the same thing.

As she drew closer to the diner, she stopped to take in the little town of Indigo Gap, so lovely, historic, and quaint, built right along a ridge in the surrounding mountains that dipped and rolled all around the historically accurate streetlights, cobblestone streets, and pretty storefronts. She saw the steep gabled roof of the home where a woman and her ex-husband were murdered a few months back, a harsh reminder that even in a place like Indigo Gap, darkness existed. She whispered a wish that they would find Gracie soon.

Chapter 3

Jane tried to focus on the people around her, but she couldn't help but be worried about Cora. What exactly did the police want with her? After their last near disaster, with Jane being accused of murdering the town librarian, she was a little suspicious of the local police force. She didn't share Cora's almost blind belief in the justice system, with all its flaws.

She took in the place to ground herself. She wanted to stop thinking of all the bad possibilities. The same red-checked curtains as always hung in the windows. Familiar faces moved in and out of her vision. Even a few unfamiliar ones—a man stood at the register and caught her looking at him, then shifted his focus quickly. With stringy, long brown hair, thick glasses, donning his favorite old gray sweatpants, the man came across like a reject from *Wayne's World*. Must be a tourist, she thought.

"So, Jane, I have one of your pieces," said Sheila Rogers, a scrapbooking expert, paper crafter, and award-winning paper doll designer. She was small and wiry, with blue glasses framing light brown eyes, and had a wide smile. "The Venus vase. It sits in my foyer. I love the way you combine mythology, artistry, and utility."

Jane smiled as she felt a blush coming on. "Thank you."

The waitress walked up to their table. "Have you made up your mind?"

Jane hoped Cora would show up in time to order with the others. But she could see that the group was hungry and she could no longer delay ordering.

"Yes, I think we're ready," Jane said. London snuggled up to her as the others placed their orders.

"I don't feel good, Mommy," she said. "I'm so tired."

Sheila was ordering a Greek salad and asking about the dressing. Jane's hand went to London's head. She was warm—not hot, but still, she'd take her temperature when they could get home.

"Oh, sugar, I'm sorry. How tired are you? Do you need to go home? We can go home as soon as Cora gets here," Jane said.

Sheila's daughter, Donna, was asking about the strawberry-walnut-spinach salad. Did it have feta cheese or blue cheese in it?

But Jane focused on London. The child's eyes appeared glassy. If she was sick, what would Jane do? She was scheduled to teach a class this weekend. Who could she call to watch her? Gracie was supposed to sit with her. Normally, London could just tag along during class. But not if she was sick. Could Jane cancel her class? Oh no, that would be letting down Cora and the crafters who were coming here, paying good money, just for her class. Shoot.

"Let's get something to eat and see how you feel," Jane said.

London nodded. "Okay," she said.

"What can I get you," the waitress said to Ruby, who had been in what appeared to be in an intense conversation with Marianne Wolfe, the basket maker. Jane had taken a weird dislike to the basket maker. This was a rarity, but something disturbed Jane about her. Off-putting. She held herself with a stiffness that made Jane uncomfortable. True, she made some gorgeous baskets—but Jane found herself wondering how such a cold and stiff woman could fashion such lovely things.

Ruby, the other regular teacher in the craft retreat, was spouting off her order when Cora walked into the restaurant, flushed and overheated. She must have been running to get there. What was so important that Officer Glass kept her so long?

"Glad to see you could make it," Ruby muttered under her breath. Ruby was an acquired taste. She was grandfathered into the contracts when Cora purchased the house, as Ruby had worked for the previous owners. Good thing her talents as an herbalist, crafter, and gardener aligned with Cora's goals. Otherwise, they'd have their hands full with an opinionated woman of a certain age living on the property.

Cora took a chair next to Jane, her red face almost matching her red curls. "I'm sorry I'm so late," Cora said, sitting down next to Marianne, who was quiet, unassuming, and probably the most gifted person at the table. Jane reminded herself of this and tried to tamp down any unwarranted bad feelings about the woman.

"It's okay," Jane said quietly. "We're just now ordering. No worries."

"Can we get a couple bottles of house wine? One red and one white," Cora said as the waitress approached her. "And I'll have the veggie burger on a whole wheat bun."

Few places in Indigo Gap offered vegetarian options, but this place did, which is why Cora liked it so much. She wanted to make certain everybody could get something.

Jane sensed something was wrong—it probably had to do with Officer Glass's visit—and she couldn't wait to get the scoop. But she was worried about London, hoping that she was just tired and needed to eat and sleep, and was not really coming down with something. This was a big weekend for her, the first that she'd be teaching at the craft retreat.

They were not prepared for pottery classes during the first retreat. But since then they had been working hard to transform half of the downstairs of the carriage house into a proper teaching studio. They had purchased a new kiln as well. The other half of the downstairs was growing into a pottery shop. Jane loved living in the carriage house and was beginning to love living in Indigo Gap, a place so different from any of the other places she had lived—London, Pittsburgh, New York. The pace was more manageable, sure, but it was also the lifestyle. Artists and crafters populated the town. People appreciated art and crafts and antiques. The active historical commission made certain that the historical integrity of the town thrived.

She felt her daughter's body slump against her. London had fallen asleep.

"Is she okay?" Cora asked.

"She said she's not feeling well," Jane said. "I think I'm going to need to find a sitter for her when I teach. She may not be able to tag along. Since Gracie's not around, I thought London could come with me to classes. But now, I just don't know. I'm sorry."

"We'll manage," Cora said with a lowered voice. "Don't worry. Your sitter is still missing."

"Was that—"

"Yes," Cora said.

Why would the police be questioning Cora about Gracie? Why not Jane since she was the person who had hired Gracie? Not that she really wanted to be questioned by the police. The thought of it made her nauseated. Jane just wanted to be a mom, an artist, and a friend. Yet, trouble kept finding them.

"Is Adrian still out of town?" Jane asked.

"I'm afraid so," Cora replied, vaguely. "I'm not sure when he will be back."

Jane wished that Cora would open up a bit more about what had actually gone down with her and Adrian, the new school librarian. But Cora kept her own counsel.

Chapter 4

Cora preferred not to think about Adrian. Very Scarlett O'Hara of her. And she delighted in Jane's unspoken curiosity about Adrian. The truth was probably more mundane than Jane could imagine.

Cora and Adrian had gone on one date, which went well, even without a kiss good night. A little awkward fumbling at her front door prompted her to let him off the hook and slip inside the house. She planned to take matters into her own hands on their second. However, the next day, a huge snowstorm blew in, so they had canceled. By the time he called to arrange another date, his mother had gotten sick. Within a week or so, he'd been called home to take care of his ailing mother. He was still in New Jersey, being a caretaker. Jane knew all of this, but Cora had not revealed anything else about the future of their relationship.

But there was hope. Cora liked Adrian. She really liked him. Everything from his horn-rimmed glasses framing his jade-green eyes to the one-dimpled grin and those beautiful hands—with slender but strong looking fingers that she imagined lost in her messy red hair. And he was sweet and geeky and kind. He was home taking care of his mother, after all. He was the kind of man you could imagine as a father, a sort of perfect mix of sexy and sweet. But . . . There was no kiss. She tried not to make a big deal of it in her mind. But it was worrisome. She really liked him—but what if there was no sexual chemistry? What if their first kiss went badly?

She felt her eyebrow raise and she bit her lip as she imagined leading the way to that first kiss with Adrian.

"Hey, what are you thinking about?" Jane poked her.

"Who, me? I was just thinking about all the lovely paper we organized today," Cora said. They had boxes and boxes of paper for the craft retreaters. And boxes of ribbons, thick, silky black thread, and fabric, along with doodads for Sheila's paper doll class. Not only was the paper in every color imaginable, but it also came in different textures, such as the rough mulberry paper, the delicate rice paper, and handmade paper from different fibers.

"I can't wait to learn how make your charms," Sheila said to Jane with enthusiasm. "We've always been so into paper in our house. It will be wonderful to learn a new craft."

Jane planned to teach a clay-charm class, which was a different take on regular pottery classes. The sample charms were lovely, of course, showing how versatile the charms could be; she mostly used them for necklaces and bracelets, but she made samples showing them as adornment for gift packing, earrings, and bookmarks. She made a big fuss picking out complementary beads and other embellishments for her students' projects. She'd gotten a deal on some beads from a new company—they came in earth tones, with gold flourishes.

"I'm excited about the nature walk," Donna said. She and her mother, Sheila, had started a paper doll company and were teaching a paper doll–making class. Cora was utterly charmed by the dolls—and Sheila was a friend of her aunt and uncle, so she had agreed readily to come teach at the retreat.

"It'll be fun," Ruby said, her gray eyes shining with excitement. "You'll be amazed at the crafts you can make from what you can find in these mountains. I grew up in these hills wildcrafting. My mother used to make some gorgeous herbal wreaths. Oh, and sometimes these beautiful floral swags."

"I've always loved pressing flowers," Cora said.

"You know, I once saw a scrapbook made with pressed flowers and herbs. It was a kind of a Book of Shadows," Sheila said. "It was absolutely lovely."

Ruby dropped her fork of spaghetti and swiveled her head toward Sheila. "We need to talk more about that. I have something similar that's been handed down through my family. My great-grandmother planted according to the moon and she recorded all of her observations in this book, along with flowers and plant clippings and herbal remedies."

"Fascinating," Sheila said, sitting up straighter. "I'd love to see it. What a wonderful keepsake for you to have."

"I come from a long line of women who craft, but we didn't take pictures or keep a book about it," Marianne, the basket maker, said. "I suppose your ancestors were herbalists?"

Ruby nodded and clucked her tongue. "That's one way of putting it."

"Are all of your ancestors basket makers?" Sheila asked Marianne.

Marianne smiled slowly. "Of a sort," she said.

"I wish more of my family were into scrapbooking," Sheila said as she scooted some salad around on her plate. "I think that's one reason I find scrapbooking so compelling. I have no real answers about my family. My mom died young. I'd really like to know some things, but there's no real record of anything."

"Well, Mom, I'm glad you've kept such beautiful scrapbooks for us," Donna said, and held up her glass. "To the record and memory keepers!"

"Hear, hear," said Cora.

"Things are changing so quickly with all the digital scrapbooking and blogging and so on. I wonder what the record keepers of the future will be like," Sheila said.

This brought Cora's mind squarely back to Gracie and the police and wondering exactly what was going on. She was amazed the cops could trace her phone number from a completely anonymous texter, but it still made her antsy.

"It's very strange," Marianne said. "I think about it sometimes, too. I'm not a big blogger or anything like you are, Cora. I've hired someone to do my blog. But I suppose we're leaving records for future generations in a completely new way."

"Blogs, my butt," Ruby said, after sitting her wineglass down. "It's not the same as a handmade record. Something your ancestors have touched. I think we are just making it easier for the man to track us down by putting everything online."

The group chuckled.

Cora would have asked Ruby who The Man was, but she knew exactly what Ruby was talking about—and given what had just happened to her, she feared that maybe Ruby, even given her usual paranoia against all things virtual, was just a bit right.

Chapter 5

An hour later, with everybody off to their own rooms in Kildare House, Jane and Cora caught up on the day's events in Jane's refurbished carriage house. Jane woke London up long enough to give her some ibuprofen before the child slumped into bed.

Cora told Jane about the evening's odd happenings, while she was working on an embroidery project she brought along with her.

"Man, that is some scary stuff," Jane said. "How did they track you down?"

"Did you give my name as an emergency contact to Gracie?" Cora asked, then took another sip of dandelion wine, one of Ruby's concoctions. It wasn't bad at all. She then went back to her stitching.

Jane appeared to think a moment. She twisted strands of her long dark hair around her finger. "I think I must have. Who else would I use?"

"That's got to be it," Cora said. "It must be some kind of hoax or prank. Why would a real kidnapper send out a text message announcing they kidnapped someone? That doesn't make any sense."

Jane sat her wineglass down. The light reflected in the amber-colored liquid. "Let's hope it was a hoax and Gracie's okay. She seems like a young woman who can take care of herself. Very together, just doing this nanny thing until law school."

"Just what the world needs, another lawyer," Cora said. She rolled her eyes. She clipped a thread.

Jane laughed. "Well, she's planning on corporate law. So chances are she'll end up in New York or someplace like that. If she's okay. I mean, she has to be okay, right?"

Fear seeped into the edge of her voice. If someone could kidnap a young woman right out from everybody's noses, they could kidnap anybody.

"She's young," Cora said. "Even though she's smart and has it together, young women do stupid things sometimes. Run away to get married. Stuff like that. Maybe that's what happened. Maybe she was swept away in some romantic getaway." She threaded her needle with bright yellow thread. Her embroidery project, a detailed sunflower, was almost finished. When she came to this point in a project it was hard to put it down.

Jane laughed. "Girl, you are such a silly romantic."

Cora shrugged. "It's just that I remember what it was like to be that age—don't you?"

"Yes, sure," Jane said. She gazed off into the distance briefly, as if remembering something or someone. Cora didn't want to push. But she knew things hadn't worked out with Jane's latest romance. She found out the man had a drug problem—and even though he said he was clean, Jane cut him out of her life for the sake of her daughter and herself.

"She has a boyfriend, right? That's what Glass said today. I remembered meeting him when he painted your kitchen. I wondered if she went off with him or if he was the one who sent the text. He said no. Something about that would be too easy," Cora said.

"Yeah, that's right. She does have a boyfriend. They went to school together. She's so special. I mean, London loves her, so does Jillie. I just hope she is okay," Jane said. The worried edge crept in her voice again. Cora knew it well.

A knock came at the downstairs door. Cora dropped her embroidery in her lap and peered at Jane. "Are you expecting someone?"

"At this time of night? No," Jane said. Her deep blue eyes flicked with impatience. "Who'd be coming here at ten at night?"

She peeked out of the window and drew back quickly. "It's Paul with some strange man."

Paul was Gracie's boyfriend, Cora remembered. Cora set aside her project and walked over and peeped out the same window. One of the young men had his face turned away. When he glanced back and knocked again, Cora recognized his youthful face immediately. "We'd better let him in."

Jane stopped her. "What did Glass say about him?"

"Glass said he wasn't a suspect," Cora said. "I'll come with you, just in case . . ."

"In case?" Jane said as they made their way downstairs. She flicked on the outside light once they reached the front door.

"I'm here no matter what. That's all I mean. For goodness sake, open the door," Cora said.

Gracie's boyfriend was pretty close to their age, Cora surmised, and he oozed sexuality and charm— or perhaps it had been way too long and every good-looking guy oozed it for her. But judging from Jane's flushed face, that wasn't it. The other young man stood in the shadows, so Cora could not see his face.

"Jane?" Gracie's boyfriend asked, after making eye contact with her.

She nodded. "What's wrong, Paul?"

"I'm just going around talking with people and kind of, you know, tracing Gracie's footsteps," he said. "You know she's missing, right?" His voice cracked and suddenly Cora saw unfathomable rawness and fear in him. He looked weary. And frightened.

"Hi, Paul. Why don't you come in?" Cora said, leading them inside. She caught a glimpse of Jane's open mouth. She smiled back reassuringly. *Yes, I've just let two young men into your house and it will be okay. Trust me.*

Chapter 6

"Let's have a seat here," Jane said, gesturing to her studio couch and the few chairs she had in the room. Cora loved the old hot-pink couch—it was 1950s retro, and still in great shape.

Now that the other man was in view, Cora saw that he had mocha skin and dark, almond-shaped eyes. She wondered if he was part of the local Native American population, but it was hard to say just on the basis of appearance.

"This is my roommate, Henry," Paul said as he sat on the pink couch.

Henry nodded. He too appeared exhausted and frightened.

"What's going on?" Cora said, folding her embroidery cloth. "Have you found out anything yet?"

Paul's large hands turned upward. "Nothing." He pulled out his cell phone. "We know she went to get her hair cut early yesterday," he said, glancing over his phone. "Then she stopped in at LuLu's for a smoothie."

"Oh yes, she brought London and me each a

raspberry smoothie yesterday morning," Jane said. "She stayed for four hours or so while I prepared for my workshop this weekend. But I've already told the police all of this, right after Jillie's mom called me. I called the police and told them everything I know."

Henry cleared his throat. "She was scheduled to be here tonight. We wondered if she might have said or done anything odd. Mentioned a place. Or something."

"I wouldn't know," Cora said. "Jane?" Cora stuffed her craft tools and cloth into her bag.

Jane squirmed in her seat a bit. "Look, I left her with my daughter. We didn't talk much. I was so distracted, making certain I had all my supplies in for the class. I don't think we spoke much at all."

The two young men looked at one another and sort of nodded.

"How about when you came back?" Paul asked.

Cora's intuition stated to ping.

"When I came back, she'd fallen asleep on the couch. She was holding a book in her hand," Jane said.

"Book?" Henry said. "It wasn't *The Wonderful Wizard of Oz,* was it?"

Jane's face fell. "What—"

Cora sat forward. "What's going on here?"

"How did you know what she was reading?" Jane asked as she regained her composure.

Paul glared at Henry. Both young men remained silent.

"If you know something about this, or if it has anything to do with her disappearance, I think you should go to the police," Cora said with gravity in her voice.

"No, no," Paul said. "It's not like that. It's just that we've been playing this *Wizard of Oz* game and she was really into it. It's an app. You can play it on any device. She'd been reading everything she could get her hands on about the book as well."

"We told the cops about this game we've been playing and they didn't pay any attention to us," Henry said. His voice cracked. Cora thought she saw a slight tremor in his cheeks.

They sat in uncomfortable silence for a few seconds. Cora wondered what the game had to do with anything. But if the police had dismissed it, they must have a good reason. But obviously the young men were distressed and needed someone to talk to. *You can't save the world,* she heard a little voice in her head say. But it won't hurt to listen for a few minutes, she told the voice.

"Back up," Jane said. "What the heck are you two talking about? Gracie is missing and you're talking about a game?"

Leave it to Jane.

Paul cleared his throat. "The thing is—maybe it's stupid, I don't know," he said, and shrugged. "But we've been playing this computer game. Then all sorts of weird stuff started happening."

"At first," Henry interrupted, "we didn't make the connection."

"What kind of stuff?" Cora said. Her intuition barked wildly at her now. Even if this had nothing to do with the missing girl, obviously these two were in some kind of trouble.

"Weird untraceable text messages—not just notifications from the game," Paul replied. "Quotes from the book, for example."

"We thought nothing of it until I tried to shut it off," Henry said. "But it wouldn't allow me to shut it off. It behaved like a virus."

"Okay, guys, sounds like you got into a weird computer game, which has some glitches or something in it," Jane said. "We're not computer experts, so we can't help you. If you can tell us what this might have to do with Gracie disappearing, we can get the cops involved and go from there."

Cora beamed. Jane had a handle on the situation.

"Gracie was brilliant at the game," Paul said. "She'd moved further ahead than either of us. She started getting more insistent messages."

Cora felt the hair on the back of her neck prickle.

"Yeah, directions to meet the Tin Man, for example," Henry said.

"And when she didn't show up for the meetings, she started getting threats. I was, like, what kind of a messed-up game is this?" Paul said. "Right?"

"Threats?" Cora said. "What kind of threats?"

"Creepy stuff," he replied. Suddenly the young man's face crumpled and his chest heaved. "Oh my God, if anything happens to her . . ."

Cora's arm went around him. He smelled of peppermint and old socks.

He pulled away after a few minutes of awkward almost silence.

"I'm sorry," he said. "I just love her so much. I'm so worried."

"Of course you are," Cora said. She felt okay wrapping her arm around strangers and offering comfort, but he seemed a bit uncomfortable. His back stiffened at her touch.

"So what are you saying?" Jane said. "Are you saying that someone from this game might have tracked her down and kidnapped or hurt Gracie?"

"That's what we're afraid of," Henry said.

Jane shot Cora with a dubious look.

"It sounds far-fetched," Jane said. "Sounds like you might have better luck searching for her on foot with the search team than following up with this computer stuff."

"There's no search team yet. Their efforts are focused on finding the guy who sent the text," Paul said.

"I agree with Jane," Cora said. "But one thing doesn't make sense to me. Why would someone want to kidnap her? I mean, I assume her family doesn't have money since she's working her way through school as a nanny. If not money, what else could they want with her?"

"That's what I want to know," Paul said in a hushed voice.

Chapter 7

Jane tossed and turned through the night.

Money wasn't always the reason for a kidnapping. As Cora pointed out later that evening, parents were often the first to be suspected for children, but Gracie was not a child.

Cora also pointed out that a missing person was really just abducted, not necessarily kidnapped—the technical or legal difference being that in kidnapping, the perpetrator wanted money (or something) for the return of the victim. The only reason the police were calling it a kidnapping was because of the text message calling it so. Which was weird enough as it was. Of course, maybe Gracie's family had gotten a message about a ransom by now? Maybe it was a true kidnapping after all.

Jane thought about her own daughter and the fear that not only she, but every other mother had that someone would abduct her child. Knowing that Neil had gotten out of jail for possession of illegal substances and was back in the States—living in close-by Virginia—did not help matters. He was petitioning the court for chaperoned visits with London. They were married for four years, and at first they were they happiest years of her life, then came his heroin addiction and the violence. Her dreams had turned into living nightmares.

Jane took a deep belly breath in and then out. Deep breathing was supposed to help you fall asleep. But it didn't seem to be working.

Would Neil ever be so foolish as to try to take their daughter from her? Just the thought sent jolts of panic through her.

She turned over to her side, fussed around with her pillow, then dropped her head back onto it. She felt for Gracie's parents. Where were they? She assumed they were local, but really had no idea. What did she really know about Gracie?

She was twenty-four years old, saving money for law school, had impeccable babysitting references. She knew CPR, spoke Spanish fluently. Loved to read. Loved her London.

London loved her, too, which said something. There had been sitters whom London hated, and Jane always honored her daughter in that regard. She respected her daughter's intuition.

But when Jane came right down to it, did she really know Gracie? She knew all these things about her. But did they ever really have a conversation about anything other than London? Now that she thought about it, it sort of embarrassed her. How could she leave London with a young woman whom she barely even knew?

But Jillie's mom knew her, right? Another mom's

word is a good thing—especially a mom like Chelsea. She was no slouch. She was a divorce lawyer and her husband was a DA, which is why they'd hired a nanny. They'd really needed one, given their busy work schedules.

Jane loved that Jillie and London were such good pals. They seemed to like each other a lot, and they played well together. So the fact that Chelsea liked Gracie and highly recommended her meant a great deal.

Jane sighed and tried to remember if she'd ever really had a conversation about their shared sitter with Chelsea. She closed her eyes and started to drift off.

Bam! She remembered something. It happened a few weeks ago.

Gracie shoving her phone into her bag in a huff.

"You okay?" Jane had asked her.

"Yeah," she said. "It's just my boyfriend. He's being a bit too clingy these days."

At the time, Jane was rinsing off dishes and trying to get them done so she could go downstairs and start working, so she was only half listening. "How long have you been dating?"

"A couple of years," she said.

"So why is he so clingy?" Jane asked, wiping her hands on a dishtowel.

"I don't know. It's kind of a sudden thing. I don't know what to think about it," she said with an air of winsomeness. Then she seemed to snap out of it. "Oh well, I'll get to the bottom of it."

"If not, there are other guys out there," Jane had said, moving toward the stairs. She stopped and turned around to look at the young woman. Gracie stood with a sunbeam coming right in on her, lighting her youthful, almost angelic freckled face. Unlined, smooth skin, and clear hazel eyes. But she seemed forlorn as she stood and watched her go.

Jane eyes popped open. She stared at her dark ceiling. She had liked Paul and Henry. But maybe they knew more than what they let on. And Paul was a bit too crazy about Gracie.

It seemed too sudden when the alarm clock went off the next morning. Jane had no idea how much sleep she had gotten, but knew she wanted more. Seven AM and London was not up and around. That was odd.

Jane sat up quickly. Something was wrong. Her daughter always woke her up before the alarm went off. She hightailed it into London's room. London, still asleep, was curled into a ball. Sweat glistened on her forehead and her breathing was labored. Jane put her hand to London's face, which was warm to the touch.

Jane went into the next room and texted Cora: London has a slight fever. I'm going to have to take her to the doctor. I should be back by brunch.

She rushed around the carriage house apartment and readied herself for the visit to the doctor. She made certain she had the insurance card, a book to read, and that her phone was charged.

Her phone dinged, alerting her that she'd gotten a text back from Cora: Take your time. We will figure something out. XO, Cora.

It was at times like these she wished she could turn back time.

How many times over the past few years had she wished that things turned out differently with London's father? Too many to count. And sure she'd missed having a partner in her life—but she couldn't ask for a better friend than Cora Chevalier.

Chapter 8

Cora expected twenty-two guests for the weekend craft retreat. Only fourteen of those guests would be staying at Kildare House. A couple of those were sharing a room; though the house was large enough to accommodate them all with private rooms, she'd offered a discount to those sharing a room. It was less work for Cora.

For the first retreat, the rooms were done just in the nick of time, and Cora and Jane had barely had time to stamp their own style onto the décor. Each room was now coming together, though they told themselves that they were a work in progress. The only guest room that Cora considered complete was Mémé's Boudoir, which sounded sexy, perhaps, if one didn't know the French translation—literally "Grandmother's Bedroom."

Cora had inherited a trunk full of French linen from her grandmother, who in turn had inherited them from her in-laws. Since the sheets were old, they were incredibly soft. Fine linen grew softer with age and even more elegant. But Mémé never had used the linens because she was afraid of ruining such fine linen. She saved them for Cora, and Cora wasn't one for hiding away beautiful things. She washed the sheets, pillowcases, and duvet cover and placed them on the four-post queen bed with ornate iron work on the headboard, much the same as her grandmother's bed.

The embroidered initials added a further touch of homespun elegance. The pillowcases had pink scalloped edges, soft and pleasing to the eye. Her Mémé's collection of handkerchiefs donned the walls in elegant French country-style frames. Her linen tablecloth covered a table sitting beneath a window. The table held old family photos and a Monet print. Monet was her Mémé's favorite artist. She felt a kinship with him since her husband and she were from the same region in France.

A young woman named Liv had booked the room for this retreat. She was already settled in. When Cora first met her, she was surprised by the woman's appearance. She was young with a Goth style—pierced nose and black-purple dyed hair. She sported a tattoo running the length of her arm. She didn't look like their usual crafter, but then again, crafters came in all types. But it was odd and intriguing that she'd asked for Mémé's Boudoir, perhaps the most old-fashioned room they offered.

The only class scheduled for today was the mother-daughter paper doll class with Sheila and Donna. This class was really meant as a way to get things started, to give the crafters a little something to work on as they were getting to know one another. Sheila would also be teaching another class later in the weekend, but it focused on using some of the plants and materials the crafters would be gathering on their hike early tomorrow morning.

This retreat was all about wildcrafting and how you could blend elements from nature into many forms of crafting. Cora was so excited—but not more so than Ruby, who was definitely in her element.

Ruby had lived in Indigo Gap her whole life. She knew the plants—particularly the herbs—and had always crafted with them. Her home was full of handmade crafts from the area—many of which she made herself from the nature around her. Herbal wreaths and swags. Framed pressed flowers. A gorgeous dream catcher made from local fallen branches and twigs and found bird feathers.

Glancing across her attic apartment, Cora saw that Luna had finished breakfast and was already curled into a ball on the couch. Cora walked out of the apartment and made her way downstairs, where the group of teachers and some early-arrival retreaters were sitting in the living room along with several new faces.

"Hello there," Cora said. "Good morning."

"Hi, Cora," one woman said, and stood. "I'm a big fan of your blog!" She moved forward and shook Cora's hand. "I'm Maddy."

"Nice to meet you, Maddy," she said. Short and thin, Maddy resembled a wren with her chestnut brown hair and matching eyes. She had small features—except for those large eyes. "Thanks for your kind words about my blog."

"I bet it's a lot of work," Maddy said.

"It is, but I love it," Cora said, shifting her attention

to an older woman sitting on the chair next to the red velvet sofa.

"Hello, I'm Lucy Rester," she said with a Boston accent. "I'm so thrilled to be here. I've never done anything like this in my life."

"Happy to have you," Cora said.

"I've been a fan of Sheila's for a long time," Lucy said.

Sheila beamed.

"The scrapbooking, the paper dolls," the woman went on. "I just love your designs."

"Thank you," Sheila said. "Aren't you sweet?"

"I was hoping to meet Jane Starr," another woman said. She was sitting behind Cora and she turned to look at her.

"I'm Liv," she said. Cora noted that she was once again wearing heavy Goth makeup. "We met last night, but it was late. I'm mostly here for the clay-charm class and to pick Jane's brain. I'm a student at BMU."

"Aha," Cora said. "I remember. Jane will be here anytime now. If you want to learn about pottery, this is the place. Jane is so talented."

"Yes, I've bought a couple of her pieces," Liv said, the sparkling gem in her nose catching the light.

"Well, if you'll excuse me, I'm going to check on a few things," Cora said, leaving the group to chat amongst themselves.

Cora walked into the craft hall, where she, Ruby, and Jane had already set up for the weekend with baskets full of crafting supplies. The baskets held paper, several kinds of scissors, tiny hammers, glue, tiny bags for collecting items in the wild, buckets, and delicate glass frames with no borders. The students would press some of their wildflowers in between the glass and create lovely mobiles or wall art from it. Cora had crafted paper flowers out of coffee filters for each basket to add a festive note—and they turned out better than she had expected. Several people remarked about the paper flowers.

The room was large—a wing built on to the main house—and it was well lit by natural light. One side of the room faced the front yard and down onto the street. The other side of the room faced the back of the property. The views were of the estate's lovely gardens and several outbuildings in addition to Ruby's garden cottage and Jane's carriage house. Cora could see the carriage house through the trees.

She hoped that London was okay. This weekend was so important to Jane, as it was the first time she'd be using her new teaching studio. Cora supposed if anybody could handle a sick child and a studio full of students, it would be Jane.

Jane was a little off last night—well, they all were. The abduction of a local young woman was scary, especially when it was someone you knew, however vaguely. Cora did not know Gracie well, but Jane did. Jane must be horribly worried about her.

Satisfied with her inspection of the crafting room, Cora proceeded to walk through the dining room where the caterers were setting the table with a brunch buffet. The floral centerpiece on the dining table caught Cora's eye. Consisting of local wildflowers, it made a spectacular focal point for the table. Cora had learned from their local florists that this part of

North Carolina offered one of the longest seasons for wildflowers. She planned to take advantage of it.

Wild columbine, bellflowers, Turk's-cap lilies, and rhododendron provided orange, purple, and white exuberant colors couched in the greenery. Plates holding gorgeous, delicious-looking food surrounded the flowers. On either end of the table sat huge carved watermelons with cut fresh fruit heaped inside. Platters of chunks of local cheeses beckoned to Cora. Cucumber sandwiches, pasta salad, and miniquiches filled the rest of the platters.

She was called away by the ringing of the doorbell. She expected to see more crafters, but when she opened the door, there stood the man she'd seen the night before in the restaurant. Today, he wore blue jeans and a tie-dye shirt. He still could have used a bath.

"Can I help you?" she asked, hoping to get rid of him as quickly as possible. What could he possibly want with her?

"Hi there," he said, and handed her a flyer. "I'm starting a new computer repair company. Just thought I'd give you my information, and if you ever need someone . . ." His voice trailed off.

Cora managed a smile. "Well, thank you," she said, taking the flyer. "I may give you a call." She turned to go.

"Uh," he said. "What kind of computer do you have? I could give a free maintenance check."

"I'm sorry," Cora said. "I'm a little busy right now. I have a houseful of guests. I'll call you if we need help."

His eyes shifted to the floor of the wood porch. "Okay," he mumbled.

"Good day," she said. Normally, if someone came to her door like this during a retreat reception, she'd invited them in. But for some reason, she just wanted him to go away. She gently closed the door.

She must be more nervous than she thought. She wanted this retreat to go off without a hitch this time. She didn't mean to be rude to the man. Perhaps she should invite him in? A pang of embarrassment shot through her, then mild regret. But when she reopened the door to ask him back in, he had already left.

What was wrong with her? Why had she let her nerves get the best of her?

She turned her focus back to the lovely table and her guests. This is what was important right now. She'd deal with this man and his computer business another time. She didn't want to have to worry about computers right now.

Cora hungered for a simpler time—and that was what she was trying to create for herself and these women. A simple, relaxing weekend, space to breathe, dream, and create. Even for just a few days.

Chapter 9

I can't make it to brunch, Jane texted Cora. Sorry. I've not been able to find a sitter and London is out of sorts. She's feeling better, but not quite herself.

That was the second time this year, Cora noted, but elementary schools were notorious for attracting germs. Five-year-old London was used to tagging along with her mother while she taught classes. It was not ideal, but since London's babysitter was missing, what could they do?

Cora showed the text to Ruby, who sat next to her on the couch.

"Oh dear," Ruby said, shaking her head. "I hope she feels better soon."

"I have to wonder if she's just upset because of Gracie," Cora said.

"It could be," Ruby said, after a minute. "It's a scary thing, even for us grown-ups."

A group of their guests was discussing quilting in another corner of the room, which reminded Cora of her plans for a felt and fiber-arts retreat. She needed to follow up with several of the potential teachers.

Quilters and felters were a busy bunch. But she would persist, especially with the felters, as they were practicing an extremely popular craft—one that Cora wanted an opportunity to learn.

The doorbell sounded and Cora rose to answer it. She was surprised when she opened the door to find Detective Brodsky, Paul, and a man in a suit and tie. Brodsky himself never seemed to wear a tie, but today he was wearing a smart jacket.

"Cora," he said, and nodded.

"Nice to see you, Detective, Paul," she said, smiling, but wondering what the heck was going on and why they were here. At the same time, she'd much rather deal with Detective Brodsky than the uniformed Officer Glass.

"This is my new partner, Joe Dell," Brodsky said.

Cora shook the man's hand. "Nice to meet you."

"May we come in?" Brodsky asked.

Cora couldn't tear her gaze away from Paul—so drained, pale, and his eyes rimmed in red.

"I'm sorry," she said. "What did you say?"

"May we come in?" Brodsky repeated.

"I have a houseful of teachers and crafters," she said. "Is there a problem?"

"We should really go inside," Detective Brodsky said with an apologetic note in his voice. "How's the paper-arts room? Anybody in there?"

Brodsky had been to Kildare House and therefore knew about the various rooms. An image of the detective and his previous partner, along with several uniformed officers, sitting in the paper-craft room among all the pretty paper and embellishments flashed in Cora's mind. But that had been about a murder case. Surely there hadn't been another killing? Her heart began to race. Had they found Gracie?

"Sure," she said. "Okay. Come on in."

A few of the crafters raised their heads and watched them as the group walked by the door of the crafting room, but no one spoke.

"What's up?" Cora said, once they were all seated at a table in the paper-arts room.

"Paul here tells us that he visited with you and Jane yesterday evening at about nine-fifteen," Brodsky said.

"That's right," Cora replied.

"We stopped by Jane's place and she's not there," he explained.

"She's at the doctor. London had a slight fever this morning. She . . . She might be home by now."

"Thanks," said Detective Dell. "We'll try her again later."

"Was Paul alone when he visited you?" Brodsky asked.

Cora thought of the detective as being much younger than her, but he wasn't really. Only five years or so separated them, she reckoned, but there was something boyish about him. "No," she replied. "His friend, Henry, was with him."

Paul covered his face with his hands and rubbed it. He breathed loudly, almost as if he was hyperventilating.

"Henry is missing," Brodsky said.

"What?" Cora's voice raised. "What's going on here? Two people are missing? From this small town?"

"Henry is not from Indigo Gap," Brodsky said. "His family lives right off the Cherokee reservation, outside of our jurisdiction, normally. But we are combining efforts. It seems like he disappeared late last night. We found his car, with the door open, along an Indigo Mountain road."

"He's just gone," Paul said, his voice cracking. "How can it be? And nobody's found Gracie yet!" he added with a touch of frost.

"We have search crews looking for her," Brodsky said. "For both of them."

"What about the FBI?" Paul asked.

"Look," said Detective Dell. "I told you they don't get involved unless state lines have been crossed."

"How can I help?" Cora interjected.

"You just did," Brodsky said. "You just corroborated Paul's story."

"Henry is my best friend. Gracie is my girlfriend. What the hell do you think I'd do to them?" Paul said.

Brodsky shot Cora an expression of despair. His mouth twisted off to the side.

Cora's mind raced. If two of the three of them had been abducted, was Paul next?

"What are you going to do about Paul?" Cora asked.

"What do you mean?" Brodsky asked.

"Is he in danger? Two of his friends have been abducted. Could he be next?"

Paul sat up straighter, as if the thought had just occurred to him.

"Do you have someone watching him?" Cora persisted.

"Until this moment Paul was a strong person of interest. You gave him part of an alibi. But he still has a couple of hours unaccounted for."

"I told you I went to bed. I took a couple of sleeping pills. I was home. In my apartment," Paul said.

"So, you don't have anybody watching him?" Cora said. She suddenly felt chilled and began to shiver—which is one of the ways stress sometimes hit her. Pings of intuition were pricking at her. Greater danger existed here than what was being acknowledged.

"We don't have the manpower to watch over him or anybody else," Brodsky said. "Sorry. And we're not sure what's going on here. This is an ongoing investigation. Right now all hands are on deck to find Gracie and now Henry. Our resources are completely strained."

Cora respected Brodsky and knew he spoke the truth.

"Do you have someone you can stay with, Paul?" Cora said, directing her attention to him.

"That's a good idea. Just in case," Detective Dell said.

"I'm not from this area. I don't have any family here. I'm only here because of Gracie. Just for the summer. I freelance now and I can work from anywhere. I just don't know anybody. Just Gracie and Henry," he said.

"I have plenty of room," Cora heard herself saying, even though her brain was telling her not to get involved. Plus, she had a houseful of women—and given what had happened with Jude Sawyer during the last retreat, she had vowed not to have any more men at her retreats. But Paul wouldn't really be at the retreat, would he? "Stay here," she said more insistently.

"Are you sure about this?" Brodsky said, lifting an

eyebrow, fully aware of her past, both distant and more recent, plus her anxiety issues.

"Absolutely," she said. "I can't turn my back on him. Besides, I may have some work he can help me with. He did a great job painting Jane's kitchen."

"I don't want to impose on you," Paul said.

"Nonsense," Cora said. "It's not an imposition at all. Just go to your place and get your things. You are welcome here until this is all over."

His eyes met hers and she could see that not many people had been kind to Paul. He was genuinely touched. If she had any cause to doubt that, the next expression that came over his face solidified her feeling, for he glimpsed away in embarrassment. As if he knew she had just caught a glimpse into his heart.

Chapter 10

"Why would you do that?" Jane whispered to Cora. They were sitting in the back of the crafting hall. The paper doll class was up and running, and she didn't want to interrupt Sheila's lecture.

"Why not?" Cora whispered back. "Obviously he's in danger."

Jane rolled her eyes.

"Paper dolls have a long history," Sheila said as her daughter handed out more paper. Each crafter had a basket of paper already, along with other embellishments they might use for their paper dolls.

"Did it ever occur to you that he could be the one who abducted those two?" Jane whispered. "We really don't know him at all!"

Cora bit her lip. She hadn't thought about that. Not really. She had thought he perhaps knew more than what he was letting on—but not that he would injure his friend and girlfriend. Was there something Jane knew that she wasn't telling Cora?

"The first manufactured paper doll was *Little Fanny*, produced by a London company in 1810. The first

American paper doll was the *Adventures of Little Henry* in 1812. In the 1820s, boxed paper doll sets were popular in Europe and exported to America for lucky children. The first celebrity paper doll was a doll portraying the renowned ballerina Marie Taglioni in the 1830s. In 1840, a boxed set was done of another ballerina, Fanny Elssler, as well as of Queen Victoria," Sheila said. "Ballerinas were popular."

"If you can find any of those paper dolls today, you'd be in for some money," Donna said as she handed the last sheet out.

"I bet!" one of the crafters said.

"Even before that, paper dolls were being created in places like Japan," Sheila went on. "An ancient Japanese purification ceremony dating back to at least AD 900 included a paper figure and a folded paper object that resembled a kimono. How about that? Paper dolls as part of an ancient ritual!"

"I think we might be surprised to find out just exactly what people have used in ancient rituals," Ruby said, and harrumphed. The other crafters made noises of agreement.

"I bet," Sheila said, and smiled. "As you know, some of the dolls we design are one of a kind and hand-painted. You'll note that you have some paint and brushes in your kits. It's entirely up to you if you want to try to paint the dolls and their clothes, or if you just want to use the paper to create them. We also have some feathers, seashells, and dried flowers. After all, we are making fairy paper dolls. You might even find something on our nature walk that you'll want to include."

"Mom and I just saw an exhibit of hand-painted

paper dolls at Winterthur Museum in Delaware dating back to the late 1780s," Donna said. "I loved them because they were handmade. So precious. I mean, the manufactured ones are cool, but not like the handmade dolls."

"I agree," Liv said. "I have some of my grandmother's paper dolls. I just love imagining her making those dolls."

"The doll we saw was called an English Doll. It was a young female figure, eight inches high, with a wardrobe of underclothes, headdresses, corset, and six complete outfits." Sheila added, "It was so delicate and lovely."

Cora turned her attention back to Jane. "It did not occur to me that he could be guilty of abducting his girlfriend and his best friend. That seems kind of paranoid. Do you know something I don't?"

Jane focused on the paper in front of her. She started cutting out a doll form. She glanced at Cora with her dark blue eyes, bright with concern or fear. Cora couldn't say which.

"I don't know him. But I do know he was getting a bit obsessed with Gracie," she said in a low voice.

The women were chatting amongst themselves now about playing with paper dolls when they were little. The sound of happy conversation filled the room.

"He's in love with her. Of course he's obsessed. But she loved him, too, right?"

"I guess so," Jane replied. As Cora surveyed the crowd of crafters, she noticed a police car parked outside of her window. "It looks like we have company."

Jane lifted her head up. "Again," she said, and rolled her eyes.

"I'll take care of it," Cora said. "You stay and enjoy the class."

Cora left the room and headed for the front of the house. When she opened the door, she faced a weeping Paul and two uniformed officers.

"He's dead!" Paul wailed. "Henry is dead!"

"What?" Cora said. "What's going on?"

"I'm sorry, Ms. Chevalier," the officer said. "We found Henry's body about an hour ago."

"Oh, Paul!" she said, her heart splitting open as he fell into her arms.

"What happened?" she managed to say to the officer.

"It's an ongoing investigation," he said.

"He was killed!" Paul said. "Just say it!" he said as he twisted himself out of Cora's arms. "What's going on here that you can't say a man has been killed?"

The officers grimaced. One shook his head. "We don't know that for sure."

They were standing in her foyer, surrounded by the beauty of Kildare House with its gleaming chestnut floors, lace-covered windows, and well-appointed, but slightly funky, furnishings. It all seemed surreal to Cora. How could this be? Henry was just here, less than twenty-four hours ago. Now he was dead.

"We'll take Paul to his room," one of the officers said.

"We'll stay until he falls asleep," the other one said. "He's just been given something to calm him down. He's despondent, as you can tell. We're trying to track down his folks."

Just then, Cora realized that Jane was behind her. How long had she been there?

"Certainly, please follow me," Cora said as she led them up the stairs to the third floor, but first she stopped and regained her breath on the landing, where the stained-glass window of the goddess or saint named Brigid kept counsel. From the moment Cora first saw the window, she knew she wanted this place for her craft retreat and her home. Ornate Celtic knots gleamed in the corners of the window. Brigid held a chalice with a huge flame in one hand and a book in the other hand. Her flowing green robes covered layers of white and gold garments. Crimson, gold, green, and shades of blue glass formed an image of Brigid, whose face conveyed a sense of peace and comfort. Cora whispered a little prayer that the goddess of poetry and crafts would send some safety and healing to Paul.

Chapter 11

"Do you still think that we shouldn't help him?" Cora leveled at Jane after the police had gone.

Jane gave a long, frustrated sigh. "Look, Cora, I admire your wanting to help. But here we are in the middle of a retreat. And look, at first it was just to give him a place to stay because you thought he was in danger and now, now . . ."

"Now, we pretty much know he's in danger. If someone abducted Gracie and killed Henry, then could he be next?"

"Precisely. Do we want to get involved in this?" Jane asked. "I mean, we don't really know him. We don't really know what's going on here."

They were standing in the kitchen, waiting for the French press coffee to be finished. The scent of the coffee filled the room.

"Maybe you're right," Cora said. She was always so quick to help, sometimes without thinking things through. "Like it or not, we're involved now. I just wanted to give him a place to stay, to keep him safe.

Nobody is going to find him here, right? Who's going to come seeking a young man with a group of crafting women? We're protecting him. That's a good thing."

Jane crossed her arms and shifted her weight to one hip. "I don't know. I'm not as sold as you are. He was getting a little clingy with Gracie. She was annoyed with him one day. I told her there were more fish in the sea."

"Just because he was a little clingy, or insecure, doesn't mean that he abducted his girlfriend or killed his best friend, right?" Cora said, after a moment, as if trying to convince herself. "It's more likely he's in danger."

Jane reached over and began to press the coffee. "Oh God, I need this," she said as she pressed the handle down.

"How is London?" Cora asked.

"She's upset and not feeling well, but she doesn't have strep or anything like that. One of her pediatrician's daughters babysits. I don't really know the girl, but I know her mom. She's staying with London now and this afternoon during our river walk," Jane said. She reached over and slid a mug toward Cora and one toward her. She poured the steaming brew into the mugs.

Cora stirred almond milk into her coffee. "Any word about Gracie?"

A flash of worry and fear came over Jane's face, which made Cora sorry she asked. "No," she said. "Nothing at all. They're still searching for her. In fact, they were searching for her when they found Henry, from my understanding."

"Where did they find him?" Cora asked, but one of the crafters, Maddy, wandered into the kitchen.

"I thought I smelled coffee," she said, and smiled.

"Please help yourself," Cora said, opening a cupboard and fetching a mug from it.

"Thanks," she said.

"Are you enjoying the class?" Cora asked.

"Yes, it's interesting. I've never been into paper dolls, but this has been fun. An interesting group of women, too," Maddy said as she poured.

Jane glanced at Cora. That's exactly what they wanted to hear. The paper doll class was a good way for the group to relax and get to know one another. Tomorrow, they had the nature walk to collect items to use in their crafting. Some things had already been gathered and prepared—like the reeds they'd be using for basket making. But Marianne intended to show them the same plants growing in the wild, along with some of the plants the local Cherokee used to dye the baskets.

"That's good to hear," Cora said.

Maddy took a sip of her black coffee and rocked back and forth on her feet. "I'm a big fan of your blog," she said. "I hear you're teaching a blogging class soon."

Cora nodded. "Yes, I'll be teaching at the Big Island Beach Retreat and looking forward to it."

"I might try to get there. I have a blog, but it's not going anywhere. Maybe your class would help," she said.

"I can take a look at it for you," Cora said. "I'd be happy to give you a few pointers."

"That would be awesome," she replied. Her face lit with enthusiasm.

Later, Cora wandered through the paper doll class and snapped photos for her blog. Some of the paper dolls were extraordinary. Most were still unfinished. Judging from the laughter and chatter in the room, it had become more social than crafty. Let it be, Cora thought, as she took a photo of a laughing crafter as she glued fairy wings on her doll.

Not all of the women had chosen to create fairy paper dolls. Cora took some photos of a group of dolls that resembled little Russian nesting dolls. The crafter had used fabric and paint to create four dolls. So charming.

Another crafter had used the Cinderella fairy tale as an inspiration—but it was a dark Cinderella with a sugar skull face.

Liv, the Goth girl, had crafted the most interesting dolls. Her dolls had faces pasted in from a magazine and wore sexy corsets and slit skirts. Their wings were angelic, almost translucent, giving the otherwise sexy dolls an air of whimsy.

Another woman hand-painted a Victorian doll and used bits and pieces of real lace on her dress and over-sized hat. Someone else had created a simpler vintage-inspired group of dolls. Not hand-painted, just simpler, handcrafted paper dolls. It almost broke Cora's heart to view them—they were so delicate and sweet. This clearly was a crafter with some paper doll memories.

Cora felt a wave of excitement. This was what she had imagined when she envisioned holding craft

retreats for women. She knew that crafting was not
only fun, but it was also healing. Even if you weren't
healing from major trauma in your life, just giving
yourself time and space to make things allowed a
growth of spirit—and given everything that had
happened lately, that's exactly what they all needed.

Chapter 12

The Indigo River was anything but Indigo. It was, like most rivers, mostly brownish green, but then in spots sparkled translucently over rocks and through narrow passages. The scent of wet earth and fresh flowers and greens filled the air. Usually, the sight would cheer Jane, but today she was thinking of Gracie, who hung like a heavy cloud in Jane's heart and mind as she trudged along the riverbank.

The group of women walked quietly along the edges of the river as Jane led them to the banks she had scouted out earlier. Marianne pointed out the reeds growing alongside the bank.

"Those reeds are the exact ones we'll be using in our basket class tomorrow," she said.

"I've seen your baskets," Maddy said. "It's amazing what you do with those reeds," she said, and smiled. "I can't believe you make such beautiful baskets from those things."

Marianne nodded as a large bird flew overhead and screeched loudly. She flinched.

"Are you okay?" Jane asked her.

"I don't like hawks," she said. "They creep me out." She turned away and muttered something.

Jane stopped at the spot where they'd gotten permission to dig. Each woman had a bucket and a small spade.

"The idea behind this retreat is that we don't need to buy expensive supplies in order to be crafters. Often, we can find what we need in our own homes, or outside. But it's a good idea to ask the owners of the property before you take anything," Jane said. A breeze picked up. The trees shimmied and the water rippled as several women laughed.

"I was in trouble once for helping myself to some pinecones," one woman said. "Turns out you're not allowed to take anything from national parklands."

More laughter.

"I guess not," Marianne said.

Jane crouched down and the women gathered around her. "About eighty percent of the earth's surface contains clay."

"I had no idea," Sheila said. "I guess I just never thought about it." Her face was lined with graceful lines, but Jane wondered if they were premature. She knew that Sheila's daughter had a surprising onslaught of epilepsy a few years ago and was not doing well with it. Hence, Donna had stayed behind for the river walk, along with Cora, who was updating her blog with photos of the paper doll class.

"Does it need to be processed or something? Or do you just take it from the ground?" one crafter asked.

"Clay straight from the ground does need to be processed," Jane replied, setting down her bucket and burrowing her spade into the wet clay. "It'll need to be sieved to remove rocks, twigs, and roots."

"Oh, so that's what those screens in our kits are for, right?"

Jane nodded. "Sieving can be done either of two ways: The clay can be pulverized when dry and then sieved; or dried, slaked down in water, and then sieved. The finer the mesh used, the smoother your clay will be. I suggest using a 50-mesh screen, although a 30- or 80-mesh will do. Don't go any finer than 80-mesh. Once the clay has been cleaned and slaked down, you will want to bring it back to a working consistency, which we will do tomorrow at some point."

The women got to work digging clay from the riverbank.

Jane's cell phone blared into the peaceful scene. Jane jumped slightly, causing Marianne to look up at her.

"Yes," Jane said into her cell.

"It's Louise," her babysitter said. "I just wanted to check in with you and let you know that everything is fine. London's fever broke about thirty minutes ago."

"Is she sleeping?"

"Yes, she's still sleeping. This is the easiest babysitting job I've ever had," she said.

"I imagine. Well, thanks for checking in. I should only be another hour or so."

"No worries. Take your time. I've got a good book and music to listen to. I'm fine," the young woman said.

Jane slipped her phone back into her pocket.

"Are you always so jumpy when the phone rings?" Marianne said, standing up.

No, only when my daughter's babysitter has been abducted and her friend has been killed.

"It was my daughter's sitter," Jane said. "First time we've used her. It's a bit nerve-wracking."

She wasn't sure if the news about Henry had been released yet and didn't want to be the harbinger of bad news during the craft retreat.

"Ah yes. I have a couple of little ones. They are staying with my sister-in-law this weekend in Asheville. Going to some museums and such," Marianne said, and smiled.

"How lovely," Jane said distractedly, filling up her mud bucket.

Marianne patted her mud down and scooped a little more into the bucket.

Jane found herself wishing she and London had family around, for times like these when they needed extra help. But they didn't. It was just Cora, Jane, and London. And evidently Neil. At some point. She shoved thoughts of Neil out of her mind, for now.

Ruby walked over to her. "I filled up my bucket and I found some really nice stones over there," she said, and pointed behind her.

"Yes, I forgot to tell you all," Jane said. "If you find some smooth river stones, pick up a few for your rock-painting class."

"Have we heard anything about Gracie?" Ruby asked in a lowered voice. Even so, Marianne heard. She lifted her head in their direction. The woman must have exceptional hearing, Jane thought.

"Nothing," she said to Ruby.

"I found something!" a woman squealed, pointing between some rocks on the edge of the river.

"I'll get it," a taller woman beside her said, and leaned over to move the rock. She plucked up a necklace lodged beside it. When she held it up and brushed off the dirt, there was a glint of ruby. It was a round pendant with a ruby slipper etched into it.

"Look," she said. "It says something. *You're my home, Love, Paul.'*"

Jane felt the air escape from her body. She wanted to scream or gasp, but nothing came to her. Cold swept over her body.

"Paul?" Ruby said. "Ain't that the name of Gracie's boyfriend?"

Chapter 13

Cora pushed the publish button. Another blog post done. It had turned out better than she expected—the crafters at this retreat were a talented, interesting group. And their paper dolls showed it.

She expected the group to return from the river walk any minute now. She stood up and stretched. Luna lifted her head, blinked at her, and placed it back down on the couch pillow where she was nestled.

Kildare House was so quiet—the only other people currently in it were Donna, who was napping, and Paul, shut up in his room.

Poor Paul. He seemed so bereft. Would he ever get over losing his best friend and possibly his girlfriend all in the same week? Cora shivered. The incidents had certainly created a specter of doom over the retreat. She wasn't certain how many of the crafters knew about the news.

She wondered if she should check on Paul. On second thought, the police said they had given him something to relax him. Perhaps it was best not to disturb him.

She stood and took a deep breath. She reveled in the silence. She didn't mind the happy chatter of the guests, but silence was good, too.

Sirens wailed in the distance. This was not a common sound in Indigo Gap. Cora left her attic apartment and headed downstairs. The sirens came even closer.

As she walked down the steps, the crafters were entering through the front door, excited and chattering as they returned from their walk and watching whatever was happening outside.

"We're going to need to take the police back out there," Jane said to Ruby.

"Police?" Cora said. "What's going on?"

Jane held up a muddy, but still glittering necklace. "We found this in the river." Her blue eyes were wide with excitement and, perhaps, a tinge of fear.

"We think it belonged to Gracie," Ruby chimed in. "It has Paul's name on the back."

Cora's heart skipped a beat. "What? How?"

"We found it when we were digging clay," Jane said.

"I called the cops," Ruby said.

That explained why there were police cars with loud sirens in front of Kildare House. And it explained the excitement and agitation among some of her guests.

Cora moved through the crowd gathered in the foyer and spilling out of the front door and onto to the porch. She spotted Officer Glass walking up her sidewalk.

"Can you please shut the sound off of those things?" Cora said. "You are waking up the birds, for God's sake."

"Sorry, Cora. 9-1-1 protocol."

"9-1-1? There's no emergency here. We've found a necklace," she said.

"What?" he said, not hearing her above the sirens.

She rolled her eyes and pointed to the sirens. "I can't talk over that thing."

He walked back to the car and cut off the siren.

"Now, what seems to be the problem?" he said, with a note of impatience in his voice.

"We were down by the river, digging for clay," Jane said, coming up from behind Cora.

"And?" he said.

"We found this necklace, which we think belonged to Gracie."

"Gracie Wyke?" His face dropped.

"Yes, I remember her wearing it and it has an inscription on the back," Jane said, holding it up. The sun sparkled against its colors. He grabbed it and read the inscription.

"I'm going to need to get Detective Brodsky over here," he said, turning to his partner. "Can you call him?"

"Sure thing," the man said.

"We're going to have to go back down to the river," he said to them. "And I'm sure Brodsky will need to speak to whoever found the necklace."

"Glass." The officer came up to him and handed him the phone.

"Yes," he said into it.

Cora glanced at Jane. "Can we ever have a nice, calm, relaxing retreat?"

"Apparently not," Jane said, folding her arms. "But maybe this will help find Gracie. I wonder if she was wearing this when she disappeared."

"You saw her the day before. Do you remember?" Cora asked.

"I can't say specifically," Jane replied. "What I remember is that she seemed to wear it all the time." Her voice wavered. Her cheeks were taut with stress.

"What would she be doing down by that river?" Cora asked nobody in particular.

"A lot of the young people go down there to party, make out, and whatever," Ruby said.

"But she wasn't exactly young. I mean it's the high schoolers who party down there," Cora said. "She was a responsible young college student, a wannabe lawyer."

"Well, just because they found the necklace there doesn't mean she was there. It could have come from anywhere upstream," Ruby pointed out. "That river is full of tricky currents."

The women stood silently while Glass was on the phone speaking with Brodsky. His posture tightened. His shoulders rose.

"You ladies aren't planning on going back down there, are you?" Glass said after his phone call was finished. His face seemed drained of any color.

"No, we have plans and permission to walk up on the parklands tomorrow," Cora said. "Why?"

"Brodsky would like to meet whoever picked up the necklace down there at the river. But he asked that the rest of you stay away," Officer Glass said.

"I don't think we have any reason to go there, in any case," Cora said.

"It's going to be treated as a crime scene. The river is going to be dragged," he said.

"Dragged? What does that mean?" Cora said. "They think—"

He nodded. "Just procedure. But it certainly looks like a possibility."

"What?" Ruby said. "Just because we found a necklace?"

"I'm not going to comment on a continuing investigation of this nature," he said, with his gaze moving from Ruby, to Jane, and finally to Cora. "No matter who's asking."

Cora's stomach heaved and flipped. She knew enough to know the cops wouldn't use the resources needed to drag the river bottom just because one necklace was found. They must have found something else. She swallowed hard to keep from getting sick. Poor Gracie. Poor, poor Gracie.

Chapter 14

Because Maddy had found the necklace, the police asked her to go to the station to answer a few more questions. Cora and Jane, surrounded by the crafters, watched as she rode off in the police car. Thank goodness the police were moving from the front of the house—not without notice. Edgar Thorncraft, president of the local historical commission, and a man who lived in the neighborhood, walked up to them.

"Ladies," he said. "Everything okay?" He was dressed in his usual sweater vest, bow tie ensemble.

"It will be," Cora said. "How are you, Edgar?"

Jane turned to the women and gestured for them to move along into the house.

"I'm fine," he said. Cora knew that the recent loss of Sarah Waters, his longtime girlfriend and school librarian, weighed heavy on him. They'd chatted about it before and she felt sorry for Edgar, but not sorry enough to forgive his sometimes haughty attitude about all things historical.

"Too bad they don't have historical cop cars, hey, Edgar?" she said.

"What? Oh, yes." He smiled, as if he'd just gotten the joke.

"One of our guests found a necklace that may have belonged to the missing young woman. She's leading the police to where they found it," Cora told him, and watched his eyebrows raise.

"Oh," he said, then clicked his tongue. "It's too bad about the woman. Did you know her?"

"Not well," she said. "She babysat for London. How about you?"

He shook his head. "She's not from around here," he said, as if that explained everything. Cora wasn't from around here either. Which he knew.

Cora and Jane were both from Pittsburgh and had chosen to move to Indigo Gap to open the retreat because it was a beautiful town, historical, and full of artists and crafters. Cora also had fallen head over heels in love with Kildare House.

"I need to go. I have a retreat going on," she said. "As you can see."

He nodded. "I appreciate your sensitivity with the parking situation," he said. His constant concern was that too many cars were parked in front of the historical Kildare House. He was afraid it would blemish the town's most historical home.

Cora smiled at him, gritting her teeth, hating the way he sometimes behaved as if he were a benevolent dictator.

Cora walked off, leaving Edgar watching the cop car snaking through the streets of Indigo Gap.

* * *

"Well, this has all been very exciting," Ruby said as they gathered in the craft wing of the old house.

"If I can have your attention," Cora said, and the women quieted. She explained the Gracie situation and how the police were working hard to find her. She also told the crafters that Gracie's boyfriend, Paul, would be staying with them as a special guest for the retreat.

"It's just so lovely of you to keep him here," Sheila said.

"I had no choice," Cora said. "He's completely bereft and shouldn't be left alone. The police are trying to reach his family, who are traveling abroad. Until they do, he stays here."

"In the meantime, let's get on with it," Ruby said. "Does everybody have their paint and their rocks?"

"Okay, okay," Cora said. "Let's get started. After this miniclass, you're free to wander about the town, get something to eat, or just hang out here. We have plenty of leftovers from brunch."

She hoped they would all go out and spend their money in town. So many of the business owners thanked her for bringing them customers during the last retreat. The last retreat . . . when there were two murders in this small, quaint town. Cora could not get over it—and now, another suspicious death and a missing young woman. Perhaps this town wasn't as safe as she and Jane thought it was.

She brushed off that negative thought—she couldn't let it drag her down into a dark anxiety. She was here, in this new life, among other things, to get healthy, to free herself from the chains of her own anxiety disorder. Moving away from Pittsburgh and her job as a counselor at the Sunny Street Women's Shelter was the first step to a healthier life. She developed an anxiety disorder because of the incredible stress she faced every day. Some counselors were great at maintaining a professional distance. She was not—and had become sick because of her nature.

She turned her attention to the basket of examples of painted rocks that sat on the long table. The crafters were fussing over them. Cora, Jane, and Ruby had a fabulous time last weekend painting the rocks. Jane painted a series of bright-colored owls, Ruby painted herbs, and Cora painted designs full of swirls and spirals.

"Some of these are so gorgeous. I never knew painted rocks could be so pretty. I always thought of them in, I don't know, kind of tacky terms," Sheila said. "I've seen them at local craft shows and didn't care for them at all, but these are little works of art."

"I don't know about art," Ruby said, grinning. "But they sure aren't your grannie's painted rocks, are they?"

"Or your preschool student's," said Sheila.

"Have at it," Cora said. "Remember, after you are done, we'll be placing a kind of a varnish over them."

She studied the scene around the table, as the women picked and preened over rocks and paints. Where was Jane? Cora spotted her, lagging behind them, staring out a window. Oh dear.

Cora waltzed over to her. "What are you doing?" She elbowed her.

"Hmm?" she said, distracted and wet-eyed. Those deep blue eyes of hers displayed her every emotion. She could never have been an actress.

"Are you okay?" Cora said.

Jane shrugged. "I can't get Gracie off my mind."

Cora slipped her arm around her. "I know."

"The river—"

"Shhh," Cora said. "We don't know anything yet."

"But they are dragging the river. They must think—"

"Stop thinking the worst," Cora said. "Please. It will not do you good. Or her."

"Part of the angst is, well, I feel so helpless," she said.

"We're helping by keeping Paul safe," Cora said.

"You know what I mean," she said.

Cora thought a moment. "I do. I know exactly what you mean. But we have to leave this to the police and the search teams. They know what they are doing."

"I hope you're right."

Chapter 15

Paul came down the stairs just as the group was breaking up. Some of the guests were planning to go out for the evening; others settled in the living room to knit, chat, or read.

"Hey," he said to Cora and Jane.

"How are you feeling?" Cora asked.

"I'm still a bit woozy," he said. "I'm not sure what they gave me, but it really knocked me out. But I'm starving, so I'm going out to get something to eat."

Jane poked Cora with her elbow. "Why don't you stay here?" Jane said.

"Oh yes, I can fix you something," Cora said. "And we have plenty of leftovers from the brunch."

"Cool," he said, and shrugged.

"Follow me into the kitchen," Cora said. Jane trailed behind them.

"I need to get going," she said as they walked. "I'm sure the babysitter is ready for me to come home. If you need anything, let me know."

"Are you all set up for tomorrow?" Cora asked.

"I think so," she said. She turned and glanced at Paul. "Have a good night."

"Thanks," he said, and looked away. His eyes were still rimmed in red and black circles.

He sat down at the kitchen table and Cora pulled out leftovers from the fridge and placed them on the counters and the table. "Ham biscuits," she said. "Here's some fruit. Quiche. Cookies."

"A feast!" Paul exclaimed. He stood and wandered from counter to counter, piling his plate high with food. "I'm so hungry. This is fabulous."

"Did someone say food?" Liv asked as she wandered into the kitchen, still wearing her heavy makeup, but now in sweatpants and a T-shirt.

"There's plenty for everybody," Paul said, and smiled.

"You must be Paul," she said.

He nodded. "And you are?"

"Liv," she said, reaching for a plate. "I'm a student at BMU. Seems like I've seen you around."

He nodded. "My girlfriend just graduated prelaw. I've taught a couple of classes there."

"What kind of classes?"

"Writing," he said. "I haven't taught there for a while, though."

"Hmm," she said, piling fruit salad on her plate. "I try to stay away from writing classes. I'm an art student."

Cora sat quietly and drank from a tall glass of water, observing the two.

"Hey, I'm sorry to hear about your friend," Liv said. "And your girlfriend. Hope they find her soon."

He nodded. "They have to. They just have to. But thanks."

"Cora," she said. "Do you mind if I take my plate to my room? I've got something I'm working on up there."

"No, go right ahead," Cora said.

"Nice meeting you, Paul," she said, and walked out of the kitchen.

Cora sat and ate the quinoa-fruit salad while Paul downed several ham biscuits.

"So you're a writer?" Cora asked him.

"Yes, I freelance now, but I'm hoping to get a novel published someday," he said.

"That's interesting," Cora said. "How did you and Gracie meet?"

"At school," he said. "It's where I met Henry, too. Henry is . . . I mean was, a poet."

"Really?"

"Yes, but his degree was in computer science. He'd written several games."

"Games?"

"Yes, that's how he made his living. Writing and selling computer games," he said. "He knew computers really well. So does Gracie."

Just then Cora remembered the conversation they had all had the night the two young men had visited Jane's place. Mention of a computer game. What was it?

Cora watched Paul scarf down more food. She wondered if he'd eaten anything in the past twenty-four hours.

"I've never played a computer game," she said, and bit into the last bit of cubed watermelon.

"It's wild. It can be a lot of fun," he said. He sat his fork down. "I think I may have eaten too much." All the blood seemed to drain from his face. He rubbed his face.

"Take some deep breaths," Cora said. She stood up and placed her hands on his shoulders and rubbed them.

"I can't," he said. "I feel like I can't breathe."

He gasped for air.

Was he having a heart attack? A panic attack?

"Listen," Cora said. "Listen to me, Paul. You can take some deep breaths. You can and you will."

She moved his hands away from his face. "Look at me. Let's breathe together."

"You don't understand!" he said.

"Yes, yes, I do. I've had panic attacks for years and I think that's what you're having. Please. Just breathe with me."

After she got him through the worst of it, more deep breaths, more soothing words, and more gentle pats on his back, he excused himself and went back to his room.

"Give yourself some space and time," Cora said. "This is a lot for you. For anybody."

His phone beeped and he pulled it out of his pocket.

"It's my parents," he said. He still appeared pale and woozy. "I can't deal with them right now. I'll call them tomorrow. Like, I have about a million texts and messages to sort through."

"If you want, I can talk with them. They must be worried," she said.

He handed her the phone. "That would be awesome." It was still ringing as he slowly walked up the stairs.

"Hello," Cora said into the phone.

"This is Susan Garrett. I'm looking for my son, Paul Eugene." Her voice was edged in panic. Paul Eugene? Cora was momentarily confused, then figured she'd meant Paul.

Cora explained who she was and why she had answered Paul's phone.

"I appreciate all your help," Susan said. "But I really wish he'd come home."

"I don't think he wants to leave until they've found Gracie," Cora said.

There was an exasperated sigh on the other end of the phone.

"But I may be wrong. He might be better to speak with you tomorrow. He's been given something to help him sleep and I really don't think he's up to making any decisions now. But rest assured, Paul is safe here," Cora said.

"Thank God for that," his mother said. "At least he's safe. But I must insist our Paul Eugene come home. He needs to be with family."

"Believe me, I understand your concern, but he is very safe here at Kildare House with my crafters," she replied.

"What is your address?" his mother demanded.

"There's really no need for you to come here—"

"Please. It would just make me feel better to see him," she said.

Cora reluctantly gave her the address.

When Cora clicked off the phone, she found herself hoping that she had not lied to his mother. Was Paul indeed safe in Kildare House? After all, who besides the police even knew he was there?

Chapter 16

"How did it go today with Louise?" Jane asked London as she tucked her in.

"It went okay," London said. "I like Gracie better." Jane felt a wave of sickness roll through her.

"I like Gracie a lot, too," she said.

"I hope they find her, Mommy," London said.

Jane's daughter's eyes held terror in them. It was a difficult concept for a five-year-old to comprehend. Sometimes Jane hated the world for all its "stranger-danger" talks. But times like this made it easier to speak with London about it.

"I hope so, too," Jane said, brushing away a strand of hair from her daughter's face. Such innocence. The world could be such a cold place. How she wanted to keep and hold her daughter, protect her, forever, even though she knew it was impossible.

"I didn't know that grown-ups get stolen, too," London said, rubbing her eyes, then yawning.

To London, a twenty-four-year-old was a grown-up. Jane supposed most people would agree. But she shuddered to think of considering herself an adult at that age—she still had a lot of maturing to do, unfortunately. Young women were too quick to trust. She was one of them herself—but no more. Unfortunately, most people had to learn lessons the hard way, by making mistakes over and over again.

She hoped London would somehow avoid that.

If Gracie had trusted the wrong man, and gone off with him, could she still be alive?

But Gracie didn't seem the sort to trust a stranger. Not at all. Whoever got her off alone had to be some-one she knew. If that is indeed what happened.

"I hope she comes back soon," London said.

Of course, maybe Gracie hadn't trusted whoever her abductor was. Perhaps he just attacked and dragged her off somewhere. Jane felt sick again.

"Let's read," she said to London, hoping it would get them both to think about something else.

Soon the two of them were lost in the world of *Harry Potter*. London drifted off to her mother's voice and Jane placed the book quietly down on the bed-side table.

London's teacher was surprised to learn that they were reading *Harry Potter* each night. But London was such a good reader and had grown out of so many of the regular books you'd read to a five-year-old—and Jane was judicious about the "scary" parts. Sometimes she'd skip right over them and other times she's editorialize in her own words.

Jane sat for a few moments listening to London's breathing, a habit she picked up when London was a baby. When you were a tired, beleaguered mom pulled in countless directions, this was a moment to savor, a good reminder of the importance of being a mom.

Jane stood and reached over to turn off the light, taking one last glimpse of her girl and her tangled dark hair on the white pillow.

When she got back to her own room, Jane sat down at her computer and pulled up the day's news.

Henry's death was on the front Web page of the local paper. She read about him and was surprised to find he was a much sought-after gaming developer. Interesting. Hadn't he and Paul mentioned a game when they visited? A *Wizard of Oz* game?

Jane found the gaming subculture fascinating, but not enough to explore it. She knew there were several designers and artists she went to school with who found lucrative work in the field.

She scrolled through the article. Henry was from the town of Cherokee, son of a single mom, with no brothers or sisters. As she skimmed the article, something caught her eye: His body was found at the abandoned Oz World theme park. Closed a few years back because of a fire that it had never recovered from, the place had provided twelve years of happy memories for countless families

Her heart pounded in her chest. What? Was this a weird coincidence? Gracie had been reading that book and they had talked about a *Wizard of Oz* game. What was going on here?

She suddenly felt like she was in an episode of *The Twilight Zone.*

She Googled "Wizard of Oz Game" and clicked on the first link that appeared.

The site was brightly colored and the rules of the

game were simplistic. It was definitely designed for kids. So why were Gracie, Henry, and Paul playing this game so avidly? And what had upset them about it?

She dialed Cora.

When she finally answered, she sounded groggy. Had she been sleeping?

"Have you read this article about Henry's death?" Jane asked.

"Article? What article? I finished another blog post and have been kind of busy over here with the retreat."

"I'm sorry if I woke you, but this is kind of freaky," Jane said.

She explained to Cora what the article said.

"I didn't even know about this theme park!" Cora said. "And Henry was found there? This is wild!"

"Could it just be an odd coincidence that Gracie was reading the book and they were playing this game and he turns up at a *Wizard of Oz* theme park?" Jane said.

"I don't know."

"The game is for kids. It doesn't make sense that three adults would even care about it."

"You're reaching for answers. I get that. But sometimes there are no answers," Cora said.

Jane thought a moment. "Yes, I suppose you're right. All this *Wizard of Oz* stuff is just a distraction. It probably has nothing to do with what really happened to Gracie and Henry."

"And who knows if Henry's death is even linked to Gracie's disappearance," Cora pointed out.

"True. Except, of course, for their shared connection to Paul. How is he doing?"

Cora paused. "He's far from fine. I'm worried about him. But I think his parents are on their way. They want to take him home, but I have a feeling he's not going anywhere, not without knowing what's happened to Gracie."

Chapter 17

Cora roused herself out of her quilt-covered bed. She glanced at the alarm clock: 5:30 AM, too early for anything productive but a shower and coffee. But, she needed to get downstairs to set out the bagels, fruit, and donuts for her guests. They were going on an early-morning hike to pick flowers, rocks, sticks, and whatever else they could find to use for their crafts.

By the time she entered the dining room downstairs, Ruby had already laid out the spread.

"Thanks," she said. "You're up early."

"Just couldn't sleep," Ruby said, shrugging her shoulders.

Cora had tossed and turned a good bit herself last night. But when she finally did fall asleep, she slept deeply and hadn't wanted to leave her bed.

The group gathered in the dining room and filled up on coffee and goodies, and then headed to the craft room, where Ruby explained the ground rules for the day.

A loud knock sounded at the front door and Cora

excused herself. She opened the door to find Detective Brodsky. It was getting to be commonplace to find the police at her door—commonplace and tiresome.

"Good morning," she said. "How can I help you?"

"Good morning, Cora," Brodsky said, and smiled. "Sorry to trouble you, but is Paul around?"

"Yes," she said. "We talked him into going with us on our hike this morning."

"Where's that?" he asked.

"We've gotten special permission to take a nature walk through Blue Falls Park."

"Why did you need permission?" he asked as he walked through the door.

"Because we're taking things—flowers, rocks, twigs, stones, you know, stuff we can craft with. They'll catalog everything we take," she told him. "Come on in. Paul is in the craft wing with the others."

She led him through the dining room into the craft wing of the Victorian home. It was an open, yet comfortable space. Many of the crafters were drinking one last cup of coffee before hitting the trails. It quieted when the detective walked into the room.

He nodded. "Paul, why don't you come into the kitchen with me? I have a few questions for you."

"Did you find her?" he said as he stood up, nearly knocking over his chair.

"No," he replied. "But we have a new lead we need to run by you."

A new lead? thought Cora. That was wonderful. This meant that the river search, which might still be going on for all Cora knew, hadn't dredged up anything.

"Okay, yeah, sure." Paul followed the detective into the kitchen.

Cora gathered up the empty cups in the craft room and also followed the men into her kitchen. She busied herself at the sink while they talked. She wondered if they minded or even noticed her presence.

"Did you know Professor Gerald Rawlings?" Detective Brodsky asked.

"Yes," Paul said. "I remember him."

"His wife has stepped forward. She thinks Gracie and Gerald ran off together."

Cora dropped one of the cups into the sink. Well, if they didn't know she was here before, they certainly did now.

"That's absurd," Paul said. "Gracie and I were together. She loved me."

The air in the room seemed to vibrate with an uncomfortable energy.

"She was loyal. I know she was," Paul said.

The detective slid some photos in front of Paul. "She had a detective follow Gerald around last year."

"Last year? What does this have to do with right now?" Paul said, studying the photo. "Yeah, sure, they were together a lot. They were working on a paper together. They did have a brief fling. I knew about it. We've gotten past it. This doesn't prove anything."

"He's missing, too," the detective said. "Any idea about where he could be? Or maybe where they could have gone together?"

"Seriously?" Paul flung his arms out.

Could it be? Could sweet, solid Gracie, by all accounts, have fallen for a professor and taken off with him without letting anybody know? Is that something Gracie would have done?

"I don't believe it," Paul said. "I don't care what you

say. Gracie would not have left like that, with no notice. She had a job here. People here."

"But what if she were madly in love with this man?" the detective said. "Is that possible?"

"She loved me," Paul insisted.

"Not to be crass, but you wouldn't be the first young man lied to by a young woman," Detective Brodsky said.

Cora rinsed off another cup and dried it. That was true. People could surprise you. It wasn't just men who lied to women and had secret affairs. She knew several cases of just the opposite.

"Well," Paul finally said. "I almost hope that she did lie to me. That she did take off with this man. At least I'd know she was . . . alive."

Cora turned around and caught the eye of Detective Brodsky, who was looking at the young man with sympathy. He was not enjoying this line of questioning. Whether or not Gracie left with the professor, or indeed loved Paul, it was clear how Paul felt about her.

"So, you never suspected an affair?" Detective Brodsky prompted.

"No," he replied. "We were getting along fine. Better than ever."

But Cora remembered that Jane said they'd recently had a spat.

"No fighting?"

"Well, just like everybody else, we had our moments," Paul said.

"What did you fight about?"

Paul sighed. "Well, mostly it was about me being too overprotective or calling too much. But she'd complain, I'd back off, and then she'd be okay. She's just very independent—most of the time. But then there were other times . . . times she was vulnerable and wanted nothing more than to be with me. So, well, I just tried my best to make her happy. What can I say?" His voice cracked. Was he crying? Cora wondered, but didn't want to gape.

"Okay," Detective Brodsky said. "Thanks for talking with us. Once we find the professor we'll let you know. Okay?"

Cora could see him nodding and heard a slight sob. Oh no. He was crying again. She had hoped this would be a better day for him.

"The van is here." Jane poked her head into the kitchen. "Are you two ready?"

"I am," Cora said. "Are you finished?" she asked the detective.

Brodsky nodded. "I'll show myself out."

"Wait," Paul said. "What about Henry? How does he fit in to all this?"

"Fit in?" Brodsky said. "Not at all. Two separate cases, as far as we can tell. Just a coincidence that they knew each other."

Paul looked befuddled.

"We still don't know enough about the circumstances of Henry's death," the detective said. "The ME doesn't have results we need yet."

It was Friday and Cora knew that it was tough to get results over the weekend.

"How hard can it be?" Paul blurted.

"Sometimes it's harder than you think," the detective said with a wary note in his voice.

Chapter 18

Walking through the forest on a spring day outside of Indigo Gap was like walking through heaven. A bright blue sky with cottony-white clouds, shades of new green everywhere, a spot of white or purple or pink, sometimes yellow, dotted the landscape. Every once in a while a light conversation or laughter would begin among the group of crafters. But mostly the women and Paul were quiet, mesmerized by the pristine beauty that surrounded them.

Ruby stopped the group and pointed out some of the wild herbs growing along the rocky path.

"Bloodroot," she said, and pointed to a group of flowers that resembled daisies on steroids, with long white petals and a yellow center reaching out.

"Ah, yes," Marianne said. "I grow my own. It's one of the plants I use for dye for the baskets I make."

"I heard that most people are growing their own, rather than just plucking them," Ruby said. "It's such a good idea. We don't want to deplete the forest."

Marianne nodded. Her long black hair was pulled into a sloppy bun, showing off her strong chin line and high cheekbones. "We have many stories about bloodroot. It's also used for medicinal purposes. It has antiseptic qualities."

"Oh, this is lovely," Jane said, reaching down to pluck a wand-like flower stalk with tiny white buds. "What is this?"

"Black cohosh," Ruby replied.

"It will make a gorgeous clay impression," Jane said. Clay-charm class offered several variations for the crafters. Jane planned experiments with plant imprints "baked" into them.

"They're also good for snake bites," Ruby explained.

"I think our elders used it for cramps, too," Marianne said.

"I've seen it used for that as well," Ruby said.

"Oh, look at those gorgeous purple flowers," Sheila exclaimed.

"Bird's-foot violet," Ruby said. "They are lovely. I've heard it called the queen of the violets. You see the beautiful color variations, from the deep purple to almost white."

"Of course the leaves are shaped like bird's feet, Marianne said. "You see?"

"So you can see that there are a number of possibilities here. Let your imaginations run wild," Cora said. "Look at the flowers, plants, grasses, rocks. What can we do with them in class? But remember not to take too much. We'll be going to the ranger station and they will check out everything we're taking to make sure it's okay."

"Try to stay in this general area," Ruby said. "But let's meet back here in an hour. Don't do anything stupid like get lost or get bit by a snake."

The group laughed as they dispersed into the forest, over the banks, into the wooded glens.

Cora breathed in the air and decided to move forward, even farther up the mountain. Jane followed close behind. They found a huge boulder and sat down, looking over a valley and the mountains in the distance.

"We've come up in the world," Jane smiled. "You don't get views like this on Sunny Street."

"So true," Cora said, breathing in the cool mountain air. The mountains in the distance rippled into one another. Blue-hued, they were like a still ocean against the horizon. It was so beautiful that it almost hurt to look at it.

Cora thought about the Sunny Street Women's Shelter less and less these days, though she still did think about it. She'd spent a large chunk of her life there, which gave her a skewed view of life—one that she was working on reshaping every day. Sometimes the system made it difficult to have hope, when time after time, women and children were sent back into horrible situations, no matter how hard police and social workers tried.

Last night, Adrian called from New Jersey informing her he'd be back on Sunday. She found herself a jumble of emotions. She was on the edge of excitement. She really liked him. Lusted for him, even. But . . . she just couldn't make the leap. Not yet. Even though there was nothing to *not* like about him. In fact, everything pointed to him being a decent guy. Heck, he'd just spent several weeks with his sick mother. He seemed like a keeper.

But the Sunny Street Women's Shelter cynic in her

emphasized the "seemed like" part. And it niggled at her to try to find something wrong with him; anything that would be a good excuse to back off a relationship.

Which was ridiculous. Because, ultimately she wanted one, didn't she? Didn't everybody?

"I'd like to see you soon," Adrian had said to her on the phone. "Would that be okay?"

"Of course," she said. "How about next weekend? This weekend is the retreat."

"Can I stop by sometime Sunday?" he asked.

She hesitated.

"Never mind," he said. "I don't mean to push."

"Call me Sunday and we can come up with a good time for you to stop by," she said. "I like to leave a lot of space and time during the retreats for flexibility."

"Oh," he said. "Okay. I get that. I'll call you then."

His voice hinted at disappointment. But he knew that this was her job. She couldn't drop everything for him. That would set up a bad precedent. She needed to let him know that she wasn't going to build her life around him. Not completely.

She thought of Gracie and Paul. It seemed like she had been drawing her boundaries clearly for him. And he was trying to navigate them. At least, that's what Cora had surmised—but who knew what really went on in any relationship but the two people involved in it?

When the van pulled into Kildare House, Brodsky was sitting on the porch. He stood up and walked over to Paul. "I'm sorry, son," he said.

"Do you have word about Gracie?"

Brodsky shook his head. "I need to take you in."

"For what?" Cora said.

Brodsky breathed a deep, heavy sigh. "Calm down. We just have some questions for him about Henry."

"What do you mean?" Cora asked.

"We need to talk with Paul about Henry's murder. He's under arrest."

"What? That's ridiculous!" Cora said.

Paul paled.

"Don't worry, Paul. My son, Cashel, will meet you at the station. He's a lawyer. He'll get to the bottom of this absurdity," Ruby said, emphatically, pulling out her cell phone from her back pocket.

Jane and Cora exchanged worried glances. But Cora got the feeling that Jane was relieved to see Paul go.

"I'm sure it will be fine," Ruby told the group at the brunch. "My son is a good lawyer. He'll take care of Paul."

The crafters were clustered together in groups while eating; they had worked up an appetite during the hike that morning.

Cora's stomach was a mess and though she tried to rouse an appetite, she failed. The food smelled good. The scent of vegetable soup and cornbread taunted her one moment, and the next made her want to vomit. She reached for some lightly salted crackers.

A group of students encircled Marianne. Her basket class was next on the schedule. The group seemed excited about it, especially after she pointed out some of the reeds they would use for their basket making.

"Why aren't you eating? Are you worried?" Jane said.

Cora nodded. "I suppose I am. I feel bad for Paul."

Jane took a bite of cornbread. "If he's innocent, he has nothing to worry about, right?"

Cora grimaced. "You'd think."

"But maybe he's not quite innocent. Maybe that's what's upsetting you. Maybe you're worried about that."

"I don't know. It's absurd to think he would kill Henry."

"What if Henry and Gracie were having an affair?" Jane said.

Cora wanted to laugh. That would be straight out of a movie or a book, wouldn't it?

"Well, you know Gracie better than me," Cora said. "So far, we have the possibility of her running off with her professor, or, I don't know, having an affair with her boyfriend's best friend. Do either one of those possibilities strike a chord?"

"First of all, I didn't know her that well," Jane said, after a few seconds of consideration. "And secondly, what I know of her was that she was responsible, driven, and caring. She was so good with London."

"You can be all those things and still be having an affair. At her age, life and love can be confusing," Cora said. Her stomach raged. Talking this over wasn't doing her any good.

"Don't I know it," Jane said. "It's still pretty confusing even at our age, isn't it?"

Cora knew that Jane had broken it off with the

man she met and spent the weekend with a few months back. It had turned out that he was a recovering addict. Jane's ex-husband was a raging recovering alcoholic and drug addict. Just the whisper of the word made her turn tail and question why she was attracted to the same type of man all the time—which wasn't quite fair for the new guy. Not all alcoholics were the asshole kind that was her ex-husband, Neil. Still, after everything she knew Neil put Jane through, Cora couldn't blame her for being gun-shy when it came to relationships. She just wasn't ready.

"I'm not confused," Cora finally said. "I'm just cautious."

"Hear, hear," Jane said, and held up her orange juice. "Let's hear it for caution!"

"But still," she said after a few moments. "Didn't I tell you that Adrian is your type?" Her eyebrows moved up and down.

"Oh yes," Cora said. "You did tell me that. He's a good guy."

"But?"

"No buts," Cora said. "I really like him." She shrugged. "We've only had one date. Let's not have me walking down the aisle yet."

Jane laughed and dug into her soup.

Sheila walked over to them. "It's been such a lovely couple of days. What a great place this is."

"Thanks," Cora said. "Your paper doll class went really well."

"Yes, I think so. Tomorrow, a few people want us to get together to press flowers and try some things with paper. I hope that's okay," Sheila said. "I know it's not on the schedule."

"Oh, that's fantastic. That's just the kind of thing we like to hear," Cora said. "That's why I like leaving plenty of downtime in the schedule. I want people to feel free to explore."

"So," Sheila said with a lowered voice. "Do you think Paul killed that young man?"

Cora nearly choked on her cracker.

"No," Jane said. "Absolutely not. The police are just questioning him. You know, it's just procedure, you know?"

"Oh boy, do I," Sheila said. "Unfortunately, a lot of murders and strange things have happened in the town I live in, Cumberland Creek. I've been involved way more than I want to be. BeatBrice told you about some of it, I take it."

Cora nodded. Sheila and her new great-aunt BeatBrice both lived in the small Virginia town of Cumberland Creek. BeatBrice told her all about the unfortunate incidents.

"One thing I've learned over the years is that people often surprise you. I've been shocked to learn who is capable of murder. Men and women from all walks of life. Believe me," Sheila said.

Cora didn't know what to say to that.

"Mom." Sheila's daughter, Donna, walked up to the group and smiled at Cora. "One of the crafters has a question for you. Actually, there's a whole group of them in the paper room."

Sheila excused herself and Cora was glad of it. She didn't want to talk further about murder and murderers. She hoped she'd never have to think about another one ever again, let alone house a murder suspect in Kildare House.

Ruby sauntered up to Cora and Jane. "I've just heard from Cashel."

"And?" Jane said with an edge of impatience in her voice.

"And evidently it's more complicated than any of us know."

"What? How?" Cora said.

"Cashel wouldn't tell me, of course. You know how he is. Straight and narrow. I sometimes ask myself where I went wrong with him," she said, shaking her head.

"Ruby, he's a lawyer. It's his job to follow the rules and make sure everybody else does, too," Cora said, even though she'd been annoyed by him for the same reason several times in the recent past.

Cashel O'Malley was a brilliant, beautiful man. Cora had thought attraction sparked between them— but between her history with another lawyer and the fact that he was Ruby's son, she nixed it.

"How complicated is it?" Jane asked.

"Not complicated enough for them to keep him," Ruby said. "But he's definitely a strong person of interest in the murder of his best friend."

Cora drew in a breath. No. It couldn't be. She had good instincts about people, finely honed from years of dealing with problem situations in the shelter. Even though she didn't really know him, Paul seemed kind and very much in love. She caught herself. Love had been the cause of many killings, hadn't it? Love, in its most warped form, that is.

"That's hard to believe," Jane said. "He seems so normal. So average."

Ruby guffawed. "That's what they all say."

Chapter 19

"So this morning on our walk, we saw the river cane that we use for the baskets," Marianne said. She held up a stalk of river cane. "This is what it looks like in the wild."

She held up a cutting tool and split the reed. "Traditionally we use this kind of river reed. But as we discussed when we were on the walk today, we can also use vines, like honeysuckle and kudzu, and the pliable branches we collected to make baskets."

Cora noticed that several of the crafters had collected kudzu vine, wonderfully woodsy and gnarly. Cora loved it—but it was taking over all through the South and had become quite a problem in some areas. The conservation officer at the station today had loved that the women had taken some. "Take more, please," he had joked.

Marianne sat the split reed aside and picked up a pile of thick shavings.

"This is what you end up with, what you use to make the baskets. You each have these in your kits. They were soaked last night. If your materials dry out once you start to weave, you can always soak them again to make them more workable. Does everybody have these?" she asked.

"Yes? Okay," she said. "We'll start by creating the base of the basket, what we call a start. It's like this." She held up two bases. "The length of your base pieces helps to determine how large your basket is." She held up the base pieces again. "The static pieces are called spokes. If you look at this one, you can tell it's a Cherokee start because it looks like a water spider."

Marianne's long fingers ran over the edges of the round spoke, flicking the long pieces jutting out from the center. "Of course, when I was growing up on the reservation, I had no idea what they were called. We just called them starts." She paused and grinned. "We just learned how to make things from our elders. And they learned from their elders."

"Didn't you get a degree in design?" Sheila asked.

"Aha, you did your homework," Marianne said. "Yes, I am a degreed designer. Then I studied basket making even more through the years. But, the true basket makers, that's all they do. And they know what they are doing. There are stories in their fingers."

Marianne was short, thin, and on the plain side. She never wore makeup or did anything with her hair, except to pull it up into a sloppy bun. Her eyes were dark and large. Thin lips beneath a large nose, which gave her face a birdlike quality. Cora watched as she flitted from crafter to crafter. The room was full—all twenty-two guests had signed up for this class. Marianne was a popular teacher and basket maker. Her baskets were featured in galleries all over the world.

"Hold six strands of cane in each hand," she said. "Each one of these strands has been cut for you. They are about arm's length, yes? Like that." She held up one. "So, six in each hand, cross them in the middle. Try to keep it flat. Then we add in the runner, creating the round spoke. To create the Cherokee basket, we circle the runner around three times."

"How many times?" someone asked.

"Three times," Cora repeated. "Right?" Cora's fingers found their way around the tripped cane and counted three turns.

"It's moving along nicely," Marianne said, looking over Cora's shoulder as she walked around the room. "Now, once your base is set—no, no, take your time, I'm just talking. Keep working. But once it's set, you'll start to incorporate what we call weavers into the spokes. Sounds fancy, doesn't it?"

A few of the crafters laughed.

"If you look at my base, and some of your bases, you can see a spider shape, yes? My people have a story or myth about this," she said, still holding up the base. "They say that in the beginning of time there was no fire, and the world was cold, until the thunder gods sent their lightning and put fire into the bottom of a hollow sycamore tree. This tree grew on an island. Many animals had excuses for not going to see the burning sycamore tree, until at last the water spider said she would go. She can run on the top of the water or dive to the bottom." Marianne made diving motions with her free hand. "So the water spider would have no trouble going to the fire. But how could she bring the fire back?"

She paused. The women were quiet and leaning toward her.

"Get on with it, woman!" Ruby said, in a joking tone.

Marianne cracked a smiled. "Just building the suspense. You know." She grinned. "Okay. Well, the spider said, 'I can manage that.' And she spun a thread from her body and wove it into a tusti bowl, which she fashioned on her back. Like that." She held up the start again. "Then the spider crossed over the island and through the grass to where the fire was still burning. She placed one little coal of fire into her basket and came back with it, and ever since, we have had fire and the water spider keeps her tusti bowl."

"Ah," said one of the crafters.

"As soon as the pieces are in your hands, the process becomes intuitive and it doesn't much matter if the results are flawed. In fact, we think the irregularities add character," she said.

"I have a feeling I'm going to have plenty of character," said Maddy, laughing. "This is a lot harder than I thought."

"It takes practice," said Marianne. "Now, if we wanted to complicate it even further," she said, "we'd add some dyes in and some decorative patterns."

"I can't imagine!" said Liv, as she twisted strands of honeysuckle around.

Marianne chuckled. "Okay, we won't add in the decorations. A Cherokee basket maker uses no patterns, models, or drawings. So this takes practice. Her patterns are in her soul, in her memory, and imagination. They come from the mountains, streams, and forests, and the traditions of her tribe."

The crafters listened intently as they worked with their hands.

"I'm fascinated by the colors I've seen on some of your baskets," Jane said. "Are they all natural dyes?"

"Yes," Marianne said. "The colors are from roots, barks, leaves, nuts, flowers, fruits, stems, seeds, or sometimes a complete plant. It depends on what's available. As I told some today, bloodroot is used for a yellowish color; black walnut is used for a brownish color; elderberries are used for a rose color. It's like that. Very simple."

"I saw that you actually teach a class on dyes at BMU," Liv said.

Marianne appeared confused. "No, not anymore. I only taught one class there."

"I'm certain it was in the catalog," Liv said.

"That's an error," Marianne said. "I'm not teaching there anymore," she said with finality.

"My fingers don't like this," Jane said.

"That's because you are a potter," Marianne said. "A true potter. That is your tribe, your gift. You are a potter and your hands don't like to make baskets."

"That's for damn sure," Jane said. She held up her hands, which were red and blotchy. It didn't look like an allergic reaction, quite, but it also didn't look normal.

"You should soak your hands in some clay. They will be fine," she said. "Gifted women of the people are sometimes quite sensitive."

"But I'm not—" Jane started to say.

"Yes, you are," Marianne said with a matter-of-fact tone.

Jane sat her start down on the table. She appeared

stunned, then grinned. Jane had always thought she might be Native American, but she was adopted and it had been a closed adoption. Jane had no idea where she came from. Of course, just because Marianne said she was "of the people" didn't make it so, Cora realized. She was certain Jane did, too. But for now Jane was grasping at the possibility of being a part of a people, or something larger than herself, larger than her own little family. Cora's heart lifted for her friend.

"Um," she said. "I, ah, better go and soak my hands."

She stumbled out of the room just as Paul walked in.

"Oh, hey," he said to Cora. "There you are. Do you mind if I stay one more night?" he asked as the room silenced. The crafters were all looking in his direction.

"My folks will be here tomorrow and they'd prefer if I stayed with someone," he said.

Cora took him by the elbow and led him out of the room. She examined him. Disheveled and nervous, he resembled a twelve-year-old boy instead of a twenty-something man. Funny how stress peeled away the years in some people. Of course, there was a lot weighing on him—the possibility of his girlfriend running away with a professor, or missing. His best friend dead—and they were questioning him as if he were a suspect. He was troubled—and he had plenty to be troubled about. But was he a killer?

"Paul—"

"You can't possibly think that I could ever hurt Henry, right? He was my best friend. And I love Gracie.

The police let me go because they have nothing. They're grasping," he said.

"Of course you can stay, Paul," Cora said, trying to calm her stomach. She just couldn't get a clear read on this man. But she was not about to give up on him. Not yet.

Chapter 20

"You are really allowing him to stay?" Jane said, with her hands immersed in a tub of clay. The clay felt cool and wonderful on her hands, and the itching had completely stopped. She had read about the healing properties of clay but had never experienced it before.

Cora was standing in Jane's studio. She was still in her hiking clothes, bib overalls with a cute yellow calico blouse. Her red curls were pulled off her face with a yellow bandanna. Even dressed for hiking, Cora always turned out better than she did. Jane wore jeans and a sweatshirt.

"Of course," Cora said. "What could I do? His parents asked him to stay here. They must be concerned."

"His parents?" Jane said, and rolled her eyes. "He's twenty-eight years old. I'm sorry. That's just weird."

"Not really," Cora said. "Not if you think about what he's facing. Of course his parents are going to be concerned. Wouldn't you be if London was in that situation? Even if she were thirty or forty?"

Jane hadn't thought about it like that. It was just that she had been on her own so long that it was difficult to understand the adult-parent relationship. She had no idea what her relationship with London would be like in the future. She'd never really had an adult relationship with her own adoptive parents, both gone early, like Cora's but different in that her mother had gotten sick with cancer and her father killed himself a few years after. Cora's parents were both killed in an accident, gone suddenly on the same day.

"I don't know," Jane replied. "But I do know that you've got a group of women at Kildare House and if there's a chance that Paul is a killer or a criminal or whatever, you've got a responsibility to protect them. I told you that you never should have offered in the first place."

"I thought he might have been in danger," Cora said. "And to tell the truth I still think that. Isn't it weird? His girl is gone. His best friend is dead. What's the link?"

"There's no link. Didn't Brodsky tell you that?" Jane said, looking at the clock. The crafters would be heading her way soon. She reluctantly took her hands out of the clay. "Can you turn the faucet on for me?"

The water cleaned away the remnants of the clay from Jane's hands, no longer red and itching. Amazing. She held them up.

"Marianne was right," Cora said. "Look at that."

Jane toweled her hands off. "I wonder why Marianne thought I might be Native American."

"Well, you do kind of look like you could be. We've talked about that before," Cora said.

"I wonder if I could try looking into my records again."

"It's worth a shot," Cora said, peering out the window. "Your first student is making her way down the path." It was Liv, who was stopping to look at some flowers.

"Keep your eye on Paul, okay?" Jane said. "I mean, I don't know if I really think he's dangerous. But I do remember Gracie being pretty perturbed with him. He was clingy. It just smacks of possessiveness." Neil was the same way with her. It raised her hackles.

"I agree. There's a fine line there," Cora said, watching out the window.

She had seen it time and time again when she worked as a counselor—a man's obsession turning into possession, then violence. To be fair, she'd seen several women who were just as obsessive and, ultimately, as violent. She'd often wondered how a "normal" love relationship would turn into something sick and violent. Were there early signs? With a few of her clients, there were. But they were very easy to ignore when in the first swoony stages of romance.

Cora turned her attention to Liv as she opened the door.

She walked into the studio, beaming. "I'm so excited to take this class with you. I'm taking the advanced class tomorrow, too." She stopped and eyed

Cora, then Jane. "Geez, what's wrong with you two? It looks like you've both seen a ghost."

"Nothing," Jane said, gathering her composure. "I'm really glad you could make it. This class is going to be fun."

"Yes, indeed," Cora said. "I'd better get going. I've got a blog post to write up about the basket class. I'll be back around to take some photos of your pieces."

"I'll walk you out," Jane said.

"What are you really up to?" she whispered after they'd gotten outside. Other crafters were making their way up the path from the main house to the carriage house, where Jane's studio was located.

"Don't know why you think I'm up to something," Cora said.

"I know you," Jane said.

"I just feel like there's a connection we are missing. If we can find it, we can help Paul and maybe, just maybe, Gracie."

"The police are working on this, Cora. Leave it be."

"If I talk to Paul a bit more, I can get a better feel for things. And then maybe do a little research. It can only help the police, right? I mean, even Detective Brodsky said I was helpful with the murder case before."

Jane wished he'd never told Cora that. She had repeated it several times over the past few months. With her unstoppable need to help people, his compliment only added fuel to the fire.

"You lucked out with that. You lucked out that you weren't killed yourself," Jane snapped. "Cora, listen to me, don't get any more involved than you already are."

Cora bit her lip, a tic Jane recognized, which meant Cora was thinking—or trying to make a decision. "I'd better go. Good luck with your class."

And with that she turned to go, greeting other crafters as she left, while turning her back on Jane. She had so much to do—and so much to think about. But first, that blog post.

Cora was pleased at herself for updating her blog more regularly at this retreat than the last. During the first retreat, she was overwhelmed by everything— and Jane was right that she had been sidetracked by getting involved in an incident that was not technically her business. But it had all turned out well. As Paul's situation would, she told herself. Gracie would turn up any day. Perhaps she was off with her professor. And as Paul said, at least that meant she wasn't really missing or dead. Of course, if that was the case, his heart would be broken in a completely different way.

Why hadn't they heard more about the professor? Shouldn't they know something by now? Maybe Paul did. But he was resting in his room and she didn't want to disturb him. Who else could she ask? Detective Brodsky? He'd given her his cell phone number and told her to call anytime, hadn't he? Cora grabbed her cell phone and pressed the detective's number in her address book.

"Brodsky here."

"Hello, Detective Brodsky, this is Cora Chevalier."

"Everything okay, Cora?"

"Yes, but I was wondering if you could answer a question for me."

"Maybe," his said with a touch of caution in his voice.

"I wondered if you found out anything about the professor?"

He sighed an impatient, frustrated sigh. "You'd think this would be easy, right? But we don't know where he is yet. His wife seems to know nothing. She said he often just goes off on his own. I can't imagine my wife would put up with that."

"Why is it so difficult for her to know where he is? He must be using credit cards, cell phone data. Why hasn't anything turned up yet?"

"I have no idea, but I can't really talk too much about it," he said. "It's an ongoing investigation."

"Okay, but are you still looking for Gracie in Indigo Gap, too?"

"Absolutely. We really have no reason to stop. We just have one woman's word that she thought her husband left with Gracie. One woman. Okay, she fits the physical description for Gracie. But we just don't know yet. Why are you so concerned about this?"

"Well, Paul is still staying with me until his parents get into town," she said. "I have to admit. I'm a little nervous. I have a craft retreat going on here."

"He's still staying there, is he? Hmmm," the detective said. "But you offered him a place to stay."

"And now he's a person of interest," Cora said.

"Ah, well, you know, it's standard procedure to question acquaintances and friends."

"But should I be worried?" she persisted. Cashel told his mother that it was a strong possibility that Paul would be called back in. She could not tell the detective that she knew that, though, because it would be breaking a confidence. "How likely is it that Paul is a killer?"

He didn't answer right away. "You know, I can't really tell you that. But caution is in order, in any case. You have a stranger staying in your house." He paused. "Henry's death was bizarre."

"That's another thing. He was found at an amusement park?"

"Yes, the old Oz World. Right on the Yellow Brick Road," he said. "Hold on."

"Okay," Cora said, and could hear muffled voices over the phone.

"Cora, look, I have to go. Be careful," he said. "I appreciate you keeping him there. But even if he's not the murderer, at the least he's a young man who is deeply troubled now, with the loss of Gracie and his best friend. You know what I'm saying."

"Yes, I think I do," she said. Besides, someone could still be after him, she thought. Wasn't anybody concerned about that but her?

"I'll see you later," he said.

She heard him, but her mind was circling around the words *Yellow Brick Road*. Where was this place? What was Henry doing there? And did this have anything to do with this game they were talking about the first night they met?

Cora knew she should really check on the crafters and go to the pottery class to take some photos, but what she wanted to do was search around on the Internet for this theme park. It would only take a few minutes, she told herself.

She keyed the words "Oz World Theme Park" into a search engine. Soon she was reading a brief history of the now-defunct park Oz World, which was on Indigo Mountain, not too far from Indigo Gap, still far away enough that Henry had to want to be there— if he had gone there willingly, it was something he would have had to plan; it wasn't as if he would have just stumbled on it.

She clicked on the images—the Yellow Brick Road, the Enchanted/Haunted Forest, dilapidated structures, sad-looking cement munchkins, which all took on an ominous tone when she considered that Henry had been killed there. And that they had been talking about a *Wizard of Oz* computer game.

She glanced at the clock. She absolutely had to go now, or she would not be able to get any shots of Jane's class. She grabbed her camera and phone, and took off for the carriage house.

When she walked into the light-filled studio, her heart lifted. The retreaters had fashioned lovely clay charms. The pieces would not be ready until Sunday morning, but Cora envisioned the end products. The crafters had used plants and flowers gathered from their morning walk to make impressions on the small blocks of clay.

By this point in the class, the pieces were lined up neatly, glazed, and ready to go into the kiln. Some of the women had created round pendants from the clay, while others went with square or oblong, with beautiful floral and leaf imprints in each one of them.

She snapped a shot of Jane as she helped Maddy make an impression with a tiny flower.

Jane peered at Cora and forced a smile.

Uh-oh. Jane was still not happy with Cora. She took a deep breath as she walked toward her.

"It looks like it's gone well," Cora said, trying to keep the subject on the pottery.

Jane nodded. "Yes. What have you been up to?"

"I wrote my blog post."

"And?"

"I called Detective Brodsky."

Jane's mouth twisted. "Why?"

"I was just concerned about Paul staying here now and wanted some assurance."

"All right then. What did he say?"

"Just that it's, you know, standard procedure for the police to talk with him and all Henry's friends, but that we should be careful. Paul is distraught, of course," Cora replied.

"Is that it, then?" Jane said.

Cora nodded. There was no reason to tell her about her research into the abandoned theme park. It really led her nowhere. She felt foolish that she had wasted the time. She also felt helpless—and for Cora, that was one of the worst feelings in the world.

Chapter 21

When Cora entered Kildare House, it was through the back screened porch that led into the kitchen. Sheila and her daughter were at the kitchen table drinking steaming herbal tea and welcomed her with warm smiles. "I love what you've done here," Sheila said. "Beatrice was right. This is a special place."

Cora smiled when she thought of her great-aunt Beatrice and the way she took over her kitchen during the first retreat.

"Thank you," Cora said.

"I've thought about organizing a scrapbooking o paper-craft retreat and I just can't seem to wrap m mind around the details of all that," Sheila said.

"I think I can help you with that, Mom. If not me Desmond certainly could," Donna said.

"Desmond?" Cora asked.

"Her boyfriend," Sheila said. "He's just finishing u his degree at Carnegie Mellon University."

"Computer programming," Donna said. "He want to design computer games. In fact, he's already de signed and sold a few. He's had some job offers, but think he's more suited to freelancing. I'm sure he could help us out a bit, Mom."

Gaming? Cora had never heard so much chatter about gaming in one weekend.

"You seem troubled," Donna said.

"Oh," Cora said, and waved her hand. "You know the man who was killed? Henry? He was a gamer of some kind. It's all Greek to me." She pulled up a chair and sat down. "I've never really played a computer game and think I'll survive without ever doing so. But I'm intrigued because its seems like it's popular, and creative sorts might be able to get jobs there."

"Yes," Donna said. "It takes both sides of your brain—technical and creative, but there are a lot of poets, for example, who are also good with code. It's a perfect job for them."

"Oh, that's interesting," Cora said. "Henry was a poet."

"How well did you know him?" Sheila said.

"I only met him once. When Gracie turned up missing, he and Paul stopped by Jane's place and I happened to be there. And the next day . . . he went missing," she said.

"Why did they come to Jane's?" Sheila asked.

"Well, Gracie babysat for London, Jane's daughter, and was with her the day before she disappeared. They were tracing her footsteps, as it were," Cora said. "Trying to figure out what happened."

"Weren't the police searching for her?" Donna asked.

"Yes, of course," Cora said. "But some people feel like that . . . they have to do something. They can't just sit and wait." It dawned on her that she might as well have been describing herself.

"Yes, but it seems like they'd have been better off helping the police search," Sheila said, and then sipped her tea.

"I'm not certain the police welcomed their help," Cora said after a moment. "In fact, they offered the police some information and were ignored."

"What? That doesn't seem right," Donna said, setting her cup down loudly on the table.

"Wait a minute," Sheila said. "Why wouldn't the police want every bit of information they could get their hands on?"

Cora didn't know. The more she thought about it, the stranger it seemed.

"The only thing that makes any sense is that they already had the same information," Donna said.

"Or they thought that Paul and Henry were up to no good," Sheila said after a minute or two. "What was the information? Can you tell us?"

Cora shrugged. "To tell you the truth, I don't remember much that was said that night. Just that Paul, Gracie, and Henry were involved in a computer game that had something to do with *The Wizard of Oz*. And Gracie had gotten high up in the game and started getting threatening and weird messages."

"Well, no wonder the police didn't want to hear that," Sheila said. "They were worried about a computer game?"

But alarm came over Donna's face. "What exactly did they mean?"

"I have no idea, but the police didn't even want to discuss it," Cora replied. "Do you have some idea?"

"No," Donna said, "not without talking with Paul. But the gaming community can be 'interesting.'" She placed finger quotes around the word *interesting*. "It's full of brilliant, creative people, but there's an element that is just kind of creepy. You know, it just sort of attracts all types, and for some reason a lot of troubled types are attracted to gaming."

That didn't surprise Cora. Who would want to sit behind a computer all day and play or design games? Violent and sexist games, to boot. What kind of people want to "play" at that?

"But I've met some wonderful people who are into it," Sheila said.

"Oh, I know. I agree. But believe me, there are some real freaks involved," Donna said.

"So, could a gamer get, I don't know, enamored with one of the players and stalk them?" Cora asked.

"I don't know. That seems far-fetched, I have to say. A game is sold to a company who sells it to a consumer," Donna said, then took a sip of tea. "I'm not sure how a gamer would keep track of the buyers. It seems like they wouldn't even want to. I don't know. It's certainly possible."

"But your boyfriend, for example, is a freelancer."

"Yeah, I think there are some out there. But he sells to companies, not to people. You see what I'm saying?"

"Yes," Cora said. "I suppose it is far-fetched. Yet, both men were deeply troubled by it."

"Ask him why," Sheila said. "Could be a straightforward answer. I mean, I know he's having a hard time now, but it might do some good to talk with him."

That's my line, Cora wanted to say. Instead, she

willed away the chill she felt creeping up her spine as she admitted to herself that maybe she really didn't want to talk with him.

"But you want to know the weirdest thing?" Cora said. "Henry's body was found in a local abandoned theme park, the Oz World."

"Now that's not just odd, that's creepy," Donna said.

Chapter 22

A group of women were gathered in the paper-craft room and laughing. Cora walked by and waved in their direction. She was heading to the attic to download her photos onto the computer for the next blog post. She wasn't certain she'd be up for it this evening, but tomorrow was another day. Two crafters had broken off from the group and were knitting in the sitting room. The knitters always seemed to find each other.

As she walked by the living room, Cora was surprised to find Paul sitting on the couch with his laptop on his lap and Liv next to him looking over his shoulder.

"That is awesome," Liv exclaimed.

"You see, if you move the lion, this is what happens. But I can't get beyond this point," he said with a frustrated tone.

Oh, they were playing a game. Cora continued to walk toward the stairs. She was exhausted and desperately wanted to take off her shoes, lie down, and curl up with Luna.

"And you think that both Henry and Gracie got beyond this point?" Liv said.

Cora stopped moving.

"Yeah, I know they did. I think Gracie is one of the few who has made it to the Gates of the Emerald City. One of the few in the country," he said.

"So you say when she got to that point she started receiving weird text messages, not just the usual notifications from the game?" Liv said.

"Yeah," he said.

Cora walked toward them and sat on the edge of a chair. Was she invading their privacy? She couldn't think this was a private moment—after all, they were in the most public space in the house.

"The messages were from the actual game? That's wild."

"Well, we all get them, and it's a part of the game. Some of them are kind of threatening, but it's a part of the game. But hers were personal."

"What do you mean?" Liv questioned.

"Talking about personal things," he mumbled. "Like parts of her body."

"Woah!" Cora said. "That's no game."

Their attention was now on Cora.

"Oh, some of these games are completely sexist and masochistic." Liv waved her hand.

"Why would anybody want to play them?" Cora asked. "Especially women?"

"Well, Gracie started playing this game because of the gorgeous graphics. Henry and I were playing and she liked to watch. Finally, she started to play. I don't think the game was sexist at all," he said, looking at Liv. "Not until she reached the Gates of the Emerald City."

"Could another player have gotten ahold of her phone number?" Cora asked.

"I suppose that's possible," he said. "You know there have been credit card scams and theft associated with some of these online games, but this is supposed to be highly protected. And it's on the Darknet, which makes it even harder for most people to get to."

"Darknet?" Cora asked, not liking the sound of that at all.

"It's a place on the Web that ordinary users can't get to. You have to have a certain app to get there. It's like the underground Internet," he said. "All completely anonymous."

She felt the hair on the back of her neck stand up as a tingle traveled the length of her spine. "What is the point of it?" It sounded to Cora like this could be a breeding ground for all sorts of criminal sorts. Or was she just being paranoid? Sometimes she thought her years as a counselor in a women's shelter had permanently scarred her—formed her into a paranoid freak, never to trust anybody or any situation completely. But pings of intuition were zooming though her at this moment.

He shrugged. "I don't know. All I know is it's supposed to be completely anonymous. People who don't want to be tracked use it. So the gamers on the Darknet are serious gamers. Some of them seem to be, I don't know, completely in character all the time."

Liv laughed. "Like method actors."

Cora never heard of any of this and she considered herself pretty tech savvy.

Paul went back to clicking around on the game. Cora was pleased to see he was busying himself with something other than moping around over Gracie. But at the same time, she found it a bit puzzling. Why wasn't he helping to search for Gracie? Why wasn't he half-crazed with worry? Or was the medication making him mellow?

Liv rose from the couch. "Well, I can only look at the screen for so long. I'm going for a walk. Anybody care to join me?"

Paul, still engrossed in his game, waved her off. She shrugged, then walked away.

Cora sat and mulled over everything she'd just learned. The Darknet. The gaming community. And Gracie being one of the top players in the country on *The Wizard of Oz* game. Had Gracie been abducted, or did she indeed run off with her college professor? And how did Henry and his death play into this, if at all? Was the fact that he was found on the Yellow Brick Road of the abandoned theme park a strange coincidence? Or did it have some meaning?

The thoughts tumbled through her brain and didn't connect at all. She sighed. "I'm going upstairs for a bit if anybody needs me," she said, but she was uncertain if Paul heard her at all. She didn't even have the fortitude to repeat herself. She needed a late-afternoon nap. And that's all there was to it.

Chapter 23

Cora breathed in the lavender-scented sheets and stroked Luna, who purred loudly next to her. She thought of her mother, who had insisted on lavender in the bedroom and on the sheets. It had just become such a part of Cora's daily ritual. A touchstone to her past. Before her mother and father died, her grandparents bore no love of lavender, but when they found out Cora did, they made certain to have plenty of it around.

She took deep belly breaths in and out. She hoped to sleep for a good ten or fifteen minutes before dinner.

Images played in her mind. The Yellow Brick Road. Flying monkeys. Talking trees. Paul. Gracie. Henry. What did all of it mean? She willed those images and questions away and focused on the sweeping hills and stunning wildflowers of North Carolina. Some of which had been pressed into earthy clay charms.

She awakened abruptly to the sound of her cell phone. Dang, she had forgotten to shut the ringer off.

It was Cashel, Ruby's son, and one of the few lawyers in town.

"Hello," she said into the cell phone.

"Did I wake you?"

"As a matter of fact—"

"Cora, is my client still staying there? I can't reach him."

"Client? Who? What?" Her brain was foggy and she just wanted to go back to sleep.

"Paul," Cashel said.

"Yes, he's here. The last I saw him he was on the couch playing a computer game," she said.

"Why is he not answering his cell phone?"

"Um, I don't know," she said, flinging the blankets off and trying to sit up. "Maybe his phone is dead."

"Do you mind checking on him? I need to speak with him."

"Is it important?" she said.

"It is," Cashel said. "It looks like they found Gracie. They are pretty sure she's in a cabin, way off the grid, with a Dr. Rawlings, a professor."

Cora's heart sank. Poor Paul.

"They think?"

"She fits the description, so even though there's been no positive identification, we're pretty certain. I'm not aware of what they are waiting for. But they have to be certain before announcing it—privacy issues and then there's the slight possibility of false hope."

"Wow," she said after a few beats. "Well, if it's her, at least we'll know she's still alive."

"Yes, but the audacity," Cashel said. "So many resources were used to search for her. Everything from dragging the river to using highly trained and expensive search dogs. She's got a lot to answer for."

"Well, she's a grown woman. I don't think she needed approval to run off with her lover," Cora said. "Looks like someone may have jumped the gun."

Would that someone be Paul?

"It's a good thing it wasn't Paul," he said, as if he were reading her mind. "I'd kick his ass myself. As it is, there's Henry murder."

"You don't think—"

"Absolutely not. And if I did—"

"You couldn't tell me," she said. "I know. I've heard your spiel before. Ho hum."

"Please tell Paul to call me," he said with a clipped tone. Cora grinned. She loved goading him. He was so easy.

The line went dead.

Cora took one look at herself in the mirror and decided on a quick shower and a change of clothes. She was still feeling tired—usually a nap perked her right up. But this retreat was taking it out of her, along with the stress of the incidents with Gracie and Henry. She had just met him and the very next day he was killed. You just never knew when something dreadful was going to happen.

After her shower, she dressed in a 1970s deep purple velvet maxi skirt and a white poplin blouse. She loved mixing the vintage styles. She ran a brush through her red curls, smeared some pink lipstick on, and she was ready for Friday night dinner.

But for now she was off to find Paul to tell him to call Cashel. Whew, she was glad she wasn't the bearer of that news. Good thing his parents were coming to collect him tomorrow. He was going to need some support. Poor Gracie—it sounded like this Gerald Rawlings was quite a player and he was a mistake for Gracie. Cora knew that because she'd made a few in her day, as had Jane. Both of them vowed to think their way into their next relationships. So far, it was working with Adrian, but then again, he hadn't been around much because of his mother's health.

As Cora walked down the stairs, she heard chanting from the living room.

Chanting? What?

When she finally entered the room, she saw that most of her retreaters were sitting in a circle around another circle. Within the center circle were Ruby, Liv, Paul, Sheila, and Marianne. A photo of Gracie was on the table in the center, along with a necklace catching glints of light. All this was placed on a bed of herbs and twigs.

> *Turning, turning, turn around*
> *Gracie's lost and must be found.*
> *Turning, turning, turn around*
> *under sky or in the ground.*
> *Turning, turning, turnabout*
> *find her, find her, search it out!*

Nobody noticed that Cora had entered the room. They were intent. The room smelled of burning candles and sage.

What were they doing? It sounded like a charm or a spell to find Gracie. There she stood, knowing Gracie had been found—but she was not to tell anybody what she knew. She found the scene before her odd, but also strangely comforting. All her crafters who were here to retreat from their usual routines, give themselves time and space, had come together to say a prayer, or make magic, for Paul's girlfriend.

Cora knew this kind of "spell" didn't work. But she also knew it could serve to provide comfort. Which it appeared to be doing. Her crafters had bonded over this. And where had she been? Sleeping.

She hated to interrupt. Paul now looked relaxed, hopeful, and calm. She knew the news that Cashel would deliver would send him into another kind of tailspin. Before she cleared her throat, she stood for a few more beats, letting Paul steep in his momentary bliss.

Chapter 24

"I don't believe it," Paul said to Cora and Jane later that night. "I refuse to believe that my Gracie ran off with that creep. I'm sorry. You have no idea what that man put her through. I mean, it was bad."

Jane and Cora were sitting with him around the kitchen table, the other crafters having mostly gone off to bed. Cora had just told him that the woman with Gerald Rawlings in the mountains probably was Gracie, though there had been no positive identification.

"Paul," Cora said after a few minutes, "sometimes it's hard to see the people we love clearly. Believe me, I know."

Jane grunted. "We both do. We've both been through some stuff with men. Why do you think we're single?"

He quieted and shook his head. "It makes no sense. Gracie said she would never go back to him. It was a very brief fling. We broke up for a while and it was intense. He tried to blackmail her for grades. I mean, when she wanted to end it with him, he told her he'd fail her."

"What?" Jane said. "I can't believe she'd put up with that!"

"Well, she didn't. That's what I mean. She went to the dean," he said. "Almost got the man fired. He was placed on probation, even though he has tenure. It was bad. Evidently, there had been several others. Gracie was livid." His jaw was firm with incredulity. "And she was scared and hurt, but here's the thing, she didn't back away. She went to the dean," he said with emphasis.

"How about a drink?" Cora said to them after a few seconds of silence. "I have this new mead I've been dying to try. Someone who Ruby knows makes it."

"I'd love to try it," Jane said, perking up a bit.

"No," Paul said. "I think I'm going to bed. My parents will probably be here early in the morning. I'm going to take a sleeping pill and get some sleep. Pills are the only way I can even think about sleeping. Sometimes even they don't work."

After he left, Cora poured Jane and her each a glass of mead.

"He's right," Jane said. "What I know of Gracie, well, it doesn't add up."

"I agree that something is off," Cora said.

"But it's really none of our business, right?" Jane said, and sipped her mead. "Mmmm, this is good. I mean, tomorrow he's out of here. Then, he and the whole sordid business are out of our lives."

Cora took a deep breath and bit her lip.

"And we don't know if that whole professor thing is

even true," Jane went on. "You know, I don't know who to believe anymore. People can make up stories about anything or anyone. I mean, he is a writer, could be he's exaggerating."

"Have you ever read any of Paul's writing?" Cora asked.

"No," Jane said. "You?"

Cora shook her head and drank some mead. A sweet, floral flavor played on her tongue. "Wouldn't you think there'd be something in the news about the incident at the college?"

"Maybe. Depends on how successful the school was at keeping it a secret," Jane replied. "But it's not our concern," she said with a bit of force. "He's leaving tomorrow. The end. Right?"

Cora wasn't so sure. Too many things didn't add up. Why shouldn't she look around on the Web later tonight? She nodded but didn't look directly at Jane. She knew that Jane considered Cora's "disease to please" a problem. And it could be. But not this time. What harm could it do to look a few things up tonight?

"We'll be finishing up that basket class tomorrow, then the pottery charm class. I think one more glazing for most of them. Some of them did lovely pieces. Liv is very talented. I'm looking forward to Ruby's crafting with herbs class later in the day," Jane said.

Cora sipped her mead. It was delicious, but she was already beginning to feel its effect. Sweet drinks went to her head a lot faster.

Her cell phone went off. It was Adrian.

"Hello," she said.

"Hey, Cora, just wanted to let you know I'm home." His voice sounded as smooth and honeyed as the mead.

"Welcome home," she said. "How's your mom?"

"She's doing much better. Thanks for asking. Is it still okay if I come by Sunday night?"

"As far as I know it should be fine."

"I've been thinking about you a lot," he said, and breathed heavy into the phone. "I know we only had the one date, but I felt a connection and I'm hoping for more."

How sweet. Cora caught Jane's eye. She was listening, unabashedly.

"I feel the same way," Cora said.

After Cora and Adrian had hung up, Jane sat there with her chin in her hands. "I want the scoop."

Cora was smiling so hard her cheeks were beginning to ache. "I really like him." But even as she said that, she felt a tendril of fear moving through her. Yes, she liked him, but she reminded herself to be careful.

Chapter 25

Jane made her way home down the path through the garden. She stood a moment and gazed at her pretty little carriage house and studio. It was all coming together: her house and studio, her life with her daughter. It was going to be okay. She wasn't certain an exhale was in order yet, since Neil was back in the picture, out of jail, and wanting to see London.

The moon was full and so bright it lit the path ahead of her. This would be their first spring in Indigo Gap. But a year ago they first laid eyes on the place—and Cora fell in love with it. Jane admired Cora for her talent in repurposing houses, objects, and even lives. Cora saw the diamond in the rough in this dilapidated old place. Jane was beginning to love it here. She was so afraid that Cora would bring them trouble with all her poking and prodding. She just couldn't leave well enough alone.

When she opened the door to the house, a scream reverberated through her whole body. London! She flew upstairs to find the babysitter holding her daughter and trying to comfort her. "Shhh, baby, it's fine," she was saying to her.

"What's going on?" Jane demanded.

"Mama!" London held her arms out to her and Cora made her way to the bed.

"What's wrong? Sweetie, calm down," she said, as the child plastered herself to her, trembling.

"She was asleep," Louise said. "I think she had a bad dream." She looked uncomfortable, like she didn't know quite what to do with herself, perched on the edge of the bed.

"Don't let him take me!" London said.

"Shh, baby, nobody's going to take you. I'm here," Jane said, willing back tears and the roaring ache inside her chest. All this talk of Gracie missing had frightened London.

"The bad man is going to take me!" she said.

"Baby"—Jane peeled her daughter from her body and looked her in the eye—"ain't nobody going to take you. Your mama is here—your sitter is here. We are here. You just had a dream."

"But someone took Gracie!" she said between sobs. "And she's a big girl!"

"Oh, honey," Louise said.

The three of them sat in silence for a few moments. Jane reached for a tissue for London. She would need one herself soon, once her daughter was safely tucked in bed again. She planned on a good cry. The world was a scary place, which she tried not to think about. She tried to cast it aside, even though she had been in the belly of it at one time in her life. She didn't want to bring that fear into her daughter's life. She didn't want fear to control her or London. There was a huge part of her that wanted to tuck London safely away from the world and its dangers. But at the same time, she knew she couldn't shield her child forever. And she had vowed not to lie to her, to help her daughter become an emotionally stable person by offering her honesty, even about the dangers in her life.

But this was hard. It was the hard road. It was the road of ogres and monsters and fighting them head-on. She preferred to dwell in the world of fairies and princesses. But that never lasted long.

Later, after London was tucked in, and Louise gone, Jane surprised herself by not pouring a glass of wine and having a good cry. Instead, she turned on her computer. She was going some check up on some of the people she allowed into her daughter's life. How had Gracie fooled them all? She was working for one of the best families in town. Everybody she worked for offered nothing but good things to say about her. Yet, she had apparently been involved in some questionable things.

Wait a minute, she told herself, why are you doing this? Hadn't you just told Cora this was no longer our business?

Yes, but now she saw how this was affecting her daughter. Now, she simply had to know more about this young woman. If for no other reason than to explain things to London.

She keyed in "Gracie Wyke" on her laptop. The search engine brought up a list of links. Jane took a deep breath. It was going to be a long night.

Chapter 26

"I can't find anything bad about Gracie Wyke," Jane said.

"What?" Cora managed to say, glancing at the clock. Was it really 1:35 AM?

"Gracie Wyke appears to have lived the perfect life, except for the professor thing," Jane said.

They had always called each other any time of the day or night, but late-night calls had gotten to be a thing of the past since they had moved to North Carolina and were close "neighbors," essentially living on the same property.

"I couldn't sleep," Jane said. She sounded bright and chipper, which Cora found irritating. "London had this nightmare about a man stealing her. I started thinking about how this is affecting her, and probably a lot of the kids that Gracie sat for."

"And then there's Henry . . ." Cora interrupted. Luna lifted her head from her spot on the bed toward Cora, with an air of confusion.

"Yeah," Jane said. "I'm not so certain one thing doesn't have to do with the other."

"The police are certain," Cora said.

"I need to find out," Jane said after a minute.

"What? Find out what?"

"I really need to know what's going on here. I feel, I don't know, personally invested here because of London and her relationship with Gracie," Jane said. "I need to know what is going on."

Cora noted an edge of panic in Jane's voice.

"Look, all things will be revealed soon. I'm sure," Cora said. Usually it was the other way around, with Jane talking her out of pursuing one thing or the other. "I think it's sweet that Paul has so much faith in Gracie. Don't you? I mean, it's endearing."

"Or stupid," Jane said.

"Oh, the man is not stupid," Cora said. "I've read some of his writing. While you were digging up info on Gracie, I was reading some of the most beautiful writing I've ever read. Paul is a brilliant writer. He's won all kinds of awards—so I'm not the only one who thinks so."

"Yes, but writers are fragile sorts," Jane said.

"I'm not sure about that. I mean, yes, he does seems rather sensitive. But I don't think he'd blindly believe in Gracie if there wasn't good reason, even if he is madly in love. After reading his writing . . . I just don't know what the hell is going on here. But I'm with you. We need to find out."

"What should we do?"

Cora thought a moment, yawning. "The first thing we need to do is get a good night's sleep."

That may have been a steep order. Cora tossed and turned the rest of the night. Sleeping fitfully was worse than not sleeping at all. Finally, at 5:30 AM she gave up and decided to get her day started. Coffee. Cuddles with Luna. And writing a blog post.

She curled up in her window seat, holding a big cup of hot coffee, and gazed out over the town of Indigo Gap and the surrounding mountains. It was almost as if the town were scooped out of the mountainside. Luna curled up on her lap, kneading her flesh and circling around before settling down. The conversation with Jane played in her mind. London must be deeply disturbed by Gracie's disappearance to have had a nightmare about it. And then Jane in turn was upset enough to start doing research online.

Cora herself was careful about what she shared about herself online. A resourceful person could create a whole false identity online. It was easy enough to do.

It wasn't as though Cora lied about herself. A part of her was exactly the person she portrayed online. Aware. Upbeat. Crafty. Caring. Vintage. But, she mused, nobody would want to read about the depth of the darkness in her previous life. Which led her to the anxiety attacks and ultimately to her early retirement from the Sunny Street Women's Shelter. No. People didn't really want to know about that—and why should she tell them? She wanted an upbeat, positive personality—at least online.

She drank from her coffee and wondered what truth Gracie could be hiding from people online—if any at all. But everybody had secrets, private matters. For example, this professor whom she had an affair with.

Love made people do all kinds of crazy things. Twisted love. Obsessive. But it was still love, wasn't it?

Cora wished she knew.

"It was definitely a murder." Cora heard Detective Brodsky's voice in her head.

She felt a chill, but assured herself it was nothing more than the dilapidated old window allowing the spring air in. Outside, the rising sun shone crimson on the horizon.

Chapter 27

Cora and Jane took advantage of the morning lull, during which some of the crafters were still sleeping and others met with Sheila and Ruby pressing flowers. Brunch was planned for 10:30. They had plenty of time before then.

Jane called Chelsea and they planned to meet at the coffee shop. After she and Cora had put their heads together in the early-morning hours, they'd decided she'd be a good place to start to find out more about Gracie, which might lead to so much more.

Chelsea was dressed in a pretty blue shirtdress with a splash of light blue eye shadow on her lined eyes. She smiled a pretty, perfectly white, toothed smile. Cora hated her immediately.

Get a grip, she told herself. You don't know this woman at all.

"Hello, Chelsea, this is my friend Cora," Jane said.

"Nice to meet you," she said with a soft, lilting Carolina accent.

Cora nodded. The waitress appeared and turned

the coffee cups, already placed on the table, over and filled them with coffee.

"What can I do for you, ladies? You said something about Gracie. Jillie is so upset. I'm upset. Hell, we're all upset," Chelsea said.

Cora relaxed. She liked her a wee bit more.

"It's just that we've been trying to make sense of this. As I told you, London had a horrible dream last night. It's hard to be honest with our kids when we don't know what's really going on."

"You're telling me," she said, and took a pink pack of artificial sweetener out of her bag. She opened it and poured the whole thing in her coffee. "I am really at a loss. She's worked for me for two years. Jillie thinks of her as a second mother. I've had my hands full, I can tell you." She stirred in the powder. "Her parents are in town and have been all over the TV. Have you seen them?"

Neither Jane nor Cora owned a television. Jane streamed TV shows for London over the computer.

"Did Gracie ever talk about Paul?" Cora asked.

"Talk about? Yes, he spent a lot of time at my place. They were sweet together. He must be devastated."

"He is," Cora said.

Chelsea sat up a bit and puckered her mouth. "Something fishy is going on."

"What do you mean?" Jane said.

"I mean, I remember the incident with that professor. I offered her legal advice at the time. She was torn up about the whole thing, of course, but I never thought she'd go back with him. In fact, I find it shocking," she said.

Cora's stomach began to churn. Was it the coffee on an empty stomach—or was it what Chelsea said?

"Young women do stupid thing sometimes," Jane offered. "Especially when it comes to romance."

"She's not that much younger than you," Chelsea pointed out. "And she's very bright. Dependable. Seemed to have her head on straight. I'm a good judge of character. I don't get it. It makes no sense."

"Well, we are all agreed, then," Cora said. "That something is off."

"What about Paul?" Jane asked. "She seemed to be annoyed with him from time to time."

Chelsea nodded. "I often wondered about that. He seemed obsessed with her."

"Maybe he was just madly in love," Cora said, with hope in her voice.

"That's what I always came back to."

"But what about Henry?" Jane asked. "Did you know him well?"

"Not really," she said. "Shame about him, and the timing is weird, right?"

She was justifying all their feelings about everything. But now what to do about it?

"What if the woman in the cabin is not our Gracie?" Jane said after a moment. "Cashel said she fit the description. But did he ever say it was her? Positively?"

Cora thought a moment. "No," she said. "He said there was not a positive identification."

"You're right," Chelsea said, checking something on her smartphone. "No positive ID yet. The local cops probably know positively, but they are out in the middle of nowhere. There's probably no Wi-Fi or maybe even cell phone service. It's probably just a matter of time."

"I'm betting it's not her," Jane said. "I just have a very strong feeling about this."

"Okay, so let's assume it's not her and that Gracie is still missing," Cora said.

"This could be a matter of life and death," Jane said. "I mean, if the police think the woman in the cabin is Gracie and it's not really her and they stop searching for her. She could still be in danger."

"But Brodsky said they haven't stopped," Cora said.

"They might. Any minute," Chelsea said.

"I have a little girl who is torn up about this and not sleeping. I want answers. And I'm going to get them," Jane said.

A large group came into the diner, followed by a man alone, who walked by their table. His stench wafted by Cora, who wrinkled her nose and turned her head.

"Indigo Gap's finest," Chelsea said, and rolled her eyes. "If the man had a bath, it might kill him."

"I've seen him in here before," Jane said. "He wore sweatpants that day. I guess the camo is a step up?"

Cora didn't care what a person wore, usually, but he was filthy. Long, stringy hair fell down his back— the least he could do was pull it into a ponytail.

"I know his family. Very odd situation," Chelsea said with her voice lowered.

"He came to Kildare House," Cora said, just then recognizing him. "He was looking for work. Said he's starting a computer business."

"Best to avoid him, believe me," Chelsea said.

Poor man, Cora thought, wondering what his story was. But for now the image of the ruby slipper charm played in her mind, as she imagined it collecting the sun's light and reflecting in the water as Maddy pulled it out of the river.

Cora dialed Brodsky. "I can't talk," he said. "I've got to go. There was a break in Henry's murder case. A meeting this morning."

Cora gasped. "Please let me know."

"Will do," he said with a kind of glee in his voice, which was not like him. *Nothing like a potentially solved murder case to put a song in your voice.*

Chapter 28

Cora and Jane agreed that they needed to speak with a few more people about Gracie—and maybe Henry. They were going to come up with a list over brunch. In the meantime, they each would also do research online.

The two of them walked up the stone sidewalk to Kildare House and up the stairs to the wraparound porch. The porch was one of the many things Cora loved about this old house—she loved the way it seemed to smile at people as they walked along the sidewalk. The day she moved in, she spruced up the front porch immediately with potted plants and wicker furniture. Jane had insisted on painting the door red. She also loved the many window seats the house held and certain creaks and moans of the house depending on where you stood and walked. She loved it. She was beginning to know this place intimately. As if it was home.

She turned toward the town before opening the door, gazing over the pretty little historical town, and out into the distance at the mountains. Mountains with caves, and rocky ledges, and all sorts of water holes. Places Gracie could be. She shuddered and willed away images of dread.

They opened the door to the scent of cinnamon, nutmeg, and coffee. Cora felt like swooning. She hadn't realized how hungry she was until now. She breathed in deeply and headed for the dining room table, which was full of brunch food: French toast, berries, croissants, marmalade, miniquiches, and fruit. She piled her plate high as she smiled at Liv, who was just coming to the table.

"Good morning," Liv said.

Cora nodded back. "Sleep well?" She didn't really want to make chitchat, as the food was calling to her, filling her senses.

"Yes. In fact, I don't think I've slept so well in such a long time," she said. "It's so relaxing here."

"I'm glad to know that," Cora said, as Ruby came up beside her.

"That's what we like to hear," Ruby said. "The class this morning went well."

Cora couldn't wait anymore. She took a bite of the French toast. Cinnamon and nutmeg flavors swirled in her mouth. She was in breakfast heaven.

"I'm sorry we missed it," Cora said. "I would have loved to make some herbal crafts this morning. Especially the wreath. Your wreaths are gorgeous."

Ruby beamed. "Thanks. And little London did a fantastic job. What a kid."

Cora nodded. "I'm going to sit down," Cora said. "Catch you both later." She simply had to sit in order to tuck into this French toast. She wanted the recipe—she made a mental note to ask the caterer about it.

The caterer was new to Cora, but everything was working out so well she might use the company again.

Cora walked into the kitchen, where Jane was already sitting with London. She sighed. She was hoping to renovate the kitchen soon, but she didn't think it would happen anytime this year. The kitchen was too small for her plans. She envisioned holding baking classes. The room was large enough, but the space wasn't convenient for even one baker, let alone ten or twelve.

London stood and ran to Cora, hugging her. "Hi there," Cora said. "I heard you made a wreath this morning with Ruby."

London held up the wreath to show her.

"Wow, how did you do that?" Cora asked. It was lovely—full of different shades of green and a variety of textures.

"You have to use long herbs," she said. "See, this is sage. This is rosemary." She ran her fingers over the wreath and its scent filled the room. Fresh herbs.

"I love it," Cora said.

"Me too," Jane said. "I'm going to hang it on the front door."

London grinned and then took a bite of a croissant.

Marianne entered the room. "I'm getting ready to start class. Just wanted to let you know."

"We'll be there soon. We've gotten a bit of a late start," Cora said.

Marianne shrugged. "Well, today is basically about

how to finish baskets. I'm sure you two can figure that out. Quite a gathering of women you've got here."

"Yes, it's going well," Jane said.

"I've met some talented basket makers. Liv is doing quite well," Marianne said. "You look at her and think . . ."

"I know," Cora said. "But she's very gifted."

Liv, with her tattoos and black-purple hair, didn't look like your usual crafter. But she was—and she was incredibly talented.

"Maybe it's just me. That Goth look is kind of scary. But she's the sweetest thing," Marianne said.

"You shouldn't judge people on how they look," London piped up.

Startled, Marianne laughed. "So true. I wouldn't like it if someone judged me on how I looked."

London's head tilted and she grinned.

"It smells so good in here," said Paul as he walked into the kitchen.

"You better get some food before it's all gone," Cora said. The catering staff was in and out, moving all around the place.

"There's plenty," one of the servers said as he passed by.

"Thanks," Paul said, and meandered off to the dining room, where there were stacks of muffins, bagels, rolls, and two huge pots of soup—vegetable and chicken noodle.

"Quite a nice young man," Marianne said after he left the room.

"I'm curious," Cora said. "Have you ever seen him before? I mean around campus?"

"No," she said. "I'm no longer at that school and I don't know why they insist on putting my name on their catalog."

"Probably an oversight," Jane said.

"Yes, but it's annoying," she said. "I do remember Henry, though."

"Really?" Cora's heart sped.

"Yes," she said. "He was a poetry fellow. A distinguished post. Then he turned to computer programming and gaming or some such thing. People were shocked. When I was leaving my post there, he was the talk of the school for giving up that prestigious fellowship to become a gamer."

Games. Again. Cora wanted to scream.

"I checked out the game they were playing," Jane said.

"What game?" Marianne said.

"Some kind of *Wizard of Oz* game," Jane said. "I don't know what the big deal is."

"I don't follow," Marianne said.

"All three of them were into this game. I tried to play it. It's like a kid's game."

"Wait," Cora said. "The game I saw was definitely *not* for kids. Are you sure it was the same game?"

"I don't know," Jane said. "I'll show it to you later."

"Well, I imagine if it was a game they were playing, and it was very sophisticated, it might have been on the Darknet," Marianne said. "It's all the rage with the young gamers."

"What?" Jane said.

Just then one of the crafters walked by with her basket-in-progress.

"Oh, I'm sorry, I have to get to this class. We'll talk later," Marianne said.

"Darknet, what is that? It sounds, I don't know, scary," Jane said.

"It is," Cora said grimly.

Chapter 29

Jane made her way back to the studio. Liv was already there, fussing over her clay charms.

"I think they're done," she said. "It's hard to know. I could play with the glaze forever." She smiled at Jane and Jane was reminded of how young Liv was. Her youth came through as she "played" with her charms. Jane was happy to see it. Some took themselves so seriously and sucked all the playful energy out of the process. She had been there, a "serious" young potter, had so much stress and pressure in her life that she hadn't noticed her then-husband's alcohol addiction. Until the arrival of London.

Some of Liv's charms were deep red. Jane always liked that color. The imprints of the flowers and leaves on the clay left delicate designs. Liv elected to not use the gathered natural materials for some of her charms. She etched swirls and circles on them.

"I really like these," Jane said.

Liv grinned. "I'm all about swirls these days."

"When are you graduating?"

"Next year," she said. "I need to make up my mind what to do next."

Just then London walked in with the iPad. "Is this the game you were talking about, Mommy?" She held up the iPad to Jane.

"Yes, that's *The Wizard of Oz* game I played the other night. Is it fun?" she asked.

London shrugged. "It's kind of easy. Gracie was smart. She wouldn't play this game."

"No, she wouldn't," Jane said with a sinking feeling in her stomach.

"This is not the game that she was playing," Liv piped up. "Paul and I played it yesterday. It was challenging . . . and gorgeous."

"Can I play it?" London asked.

"I don't think it's for kids your age," Jane said.

Liv nodded. "I'd say so."

She helped Jane as they scraped the clay charms from the pan and London plopped onto a couch with the iPad, intent on playing the game.

"Can you show me this game sometime before you go?" Jane asked Liv.

"Sure," she said. She was drilling a small hole into one of her charms. "Or Paul will show you. He's such a great guy, huh?"

Jane nodded. "From what I know of him."

Was the woman in the cabin Gracie? And why was it so hard for them to find out? Why were the police being so secretive about it? Was it, as Chelsea had suggested, just because the cabin was so far off the grid?

"What? What's going on?" Liv said. "There's something else going on, isn't there?"

"I'm not at liberty to say anything," Jane said, tilting her head in the direction of London.

Liv nodded.

Other students began to trickle in, as class was about to get started. Well, it wasn't actually a class. It was more like a "finish up your clay charm" session. Jane stood back and surveyed the table, full of charms, some still warm.

They were all different colors, different impressions, designs. A feeling of calm came over her when she examined them and her studio. She had done well this weekend. Her students had learned a lot and produced a lot. She'd hang on to this feeling of accomplishment. She'd try not to think about the news they were waiting on—and that Gracie's life was hanging in the balance.

Chapter 30

Cora was about to crack. She paced the length of her attic apartment. Was Gracie in a mountain cabin somewhere? Should she hope for that? This would break Paul's heart, but at least they'd know she was still alive. If she wasn't in there, where was she?

She sat down at her computer, mulled over what they knew, grabbed her notebook, and wrote:

Gracie missing.
Police search for her.
Paul and Henry visit Jane's place.
Henry missing/then murdered.

Cora tapped her pencil on the table. What could she do? Who could she talk to? The one person she hadn't talked with was Professor Harding's wife. Hmm.

She clicked on the computer and within minutes had her name and address. She lived only a few blocks from Kildare House. Good. She'd take a basket of muffins or cookies or whatever was left over from their brunches and introduce herself and poke around, just a bit. She imagined the woman was a mess, knowing her husband was in a cabin in the woods with a much younger woman, let alone a student. Or maybe he was back by now?

Maybe the woman knew something that would lead them to some answers about where Gracie was—was she really with her husband, or was she still missing, somewhere out in the wilds of the mountains? Or worse?

Should she butt into this situation?

No, probably not. She bit her lip. But it could take forever for them to come up with the answer, couldn't it? And if they went and talked with the police, going through proper channels, it might take too much time.

Cora searched around the room for her purse and grabbed it from the edge of the bed, which prompted Luna to look up at her, blink, and then lay her head back down.

Cora glanced at herself in the mirror, just to make certain she was decent-looking, and saw a button on her shirt was undone. She buttoned it and smoothed over her denim skirt, ran her fingers through her hair.

She opened the door and Paul was standing there, just about to knock on the door.

"Hi," she said.

"Hey, I was just about to knock," he said, and grinned. "They told me this is where you lived. Very cool."

"Thanks," she said. "How can I help you?"

"I was wondering if we could, um, maybe talk," he said.

She wanted to tell him that she was on her way out, but as she studied his kind eyes, she found that she couldn't.

"Sure," she said. "Please come in."

He walked into her apartment and scanned it. "This is cool."

"Thanks," she said. "I've made a lot of the stuff myself, or other people made it and gave it to me."

"I love that rug," he said, pointing to her pom-pom rug.

"That's new," she said. "One of the women I used to work with made it for me. Isn't it great? Please have a seat."

The rug was made up of purple, pink, and brown two-inch pom-poms. Her friend's grandmother had recently died and she inherited bins of yarn, and she decided to make pom-poms with it. Cora adored the rug, though she never walked over it.

Paul sat down on her sofa. It struck her then that he was probably the first guy who graced her place—other than the detective and Cashel. It was such a feminine place that most men seemed a little out of place.

Decorated in a sort of upscale Bohemian mode, the place made her feel creative and relaxed. She had just painted the old kitchen cabinets a light shade of pink. She planned to paint some of the trim black. She loved pink and black together, but she'd not gotten to it yet.

"Can I get you something to drink?" she asked.

"Nah, I'm good," he said, and dropped his arm onto one of the many pillows on her couch.

She sat down on the papasan chair next to the couch. The rattan creaked as she sunk into the floral pillow. "What can I do for you?"

"I'm just, ah, really, I don't know, kind of freaking out," he said. His hands went to his face and he took a deep breath. Was he going to cry?

"You've been through a lot. More than most people in a whole lifetime," Cora said. "It's okay to feel overwhelmed. Be gentle with yourself."

His hands fell on his lap. "I just don't know what to think. How to feel. I just can't believe that she's with that jerk."

Cora bit her lip.

"I refuse to believe it. She loves me. I know it."

They sat in silence a few minutes. Cora reached out and touched his hand. She had no answers for him.

"Okay. Let's say she does love you, not him," Cora said. "Is there another reason she'd be off with him. I'm just saying, let's play devil's advocate here. But with logic."

"What do you mean?" he said, his head tilted.

"Logically speaking, we know she loves you, right?"

He nodded.

"But all the evidence says she's off with him."

"Right," he said.

"What would she be doing there?"

He appeared to think a moment. "Do you mean, maybe, she's there against her will?"

"Maybe," Cora said. "Maybe that's it."

He nodded. "I hadn't thought of that."

"It's hard to think in such an emotional situation," Cora said. "But we just need a little time. We'll find out the answers soon."

Oh, she wanted to tell him how strongly she felt that the woman in the cabin might not be Gracie. But she promised to keep her mouth shut. Besides, nobody knew anything for sure. It would be cruel to give him any kind hope at this point.

"That must be it," he said. "She must be there against her will. It's the only thing that makes sense. It's all going to turn out okay, isn't it? As soon as she's back, we'll get to the bottom of this. Everything is going to be okay."

Oh no, she had just given him another kind of hope. "Wait," she said. "It's good to have hope, but we need to be realistic, right, Paul? I know this not knowing business is the worst. It's hard to temper reality with hope. You're in a bad spot. Let's concentrate on being hopeful, but grounded in the reality of, of . . . we just don't know. Do you know what I mean?"

"I think so," he said. He sat with his face uplifted, looking a little like a puppy with those big brown eyes circled in tones of brown and gray—and so innocent and hopeful. Or was it cluelessness?

The two of them sat quietly for a few moments.

"My parents will be here today," he blurted. "That's another ball of wax." He rolled his eyes.

Chapter 31

After Paul left her apartment, Cora freshened up and headed downstairs to attend Ruby's wildcrafting mixer class. Her visit with the professor's wife would have to wait.

Ruby planned for this class to be a hodgepodge of several different craft projects—from making ornaments to bookmarks—all using the wildflowers and plants the women had collected on their hike.

Maddy and Liv were already in the craft hall when Cora arrived. A group of women who came together from Virginia Beach entered the room and sat at the long crafting table. Ruby followed them. She had already prepared the room with bins of crafting materials, and each woman had brought her own flowers and herbs gathered on the hike.

Cora smiled at them. "How is it going?" she said.

"I'm having so much fun," one of them said. "You know, it's been a while since I've been away from home with just my friends. I'd forgotten how important this is. Plus, I've made some wonderful things. My basket is almost finished. I've got two charms done."

"I had no idea how much I'd love painting rocks," another woman said. "I don't know. I just really have a feel for it." She was carrying around a basket and she sat it on the table and tilted it so that Cora could see her rocks, which were incredibly brilliant in jewel-tone colors and detailed. They were covered in swirls, hearts, and flowers. The words *Hope Love Cherish* were painted on top of the designs. So charming.

Cora held one in her hand and examined it closely. "You must paint," she said, and handed it back to the artist.

She nodded. "I used to. I used to think I would be an artist, but then the kids came along and I just didn't have the time to keep up with it."

"You obviously still have talent," Cora said.

She sat a little straighter. "Thank you."

"I'd like to take some photos of your rocks for my blog. I'll feature them," Cora said. The woman's eyes filled with water and her face reddened.

"Thanks," she said. "I'd be honored."

How many times had Cora witnessed this phenomena? Women giving up their art for their families? So many times she couldn't possibility count. Still, she supposed one only had enough time in the day to take care of things. At least this woman was finding her way back. So many of the abused women she worked with never did. It was all they could do to survive. All their energy went for that. And you couldn't blame them for it.

Cora lifted her gaze from the basket of rocks and saw the room was full. Ruby stood at the head of the room and cleared her throat. "Welcome to my mixer," she said. "This is one of the most fun classes I ever get to teach. You can just make whatever calls to you. I have several examples here and enough materials for everybody."

Ruby held up a bookmark. It was plastic, see-through, and several flowers were pressed between the layers. "We have everything you need to make these bookmarks, including the laminating machine. It's so simple you won't believe it."

"I'm afraid of machines," Maddy said. "I steer clear of them."

"I can help you," Liv said.

"We also have two different kinds of ornaments," Ruby continued.

Jane walked into the room holding a cup of coffee and sat down next to Cora. The woman drank coffee all day long and still slept as sound as a baby. Cora admired that. If she drank coffee after 3 PM, she'd never get to sleep.

Ruby held up a clear round glass circle that held one single daisy. "Some people do this with resin, but we've given you glass to press your flower into. Isn't this sweet?" Ruby said.

Murmurs of agreement rippled through the room.

"We also have these simple clay pressed ornaments. You just press your flower into the clay and bake it and voilà," Ruby said. "You don't use it as an impression, like in Jane's class. You are actually baking the plant or flower into it."

"I love those," Jane said. "But then again, I love to play in my clay. Anybody else?"

Several women, including Liv, raised their hands.

"How adorable!" Cora said, holding up a small, ball-shaped resin charm with a delicate tiny leaf inside.

"We have the stuff to make those charms as well. So let's get busy, shall we?" Ruby said, looking up in the direction of the door and beaming. "Hello, Cashel," Ruby said. "This is my son, Cashel."

He strode across the floor and kissed Ruby on the cheek. "Hello, ladies—what are you making?"

Cora tried not to look at him in those jeans that brought out his blue, blue, blue eyes, not to mention fit him very well. They were friends. It was not cool to have indecent thoughts about your friends. Her face warmed.

Maddy caught her eye and jiggled her eyebrows. Cora couldn't help but laugh.

"We're making bookmarks and ornaments," Ruby said, steering her son to the opposite end of the table.

Cora scanned the room. It was as if there was a pause in time and space as the women watched Cashel O'Malley take a seat next to his mother. He examined the craft materials in front of him, then lifted his chin in Cora's direction and winked.

Chapter 32

As soon as the class was over and the crafters scattered, oohing and aahing over one another's crafts, Cora slipped out of the room and into the kitchen, where she found a tin filled with cookies. She slid it into a gift bag. She set off for the professor's house, waving to Jane and Sheila, who were sitting on the front porch with several of the crafters. Some were working on their projects—baskets, ornaments, charms, and so on.

She tried not to make eye contact with Jane and kept moving. She could handle this herself. But Jane bolted toward her and the next thing she knew she was walking alongside her.

"Are you going to visit the professor's wife?" Jane asked quietly.

Honestly, was she that easily read?

"You are, aren't you? You have treats," Jane said. " know your techniques. I'm coming with you."

"Why? I don't want her to think we are ganging up on her," Cora said. "She's probably in a fragile state right now."

"She could also be in a dangerous state of mind. I think it's better if you have someone with you. Me," she said. "I'm going." She said it with a finality that Cora knew better than to argue with.

"Okay," Cora said. "Whatever."

"Where are we going?" Jane asked.

"Cobalt Lane," Cora said, pointing off to the left. As they crossed the street and turned a corner, they were assaulted with color.

"Wow," Jane said. "I've not been down this street recently."

The street was lined with pink and white dogwoods, in full bloom.

Cora's nose tickled. "Gorgeous," she said.

They walked along the sidewalk taking in the view. This street was lined with smaller but colorful Victorians. A blue house with crimson shutters and trim. A pink house, edged in brown. A peach house, trimmed in blue. Flower boxes and blooms were tastefully placed in an orderly manner.

Cora felt as if she'd just walked into Victorian-era neighborhood Disneyland—it was that perfect. She clutched her gift bag, thinking maybe the bag wasn't pretty enough for someone who lived on this quaint street.

"I think that's the house right there." Cora pointed to a yellow house trimmed in coral. Tulips circled two budding cherry trees in the front yard.

The two of them walked up the sidewalk and onto the front porch. Music was coming from the house. Sounds of laughter. Jane and Cora exchanged glances, how odd, the woman's husband was out in the wilds, off the grid, and it sounded like there was a party in full force.

Cora rang the doorbell. Nothing happened; nobody came.

"Hmmm," she said, and rang it again. She took a deep breath. She wanted to know all about Dr. Rawlings, and she was here to see what she could find out to possibly help Gracie—if indeed it was not her in that far-off mountain cabin. But her intuition was kicking in. She didn't feel right being here. Just as she turned to go, Jane following her lead, a woman opened the door.

She was dressed in jeans and a tunic—earthy, with Native American patterns on it. Her hair was shoulder length and curly. Her big brown eyes held a quizzical expression. "Can I help you?" she said, her word slurring just a bit. She swayed and then leaned against the doorframe.

The woman was drunk.

"Hi," Cora finally said. "I'm Cora Chevalier and this is my associate, Jane Starr."

"Ah!" the woman gasped. "Jane Starr! I have so many of your pieces. Please come in. I'm so sorry for the mess." She waved her arms around a bit as they followed her through the foyer into the living room, where a group of women were splayed about the room engaged in conversation and eating and drinking. Plates of food and bottles of wine were strewn about. If this was a party, nobody was a bit concerned about picking up after themselves.

"I'm sorry to intrude," Cora said. "I didn't realize you were having a party."

"Oh, honey," she said. "This is a party I shoulda had years ago."

"What do you mean?" Jane said.

She waved her hand around. "It's an upcoming divorce celebration."

"Oh," Jane said.

"Please come in. And check this out." She pointed to a wall of pottery on shelves—all designed by Jane.

Jane beamed. They had wandered into a fan's house. A fan who was holding a divorce party, Cora reminded herself.

"Wonderful," Jane said with a note of humility in her voice, and actually blushed.

"You are so talented," she said. "I loved to stand in front of this wall and just feel the energy. You know I feel the wisdom in her pieces. Goddess wisdom."

"That's, um, remarkable," Jane said.

"But what can I help you with?" she said.

Cora handed her the gift bag. She was completely unprepared for the joviality she felt in this room. She thought she might be wandering into a bad situation.

"I, ah," she said, and cleared her throat. "We came by to give you some cookies we made and, well—"

"Look, this is probably none of our business," Jane said. "But I'm going to put it out there. Paul, Gracie's boyfriend, is staying with us. If you know anything about the situation that would help—"

"Help?" one woman said, coming up from behind her. "Gladys, who are these people?"

Cora felt her throat constrict. This woman was more drunk than Gladys.

"Please calm down," Cora said. "We think there's a

possibility that the woman with your husband is not Gracie."

The room silenced. Even the music stopped. All the women were now gathered around them.

Cora took a deep breath.

"Which means that Gracie could still be missing. So time is of the essence," Jane said. "The police, of course, have called off the search. We need to know if you know anything."

Gladys's face reddened; tears formed in her eyes as this other woman circled her arm around her.

"Ladies," the woman said. "You have no idea what a bloody psychopath this man is. Let's hope your friend is not with him."

Gladys sobbed. "I hated her. I hated Gracie. But she was the tip of the iceberg. The more I looked into it . . . there were . . . others. I don't know how I could have been so stupid. I wasted my life on him."

"Him who is now living in the Blue Note," her friend said. "Don't let him come back. I'm telling you."

Gladys responded with a sniff.

Cora's heart flipped around in her chest. She ached for her.

But she made a mental note: Rawlings was in town and staying at the Blue Note B & B, which she and Jane had passed on their walk here—and would be passing on their way back to Kildare House.

"You've got a lot of life left in you, honey," one of the women said.

"Indeed," the woman said. Her arm still wrapped around Gladys.

"How did you know the woman who was with him is Gracie?" Jane asked.

"How would I know who she was?" Gladys appeared as if she suddenly heard what they said.

"Well, what led you to think it was her?" Jane asked again.

"I didn't know who it was," she said. "I just told the police he'd left with a woman. I gave them a list of names of women that I knew about. Most of them students."

"Aha," Cora said. "And she fit Gracie's description."

The woman shot them a wry glance. "They all do, honey. Every one of them."

Chapter 33

"Well, this is an interesting twist," Jane said as she and Cora walked toward Kildare House.

"It's not even dinnertime and those women are drunk," Cora said, almost to herself.

"If anybody deserves to be drunk, it's her," Jane said. "Sounds like the professor is a nut job."

They continued to walk along the streets of Indigo Gap, and cut through a cobblestone road, which led up to Kildare House. The stone road was cut off to traffic, but walkers used it frequently. Flower boxes lined the street and were filled with spring flowers. They started to walk by the Blue Note B & B.

"Could the professor have killed Henry?" Cora asked, and stopped walking.

"I don't know, but if they found Henry's killer, it could lead us to Gracie," Jane said. To her, the two mysterious happenings—Gracie's disappearance and Henry's murder—were related. Things like that didn't just happen so close in space and time to one another and not have a connection.

Cora nodded her head toward the B and B. "Isn't this where he's staying?"

"I think that's what Gladys said," Jane responded.

"Do you think he'd talk with us?"

"Oh no," Jane said. "I'm not going to talk with him, even if he'd talk with us. He might be a murderer."

"But he's been gone this whole time. He could not have killed Henry. He's been off in a love nest in the mountains," Cora said.

Jane folded her arms. "Still," she said. "He doesn't sound like a man I want to be anywhere around."

"Look, we can talk to him together and try to suss him out, try to find out if he ever had Gracie with him. Nobody else is telling us anything," Cora said. "We may as well go straight to the source."

Jane wavered. "Well, that's true. I don't know why the cops are being so secretive. If it's not Gracie, they should tell us."

Cora opened the picket fence gate and Jane walked through, reluctantly. The gate creaked and a white-haired woman appeared on the porch. "Can I help you?"

Cora cleared her throat. "Well, um, you see—"

"May we see one of your guests?" Jane interrupted.

"Are you expected?"

"No," Jane said, as Cora stood with her mouth slightly ajar. "We just wanted to talk with Professor Rawlings, if we could."

"Oh, you must be students," she said. "Hold on, I'll call up to his room. I know he's there. He just went up with a bunch of books in his arms."

Jane and Cora followed her into the B and B, decorated unexpectedly in soft dark blue hues and jazzy posters. A shiny baby grand piano stood in the corner of the large living room. Purple orchids sat in an elegant crystal vase on top on the piano.

"By the way, I'm Zora. Pleased to make your acquaintance. Why don't you two have a seat? I'll give him a call. What are your names?"

"Cora Chevalier and Jane Starr," Jane said.

She nodded and went into another room to call.

Jane and Cora sat in the room with the baby grand piano and waited.

"It looks so quaint from the outside, so jazzy inside," Cora said.

Jane nodded.

"I'm sorry," Zora said as she walked back into the room. "He doesn't want to be disturbed."

Cora stood. "Well, that's too bad. We're not students by the way."

"No?" she said.

"No, we live at Kildare House," Cora said.

"Oh dear!" she said. "I remember your names now. I am so sorry. I've been so busy that I've neglected to stop by and introduce myself."

She was sweet-faced and plump and sported purple glasses. She fingered her dress as she nodded her head in the direction of the stairs.

"If you don't know him . . ."

"We were under the impression that Gracie might be with him. You know, the young woman who's missing?" Jane said.

"Oh no," she replied. "That's not Gracie with him. I know Gracie."

"You do?" Jane said, relieved, yet worried, to hear Gracie was not with him.

"Not well," she said. "But she used to clean for me before she got the babysitting gig."

"She used to babysit for me," Jane said. "My daughter adored her."

"I bet," Zora said. "Listen, ladies, a word to the wise," she said as she led them back to the door.

Cora and Jane stood and leaned in toward her.

"This professor. He's very odd and he's a bit of a cad," she said. "I'd stay as far away from him as possible if I were you."

"We can handle cads, I assure you," Cora said. "But thanks for the warning."

"What do you mean by odd?" Jane asked.

"I don't know. It's just a weird vibe," Zora said with drama.

Jane shivered. Cora's arm went around her. "I think we should be going," Cora said, then handed Zora her card. "Call me anytime. Or stop by. Thanks so much for seeing us."

"No trouble at all. I just wish I could help more."

Cora stopped. "You've already helped by letting us know that's not Gracie with him. But the trouble is, well, if she's not with him . . ."

Zora nodded. "I know," she said, as her gaze fell to the ground.

Jane and Cora moved along and began walking down the street.

"Where is she?" Jane said, tangled with worry. "I'm glad Gracie is not with him; as we heard from Zora, the professor is very odd and the woman at the party said he was a psychopath."

"I don't know about that. Everybody thinks they know what a psychopath is, and well, actually, there are several types and—"

Jane held up her hand. "Let's not talk about this now, okay?" Jane had heard Cora talking about all of this before.

"Sure," Cora said.

They walked down the street away from the Blue Note B & B and toward the florist shop. A group of guests from the retreat came around the corner.

"Well, hello," Cora said. "Where's everybody off to?"

"Dinner," Maddy said. "Would you like to join us?"

"Sorry, I wish I could go, but I've got some prep work to do for tomorrow," Jane said.

"Me too. We'll catch you later, okay?" Cora said.

The group wandered off in another direction. Kildare House came into view. A silver Mercedes sat in front of the house.

Cora shot a look of consternation toward Jane.

"I hope Edgar doesn't see the car parked in front of the house," Jane said, and giggled.

"Who could it be? Everybody knows to park around the side and back of the house."

A man came out of the front door, walked down the sidewalk, and popped the trunk open. He lifted a box out of it and proceeded to carry it up the side walk. A woman opened the door and seemed to be giving him directions. Who was she? Who was he? Why were they delivering a box to Kildare House?

Jane reached for Cora's hand. "What's going on?"

Cora shrugged. "We're about to find out."

They approached the gate, opened it—it still squeaked, Jane mused. Would Cora ever get that fixed?

The man came out of the door again. "Oh, hello there," he said. British accent. "I'm Gene Garrett, Paul Eugene's father. You must be Jane and Cora?"

"Yes," Cora said, reaching her hand out to him, shaking it. "Nice to meet you."

Jane did the same. But, what was going on here?

"I'm afraid we're in a bit of a dilemma," he explained. "Paul Eugene has been evicted from his apartment."

"Oh?" Jane said. He was turning out to be a real pain. And Jane wasn't sure she quite trusted him. Cora did. Cora had taken more than one misfit under her wing. But this was different. His girlfriend was missing. His best friend killed. It seemed like he may have known more about all these circumstances than what he was letting on.

"I am terribly sorry," he said. "But we had to move his and Henry's things to his room here until we can find a storage facility. There doesn't seem to be anything locally. And we've not had the time to find him another apartment. It's a mess."

"Welcome to Indigo Gap," Cora said, smiling. It was a stiff smile. Jane knew she was painting it on. "If you've finished unloading, please park your car around the side, over there," she gestured. "And please come into Kildare House for a drink. We'll get this all sorted."

"Thank you. I'll join you inside momentarily. My wife is already inside."

He walked off, got into the car, and started it up.

Cora turned to Jane. "This is turning into a nightmare," Jane said.

"But what can I do now?" Cora asked. "I can't throw him out."

Jane's mouth puckered. "No, I wouldn't want you to. He's a good guy, going through a hard time. But— look, Cora," Jane said. "We've got a business to run here. We can't be taking in every sob story that comes along, especially during a retreat. What must our guests be thinking?"

Cora sighed. "I don't know. Let's find out, shall we?"

Cora opened the door to Paul standing there with his mother, Jane surmised, along with Sheila, Donna, and Marianne, who were carrying boxes up the stairs.

Paul glanced sheepishly at Cora.

"I'm so sorry. I've a bit of explaining to do," he said to her.

"I just spoke to your father," Cora said. "No worries, Paul. You're welcome here. This must be your mother?"

She smiled at Cora and Jane. When she studied them, Jane found the resemblance between her and her son to be striking, especially the sad puppy-dog eyes. She was certain the eyes were sucking Cora in like a dog to a bone.

Jane didn't like any of this. Not one bit.

She held out her hand and shook Cora's, then Jane's. "I'm Susan. This is embarrassing, but we are in dire straits. I'll make certain you are paid handsomely for your hospitality."

Perhaps Jane had jumped to conclusions. If they were willing to pay, that would be fantastic. They could certainly use the money. They were barely squeaking by with this retreat.

"Absolutely not," Cora said. "Paul has helped me out a bit around here. If he'd like to continue to do so, that would be sufficient. I will not take money from a man who obviously just needs a safe place to stay for a few days."

Susan's mouth dropped open. She didn't know what to say. "Well, I, ah—"

Cora held up her hand. "Really," she said. "I insist."

Jane refrained from rolling her eyes. Cora! She could be so maddening! Why wouldn't she take money when they so desperately needed it?

Chapter 34

Cora knew the type. Susan Garrett was a society broad and if Cora took one penny from her, it would never have stopped. She would give her so much money until she felt obligated to the woman. Once that type hooked its claws into you, soon you'd be road kill—of one sort or another.

As it was, Paul's room was taking on its own home-life. It was growing in comfort and things. Not only his things, so it seemed, but also Henry's things. She and Jane helped drag up the last few suitcases and surveyed the room. He was staying on the third floor in what was deemed to be a guest teacher room, meaning it was large, with a sitting area, which turned out to be just what he needed.

"I want you to know I'm out of here just as soon as I find a place," he told them, as his mother entered the room behind them.

The spacious room was filled with disorganized boxes, trunks, and garbage bags filled with clothes on hangers.

"I need to go through Henry's things," he said, his voice cracking. "I just don't have the heart to do it."

"Does he have any family?" Jane asked.

"None," he said.

"None?" Cora asked.

"None that I know of," he said. "He was raised by a single mom. There was only him and his mom, and she died last year."

"So you have to go through all this stuff?" Donna said, standing next to Sheila.

"Yes," he said.

"Oh, Paul Eugene!" his mother said. "This is going to be hard for you. Shall I help?"

"Good idea," Sheila said. "I'll help, too."

"I'll stay and help, Paul Eugene," Donna said, emphasizing Eugene.

"I think that should do," Paul said. "By the way, you can still call me Paul. It's just my parents who call me Paul Eugene, even though I've asked them not to."

"It's a lovely old name," his mother said. "It was my grandfather's name."

"Glad you have some help," Cora said, ignoring the name conversation. She'd had several conversations about her own full name Coralie—she much preferred Cora, and she respected anybody's wishes when it came to their own names. "I have some work to do and so does Jane. We'll check back with you later. I'd be happy to take whatever you don't need to the Goodwill."

"Thanks," he said.

"Why were you guys evicted?" Donna suddenly asked.

"Evidently, there's a clause in their contract that if

they get into any trouble with the law, they are out," Susan replied with an edge to her voice.

"Yeah, I guess if you get murdered, you get evicted," Paul said under his breath.

"Or if your girlfriend is missing," Donna said.

"Right," Paul said, and began flinging T-shirts into a box. "I can't wear any of these. Henry was much smaller than me. If anybody wants them . . . if not, off to the Goodwill."

Cora took one last look at the room and the crew of people in it before she left. Two of her teachers, two of her retreaters, and Paul and his family. This was not something she could have planned for. Once again, some strange law in her universe was rearing its ugly head. She and Ruby and Jane had thought they had prepared for every possibility. Once again, they had not. Here she was, housing a bereft young man who might be in danger, along with all his stuff, plus his dead friend's belongings, which were being sorted right at this very moment.

"Whoa, there's a box of his notebooks," Paul said. "I don't think I can part with those."

Jane grabbed Cora's hand and led her through the door.

They walked down the stairs into what felt like another dimension. Brigid gazed over them from the stained-glass window, and a group of women were gathered in their own thoughts in the living room. Music played softly. The women chatted quietly among themselves. A few women were knitting. A few were working on their baskets. Marianne was helping to weave flowers into a basket.

"Isn't that lovely?" Cora said, and sat down on the empty chair. She needed to take a look around the kitchen to see if it needed cleaning, and she was certain the caterer left her some notes. But she thought she'd just take a while and work on her own project with the other crafters. Jane took her cue—and Cora knew Jane needed to catch up on preparation for her last class tomorrow, which was basically a finishing class. The crafters would make their necklaces, bracelets, and earrings tomorrow.

"My grandmother used to do this," Marianne said. "It reminds me of simple days when I had nothing better to do than sit next to her and learn how to make my fingers work."

Cora nodded, picking up her basket of embroidery work. She didn't know if she'd ever get this sampler done. She wasn't certain that was the point. A sampler book. She was learning and practicing different stitches.

"My grandmother and I would spend countless hours in the kitchen," Cora said. "We just reveled in that space and time. Trying different spices, different fruit. It was glorious!"

"Grandparents are so important," Lily, one of the crafters, said. "It's like they have a whole different view on time."

"They do," Marianne said. "Their time is shorter, so they know it's more important to sit with a child or cook with a child than it is to get the laundry done or whatever," she said. "I'm going to be a grandmother soon."

"What?" Jane said. "You are so young."

"I am," Marianne replied emphatically. "That's what I told my daughter. And she's too young to have a baby—eighteen years old—but she is going to be a decent mother, I think. Here," she said to Lily, "pull the stem through here."

"I'm curious," Jane said, "what you said to me the other day."

"About your hands?"

"No, about my being of the people," Jane said.

"Well, I just assumed you were part Cherokee," Marianne said. "You look so much like a woman I used to know."

Cora's heart skipped a beat. Jane always had a feeling she might be Native American. But there was just no way to tell, with the sealed adoption.

"That's interesting," Jane said. "I was adopted. It was a closed adoption, so I have no idea who my biological parents were."

"Oh, I see," Marianne said. She shrugged her shoulders. "Cherokee rarely give up their children for adoption. How long have you been a potter?"

"Forever," Jane said.

It was true, mused Cora. Jane loved digging in the mud as a girl and forming balls, bowls, and rolls she used to call snakes. When she found pottery in art class in junior high, Jane never turned back to the mud puddles and creeks of their youth.

"Intriguing," Marianne said. "It's your calling."

"Indeed," Jane said.

"I wish I had a calling," Maddy said, exasperated as she tried to shove her flower just so within the weave of the basket. "My hands won't do what my brain tells them to do."

"It just takes practice," Marianne said. "Like every skill in this life. We may be born with a calling, but we have to work at becoming skilled."

Chapter 35

Later, Jane and Cora tidied up the kitchen a bit and read over the notes the caterer left. Then they sat down to a meal of leftovers.

Jane took a long sip of her wine. In fact, it was almost a gulp. "What do you really think of everything that's going on?"

"I can't make sense of it," Cora said. "If Brodsky would return my call, maybe we'd at least know if Henry's killer has been caught. I've called him twice."

"I'm more curious about Gracie's disappearance."

"The question is, do they have anything to do with one another at all?" Cora asked.

"Of course they do," Jane replied, then took a bite of pasta salad. "Law of averages says they do. Two weird things like that don't happen to people who are so close to one another and *not* be related. I mean, c'mon."

Cora mulled it over a minute or two. "I don't know. The universe is pretty random. Many things don't make sense."

They were interrupted by Cora's cell phone ringing. It was Detective Brodsky.

"Cora, I'm sorry I've not returned your call until now, but all hell's breaking loose here."

"Did you find Henry's killer?"

"Not exactly. The DNA evidence is, well, confusing."

"What do you mean?"

"We'll talk about it later, okay?" His voice was weary. Cora didn't want to push it. She knew he dealt with an anxiety condition similar to hers.

"Fine," she said. "What about Gracie?"

By this point, she and Jane knew it wasn't Gracie in the cabin with the professor—at least not according to Zora, the proprietor of the Blue Note. And Cora was just working on that assumption.

"The missing person case is ongoing. But I'm not sure how much longer we can take our resources to continue."

Cora knew how these things worked. The police with their limited resources could only give so much time and energy to a missing person case. And, unfortunately, with each passing day, the statistics proved there was less likelihood of finding her.

"I see," she said. She just lost her appetite. Things were looking grim, both for Henry and for Gracie. She found herself wishing it was Gracie with the cad of a professor and wishing that she could have spoken with him. Maybe he could lead them in the right direction. Maybe he knew something they didn't know.

"So Paul is still staying there?" Brodsky asked.

"I'd say," she said. "He and Henry were evicted. I have all their belongings in Kildare House."

"Not all," he said. "We've got Henry's computer."

"Oh?"

"These days, that's often where the most evidence lies. Kids. Their whole lives are spent on the computer and they reveal way too much to any potential predator."

"Henry wasn't quite a kid," Cora said.

Detective Brodsky chuckled. "No, not to you. Listen, I've got to go. It's the Saturday dinner with my wife."

"That's right," she said. "Have a good time."

Cora knew that Brodsky and his wife had a standing dinner date for Saturday nights. She thought it was so sweet.

"Will do. She hopes to come to your next retreat. Couldn't make it this time," he said.

"Good. I look forward to it."

Jane had been listening to the whole conversation. "No news on Gracie?"

Cora nodded. "No."

Jane's eyes welled with years. "It's just that, well, Paul really loves and trusts her. Wouldn't it be wonderful to have that kind of love in your life?"

A tear streamed down her face.

"You're a little drunk, I think," Cora said.

Jane blew her nose into her napkin. She nodded her head. "A little."

"No more wine for you tonight," Cora said, grinning.

"I should eat some more," Jane said just as the group of crafters in the living room exploded into laughter.

"Let's go in the living room," Cora suggested. "Sounds like we're missing a party."

Jane was a bit wobbly, but she was at least able to make it into the next room. Not that drunk, then.

"Land sakes, what's wrong?" Ruby said as she glanced over at them. A ball of yarn sat on her lap and she was wrapping it around something.

"She's fine," Cora said. "We were just talking with Detective Brodsky. No word on Gracie yet."

"Poor Paul," Liv said. She tossed a yellow pom-pom in a nearby basket. They were all making pom-poms. "On top of all this, Gracie cheated on him last year with that idiot professor."

"Do you know him?" Cora asked.

"Oh boy, do I. All the women on campus know him. He's a jerk. I don't know why he hasn't gotten fired yet. He must have some blackmail material on someone in a very high place," Liv said.

What a cynical thought coming from a young art student, Cora thought.

"What? Are you drunk?" Ruby asked. "Just because a man can't keep it in his pants doesn't mean he's a killer."

Cora almost choked on her wine.

"Wait a minute," Jane said. "Did the professor know Henry?"

"Probably," Liv said. "I'm sure he knew Paul."

"Where is this going?" Ruby said.

"I'm thinking there's many ways of killing someone," Jane said. "I know he was in mountain cabin off the grid when Henry was killed. But he could have hired someone."

"True," Cora said.

"If we could prove they knew each other and had a motive for him killing Henry . . ." Jane said.

"Well, that's a tall order," Ruby said, and snorted.

"I might be able to help you," Liv said, tossing another yellow pom-pom in the basket.

All eyes were on her now.

"We're all at the same school, have access to the same computer message boards, libraries, chat rooms, and so on. I'll do some digging," she said, rubbing her hands on her jeans.

"I don't think this is a good idea," Marianne said. "I think you should all leave this to the police." She held up a group of pom-poms and placed them in the basket.

A basketful of pom-poms. What were they up to, Cora wondered.

"Why?" Jane said. "It wouldn't hurt. We're not doing anything illegal. And it might lead us to Gracie."

"I don't know about that. Gracie's been gone a few days now," Marianne said. "Don't get me wrong. We all want to see her safe and sound. But it's best not to get your hopes up, my friend."

Chapter 36

Liv's fingers moved over the keyboard like an expert musician playing a piano. She pulled up Web sites and chat rooms and dismissed this one and that one before Cora even knew what was happening.

"Okay," Liv said. "Here's the *Tattler*'s—our school newspaper's—article about the professor and look, our friend Henry wrote a letter to the editor, defending Gracie."

"Okay," Jane said. "So if I was the prof, Henry would then be on my radar."

"If he wasn't already," Cora said.

"But would he hate him enough to have him killed?" Cora said.

"Certainly not," Marianne said. "Look, as a professor, you don't hold it against your students if they have different opinions. You want that. You are hoping to educate people, not to clone yourself. Right?"

Liv snorted. "I wish you were my teacher."

"Me too," Marianne said.

"So let me search through this site and see if the professor ever responded."

Cora was impressed—within moments of searching online, Liv had her answer. "It doesn't look like he ever responded. That's pretty typical. I mean, there was legal action."

"Is there some kind of court or legal records we could look up?" Jane asked.

"A lot of it would be public record, I assume," Cora said.

"Oh wait, here's something," Liv said. "Looks like the professor was on Henry's committee."

"What does that mean?" Jane asked.

"He was one of the guys who were overseeing his master's degree. They form a committee and after Henry does all his work, he has to defend it to this committee and then he gets his degree."

"So he was on Henry's committee," Marianne said. "Interesting."

"The thing is, after Henry gave up his poetry fellowship, this committee dispersed, of course," Liv said. "Here's a quote from a student, a Ted Brice, 'What I wouldn't have given for that fellowship. It's a smack in the face to the rest of us who are scrounging.' And this quote from the prof, 'This young man has wasted this committee's time and the docent's money. It's unforgivable.'"

"Unforgivable? Just because he wanted to change majors?" Cora said. "I changed majors every year."

"This fellowship was big-time. For serious poets. There was a lot of money involved. It was a smack in the face of the school, as Ted Brice said," Marianne said. "Not that I didn't change my major a few times as well." She laughed. "Some of these academics take themselves so seriously. That's one reason I quit. I just didn't fit in. It's difficult for an artist to put up with this nonsense. Henry was an artist. Maybe he got tired of them telling him how to write. How to live."

A hush came over the group.

Ruby tossed another pom-pom in the basket, which was brimming with colorful pom-poms.

"I don't know that name. Ted Brice?" Liv said.

The name rang a bell for Cora. But she couldn't quite place it. Ted Brice? Who was Ted Brice?

"He left," Marianne replied. "He was a gifted poet, too, but disgruntled. I remember that. I think he left shortly after the Henry thing."

"What was he like?" Liv asked as she clicked across her keyboard. "According to his Facebook bio, he's in Kentucky. Must have left for the hills."

"Basically, he was harmless. I kind of felt sorry for him," Marianne said. "He wanted the fellowship so badly. After Henry left, they picked someone else."

"None of that is cause for murder, surely," Cora said.

"But nothing really is," Marianne said. "Everything can be solved without violence." Her voice was even and quiet, like a poem or a prayer.

Cora's eyes met Jane's and looked away. Violence had a rippling effect on people. Everybody responded in different ways. Cora knew those who tried to fight back; some cowered in fear and others shut down.

"But," Liv said, "we have established Rawlings, Henry, and Gracie knew each other, kind of intimately, and probably didn't like one another. They are all still in the area. Ted Brice is gone. He's in Kentucky."

Then Cora certainly did not know him.

"It is so odd," Jane said. "Don't you think? All this stuff has to have a link, right?"

"What exactly do you mean?" Marianne said.

"I mean Gracie's disappearance, Henry's murder, and the professor running away for the hills. It can't all be a coincidence. It has to be related," Jane said.

"It would seem so," Cora replied. "But it could also be completely random."

"I don't think so. Let's look back at the start."

"You mean Gracie's disappearance."

"Yes, but the very start was you getting that odd text message—"

"Text message?" Liv said. "What?"

"Hey," Donna said as she walked into the sitting room with Sheila behind her. "Look what we found."

She carried a small box full of papers and photos. Sheila carried a book in her hands.

"What's that?" Cora said.

"This box is full of poems, remembrances, letters, including several from the professor," Donna said.

"I've got Henry's journal," Sheila said. Her face was pale. Her eyes watery.

"What's wrong?" Cora said.

"Henry . . ." Sheila said. "He was very troubled."

"What do you mean?" Cora asked. The woman appeared haunted, exhausted, as if she'd fall over any minute.

"His journal is full of dark images," Donna said. "He was manic-depressive. On some heavy medicine. There's a lot of writing about death and suicide and love gone wrong."

"It's all very sad," Sheila said, with her voice cracking. "Why didn't anybody help the boy?"

"We tried," came a voice from behind her. It was Paul, with his parents trailing him.

The living room was now full of crafters and Garretts.

This wasn't exactly what Cora intended for her craft retreat. The craft classes and social succeeded. Now they were coming together about Henry and Gracie. Perhaps it didn't matter they weren't gathering over baskets and pottery, though that is what she would prefer.

"He was seeing a fabulous doctor," Susan said. "I insisted. He was like a son to me. I wanted him to get help. And as far as I know he was getting help. But his creative impulses were always dark."

"It has to come out some way," Paul said. "I've told you, Mother, writing about dark things is healthy."

"I'll never understand that," she said. "But what I do know is that he was a troubled young man. But I don't think it had anything to do with his death. That was murder. Pure and simple. Totally random."

"Murder, yes," Liv spoke up. "Maybe not random."

Click, click, click.

"What do you have there?" Jane said to her.

"I've just hacked into the campus medical records," she said.

"What?" Susan said, horrified.

"Go on, dear girl," her husband replied, walking over to Liv, with a wide grin and an approving glance.

"All three of them—the professor, Gracie, and Henry—were seeing the same psychiatrist and were even in a therapy group together," she said.

"Yeah, I knew about that. So?" Paul said.

"We've been looking for a link," Cora said. "I think we may have found it."

It turned out Paul knew more than he thought he did. It was just like Brodsky had said. People often knew more than they thought—qualified investigators knew to ask the right questions.

Susan cleared her throat. "Are those pom-poms?" She walked over to the basket. "I've not seen or thought about them in years." She reached into the basket and held one up to the light. Something about the light—or was it just the look of joy—but Susan Garrett appeared twenty years younger. Maybe Cora had jumped to the wrong conclusions about her.

Chapter 37

The locals had gone home, signaling that the night was getting late. Liv's eyes were barely open as she yawned and announced she needed to get some sleep.

The group, so intent on what was going on, hadn't realized how late it was. When Liv scampered off, they all dispersed to their own crafting corners or to bed. Cora, Jane, and Ruby gathered at Jane's cottage. They met there because her sitter needed to leave for the night.

"I have to say, wow, what a retreat," Jane said, after pouring both Ruby and Cora a glass of merlot.

"Well, we have gotten a lot of crafting in," Ruby said, and sipped her wine.

"And I was thinking, as everybody was gathered talking about Henry and Gracie, that even though we were not working on a craft project together, we were all working on something together," Cora said.

"But we really wanted to provide an escape from the real world," Jane pointed out.

Ruby snorted. "We can try our best, but none of us have a magic wand."

"I have one," Cora said, and grinned.

"I should have known," Ruby said.

"Now, if only it worked," Jane said with a flat note in her voice.

"Gracie and Henry would still be here for starters," Cora said. "But since they aren't, I'd use it to find Gracie and avenge Henry. You know, find his killer."

"So we know they were all in therapy at the school," Ruby said. "For what?"

"Well, Liv couldn't get into those records, but I assume it was for depression. Henry was manic-depressive," Cora said.

"Which means Gracie was depressed, too. I'm kind of bothered by that. I mean, I left her with my daughter," Jane said.

"Well, there was no way to know," Ruby said. "Besides, she was a great babysitter, right?"

Jane nodded. "She was. But I'm not sure I'd have felt safe, if I knew. But then again, London adored her." Jane shrugged.

"A lot of people are depressed," Cora said, after sipping from her wineglass. "Depending on what kind of depression it is, the person, and the medication, they are actually quite dependable."

"I guess babysitters don't have to disclose that kind of information," Ruby said.

"But I'd think nannies would. I mean, she lived in Chelsea's house with her children," Jane said.

"She probably knew about it but wasn't too concerned—for some reason. Gracie seemed to have her act together. Why would she worry?" Cora said.

"But some depressives are experts at looking like they have it together," Ruby said. "My sister Rosemary was like that. The next thing we knew . . . she killed herself. It was awful for us."

"I had no idea about your sister," Jane said. "How awful. I'm so sorry."

Ruby nodded. "Thank you."

"I've known way too many people who've committed suicide," Cora said. "I'm sorry for your family."

"I think about her every day," Ruby said. "You know, what could have been for her. She was so young."

Cora took another drink of her wine and mulled over the last few hours. Her thoughts turned toward the connection among Gracie, the professor, and Henry. But what did it mean? Anything? Or was it just totally random?

"So how long is Paul going to stay?" Jane asked.

Cora shrugged. "You know, I didn't even ask. I assume just until he can find a place. That shouldn't take too long, should it?"

"It's difficult around here to find rentals," Ruby said. "Especially once you've been evicted. Word gets around."

"I don't know why he should even be here much

longer," Jane said. "He was only here to be close to Gracie."

"Once we find her—" But Cora couldn't bring herself to finish the thought. Would they find her? Where was she? A chill traveled through her. What on earth happened to Gracie Wyke?

"I've been thinking," Jane said. "Henry and Paul had been tracing Gracie's footsteps the day before she disappeared. We could do the same thing. Maybe they have overlooked something."

"But haven't the cops done that?" Cora asked.

Ruby harrumphed. "Probably not. They've been searching the rivers and the forest with dogs."

"Well, that's what they do when someone has disappeared," Cora said.

"Yeah, but these cops? They could be doing so much more," Ruby said. "Like you, tracing her footsteps. Have they done it?"

"Seems like they would have," Cora said. "Brodsky is a bright guy."

"Yes, but they have such a lack of resources," Jane said. "I guess it wouldn't hurt for us to go over her movements that day."

Cora yawned. "Okay. If they don't find her by Monday, I'm in. Tomorrow is the last day of the retreat and I think we all need to focus on that."

"Sounds good to me," Ruby said.

Cora knew with each passing day, the chance of finding Gracie was less likely. But she wasn't ready to give up hope—not yet.

"But what about Henry's killer? Has the detective gotten back to you? Do we know if he's been found?" Jane asked.

Cora stood to leave. "I need to get to bed. And no, Brodsky hasn't gotten back to me. I'll call him tomorrow with the information we found, just in case he doesn't know anything about it."

"Let's hope he has some good news," Jane said.

Ruby grunted her skepticism.

Chapter 38

Morning came much too soon. Many of the crafters had been up too late, including Cora, who tossed and turned through the night with images of Gracie and Henry taunting her. Not to mention she now seemed to have a boarder.

Kildare House creaked and moaned as Cora made her way downstairs, as if she were waking the old place up with each footstep.

Her own body was creaking this morning and desperately needed coffee. As she made her way to the kitchen, the scent of coffee beckoned. Ah, someone was already up and coffee was made. Bless them.

No one was in the kitchen, but Cora poured herself a cup and started toward the living room, but laughter from the paper-craft room beckoned her.

She poked her head inside to find Sheila, Maddy, Donna, and Marianne ensconced at a table covered in pressed flowers and leaves.

"Good morning," Sheila said.

Cora drank from her coffee cup and muttered, "Good morning."

"We planned to work on this yesterday. Just a few of us were interested in scrapbooking with some of these pretty flowers and plants," Donna said as Cora joined them at the table.

"Ruby's class doesn't start for another few hours and Jane's isn't in until this afternoon, so I thought what the heck, right?" Sheila said. She was bright and cheery this morning and for some reason Cora found it annoying. Perhaps she just needed more coffee. She took another sip.

"Mom is a morning person," Donna said, and smiled at Cora. "She's been up since five, went for a run, showered, and boom, she's ready to go. In the meantime, *I* need more coffee."

She rose from the table as her mother giggled.

"I'm guilty of that," Sheila said. "Can't help it."

"I love this," Maddy said. She held up a four-by-six handmade book, made of brown crafting paper and tied with a stick and yarn. She flipped through the pages. "It turned out better than what I thought."

"Can I see it?" Cora asked.

"Sure," she said.

Cora loved the feel of craft paper in her hands. It was smooth and weighty. She flipped through the pages gingerly. Maddy chose craft tape to attach her flowers and herbs to the brown pages. Cora stopped flipping when she reached a page displaying a delicate fern leaf. Maddy had taped it with purple craft tape. The purple and the green set off by brown was eye-catching.

"You have pretty handwriting," Cora said.

"Thanks," she said. "You know, I usually type any journaling I do. But Sheila talked me into this."

"I think we get too hung up on perfection," Sheila said. "Some scrapbooks might call for it. But this is a personal reflection. Your own handwriting adds so much to it."

"It really does," Cora said. "Besides, I am like the Cherokee in that regard. I find perfection suspicious."

Marianne laughed. "I hear ya." She was sliding tiny herbs into plastic sleeves.

"No matter how we try, nothing is ever perfect," Sheila said. "It can be a vicious cycle for some of us."

"Yeah, I'm still working on it," Maddy said. "I think I drive myself a bit crazy with my ideas of perfection."

"We all do," Marianne said. "I had a hard time as a young basket maker with that. I am still a bit of a perfectionist. I take pride in my work, of course, and give it my best. But there's a big difference between wanting to be perfect in your work and wanting to be perfect in your life."

Maddy nodded.

"There," Marianne said, after a few minutes. Cora perused the pages of Maddy's pressed plant and flowers scrapbook and sipped coffee. The world was becoming friendlier by the minute.

Cora glanced at Marianne's creation. She designed a page full of plastic sleeves that included pressed flowers and herbs, with handwriting in between.

"That's an interesting method," Cora said.

"Thanks," Marianne replied. "You know, I like the way you run this retreat. Many of the retreats I've gone to don't allow the teachers to take other classes while they are there. I love that I've made paper dolls, clay jewelry, and now a scrapbook of plants. Thanks, Cora."

Cora warmed. She'd been to retreats like that, too. You never knew what to expect as a guest teacher. But respecting and complying with the rules of the person who hired you was paramount, of course. "You are very welcome," she said.

"I've not been to any other craft retreats," Maddy said. "But this has been fun. I've learned a lot. Not just about crafting—about myself. My life. It's been weird. I never think about this stuff at home. I guess I'm too busy."

"I have a group of friends back in Cumberland Creek," Sheila said. "We get together once a week to scrapbook. It really helps to give yourself space and time with friends and alone. Maybe you should start a group."

Cora was thrilled to hear all this. This retreat had made a difference for Maddy, a mother, a wife, and a career woman who didn't have time to reflect, let alone craft, until this weekend. And Sheila? It was as if the gods created her, and everything she stood for, just for Kildare House and Cora's retreats.

"One of the classes Mom teaches is a class about scrapbooking about yourself," Donna said as she entered the room with a full cup of coffee. "It's amazing."

Maddy blinked. "I think I might like that class."

Cora sat up straighter. "I'd love to have you back, Sheila. That class sounds amazing."

"It's a deal," Sheila said. "Have your people call my

people." She laughed and gestured to Donna, who raised her hand and smiled.

"I'm her people," she said.

Jane and London finished breakfast and headed down to her studio to clean up and make the final preparations for the clay-charm class. Today's class would be a finishing class where the crafters would prettify their charms—choose beads, glass, crystals, and chains or silk strings to hang their charms from. Jane couldn't wait to have a full-on pottery retreat, but in the meantime, this kind of class was perfect to introduce the concepts of working with clay.

She and London dusted the studio and swept the floor with a special broom made by Jude Sawyer, the famous broom maker who taught a class at their last retreat, just for her. Eggplant-colored straw set off by a multicolored weave at the top, the broom was not only beautiful, but incredibly sturdy. It was so sweet of him to give it to her.

"Mommy, these are so pretty," London exclaimed, and she preened over the rows and rows of clay charms.

Jane nodded. "I agree."

"Some circles, some squares, and even some triangles!"

"Which one do you like best?"

"I like the heart-shaped ones," London said.

Jane scrutinized them. Yes, they were extraordinarily beautiful and delicate. Three different colored glazes had been washed over—a slate blue, an olive green, and a tan. The imprints were teeny tiny stems with leaves on them.

And on the other end of the spectrum, someone created large, almost two-inch rectangles with imprinted leaves in purple. Very little glaze, which gave the pieces an earthier tone.

And then there was the more finished variety. Circles and squares, not imprinted, but with actual designs etched in.

All were so lovely in their own way. Jane felt a sense of deep satisfaction. Knowing these women had come here, given themselves space and time to connect with each other and themselves—and make beautiful things.

"Can you cut some of those for me, London?" Jane asked, handing her daughter a roll of black silk strings.

"Sure, Mommy. What sizes?"

"Different ones. Some long, some short. It'll just save us a bit of time so the ladies can relax and enjoy creating," Jane said.

Jane started to sort beads according to color—once again, the more she prepared in advance, the better the experience would be for the crafters. That's what it's all about.

"Mommy, who did this one?" London pointed to a *Venus de Milo*–shaped clay charm with a spiral etched into the center.

"I'm not sure," Jane said. "It could be Liv. She likes the spirals."

"Liv is nice. Liv is pretty," London said. "Almost as pretty as Gracie."

Jane's stomach fluttered a bit. "London, do we need to talk about Gracie?"

"Where is she, Mommy? Did they find her?"

"No," Jane said, dumping a batch of green beads in a tin. She wanted to have the beads sorted by color before the crafters came.

"Do you think they will?"

"It's hard to say, London," Jane said. "But the police are trying hard to find her."

She nodded. "That's good, Mommy. I hope they find her. I miss her."

"Me too," Jane said.

As her daughter cut and she sorted, Jane mulled over what they learned last night. Honestly, if she was aware of Gracie's problems, she probably wouldn't have hired her. She made a mental note to talk with Chelsea about her own awareness. Seems if you were going to hire a live-in, you'd do a bit more research. Maybe Jane would call her tomorrow, after the retreat.

She then thought of Liv and the way she took over last night. The woman really knew her computers— she supposed that was a given with today's students. But she was able to find a definite few links among Gracie, Henry, and the professor. What was the connection? Jane figured it was more involved than the fact that they shared a doctor.

Liv had felt like that, too. She was a pretty extraordinary young woman.

As the sounds of the beads filled the tin cup, the thought occurred to Jane that the doctor was the common denominator, right? If she were investigating this, she believed she'd start there. Of course, with all the privacy rules in place, she wasn't certain how much the doctor could legally tell her. But maybe there was some other way.

If she talked with Chelsea and with the doctor tomorrow, after sending London off to school, she might be able to start to piece together the mystery of Henry's death and Gracie's disappearance. Perhaps she could get some answers for everybody—most importantly London, and a few other kids in Indigo Gap who loved Gracie.

Chapter 39

The group at Kildare House was sitting peacefully, reveling in their morning coffee and their own thoughts when Liv came tumbling into the room, eyes wide, and circled, looking as if she were on some kind of extra batteries this morning—and at the same time held the guise of being completely and utterly wasted.

"Liv?" Donna said. "Are you okay?"

"No," she said. "Not at all."

She placed her phone on the table with a thud. "Look at these messages I'm getting! What the hell?"

Cora's heart lurched. "Messages? On your phone?"

"Yeah, from the Wizard game, I guess. What a bunch of asses. Who are these guys?"

Cora peeked at the messages, as did Sheila, Maddy, Donna, and Marianne. They exchanged glances of concern and horror.

"Okay," Marianne said. "You need to call the police. We've got to get to the bottom of this."

"The police? Why?" Maddy said. "What can they do? She's getting messages? So just ignore them. Change your number. Whatever."

"No, listen, you don't know," Donna said. "Those are the same kind of messages Gracie was getting before she disappeared."

Silence as the women regarded one another.

"Well, I'm not putting up with this," Liv said. "I'm not sure what the police can do, though."

"They have a new cybercrimes investigation unit over there," Cora volunteered. "I had gotten this weird text message about a kidnapping and told them about it. They still don't know what it meant." She picked up her phone. Brodsky still hadn't returned her call. Odd. But then again, he was in the middle of a messy investigation. What made her think he could stop and check in with her? She dialed him again.

When he answered, it was obvious he was just waking up or had been up all night. He almost growled into the phone. "Cora! This better be good."

He was usually so polite. She felt horrible, intruding on him like this.

"I'm so sorry to disturb you. I've tried calling several times—"

"I know, I know. It's been crazy. I planned to get back to you today."

"It's just that this morning one of my guests has been getting text messages and weird notifications. You know, like the ones that Gracie Wyke was getting before she disappeared?"

Cora heard shuffling in the background. "We'll be right over."

"We? Wait? I thought just you—" he clicked off, leaving Cora staring at her cell phone blankly.

"Hang up on you?" Sheila said with a grin. "We've

got a cop like that in Cumberland Creek. Sarcastic SOB."

"I don't understand," Cora said, shrugging. "Usually he's so polite and friendly."

"Bad day, maybe," Marianne said. "We all have them." She rubbed her fingers over her newest pressed plant page, with a satisfying look in her eyes.

Ruby poked her head into the room. "A bunch of us are going to the diner to get some breakfast. Anybody else want to come along?"

"Breakfast?" Donna said. "We've been up for hours."

The group laughed.

"Oh well, suit yourself," Ruby said, and walked out of the room.

"You've not been up for hours. Are you hungry?" Cora said.

"I've been up and down all night and finally just decided to get up," Liv said. "I think I'll have some toast or something."

"We have bagels and we also have freshly made banana bread. There's cream cheese. Oh, I think there are rosemary biscuits as well," Cora said.

Liv grinned up at her. "No plain white toast?"

"Not around here," Marianne said, and laughed.

"Okay, I'm going foraging into the kitchen. I'm sure I'll find something," she said, grinning.

Cora followed her into the kitchen. "Why were you up all night? Is there anything I could do for you?"

Liv waved her off. "I should have known better. I got involved in playing the game and my brain would not shut off. I beat Gracie's high score last night. The graphics were just compelling and I just wanted more, you know? It's not good. I know that. They say you shouldn't even use electronics at least an hour before bed. There I was, all night long."

She slipped bagels in the toaster, then reached into the fridge for cream cheese.

Cora watched her buzz around the kitchen. Was this the wave of the future standing before her? A young, talented, bright artist, up and down all night playing a game? She didn't know what to think of it, what to say, but she knew how she felt.

"Is this gaming good for you as a student? An artist? What do you think about this?" Cora said.

"Ha! No, it's not good. I don't think it is anyway. I hardly ever do it. I just don't have time for it. And every time I do it, I scold myself and say I'll not do it again. But, hey," she said, as her bagel popped up in the toaster. "This is a retreat, right? I'm on a bit of a break."

"True, I suppose everybody's idea of a retreat is different," Cora said, smiling, then wondered about some advice she'd gotten when she first opened the retreat.

"No Wi-Fi," the friend had told her. "No devices. People would complain and moan at first, then would thank her. It was magic—this world of no communication," is what her friend had told her. Cora considered it strongly now as she watched Liv.

"But these messages are not my idea of fun or a retreat," Liv said, licking a bit of cream cheese from her fingers. "So violent and misogynistic."

"I'll say," Cora said, making a new pot of coffee. This group was full of hardcore coffee drinkers.

Paul entered the room in a slump. "Morning," he said. Obviously this was not his best time of the day.

"Coffee will be ready soon," Cora said. "Why don't you have a seat?"

He sat down at the kitchen table, still half asleep. "I'm sorry about everything yesterday. My parents. My stuff." He rubbed his eyes. "I swear I'm going to get out of your hair as soon as I can."

"Paul, you are no trouble," Cora said. "I told your parents you can stay here. And you can. I'll come up with some work for you to do. When it's time for you to go, we'll know it."

He looked at her as if she'd just walked off a spaceship.

"The rest of us have to go by tomorrow," Liv quipped. "Aren't you the lucky one?"

He grunted and smiled.

"So, how are you?" Cora said after he took his first few sips of coffee.

He shrugged. "She's still gone. Nothing helps."

Cora felt chilled. She didn't know what to say.

"She may still be alive," he said. "But I know that with each day . . . statistics say she probably won't be."

"Oh, Paul," she said. "Let's not give up hope."

"No," he said. "I'm not ready to give up hope."

Chapter 40

"So, what's going on with the crafters this morning?" Detective Brodsky said, after he introduced his colleague Adam Cervantes from the digital crimes task force.

"Should I start from yesterday and fill you in, or just what's gone on this morning?" Cora asked.

"Let's talk about the cyber stuff first. Cervantes doesn't have much time this morning. So"—he turned toward Liv—"are you the one with the messages?"

She nodded. "Yes, I started playing that game a few days ago and last night I scored higher than anybody and it kept pinging me. Then I started getting these notifications, then text messages."

She handed the phone to Cervantes.

"Gamers," Cervantes said with disdain.

"But as I understand it," Cora said, "these are the same kind of messages Gracie Wyke was getting before she disappeared."

"That's true," Paul said. "We tried to tell the police about it, but—"

"We?"

"Henry and myself," Paul said.

"Henry? The young man who was recently killed?"

Paul nodded. "We've all been involved in this game. Gracie more than me. But Henry was pretty into it. And you know he was a game designer himself."

Brodsky lifted his head. "I thought he was a poet."

"Both," Paul said.

"People can be all sorts of things," Liv said.

"Is that so?" Brodsky said, amused. "How about you? What are you?"

"I'm an art student," she said. "I enjoy a good game from time to time. We're not all geeks who stay in the basement all day long."

"Good point," Cervantes said. "Not usually, anyway, but I've seen my fair share." He took Liv's phone and pushed a few buttons. "I've downloaded and sent those messages to the office. I'll look into this and get back to you." He stood to go, handing her back her phone.

"Is that it?" she said.

"Yes," he said with a clipped tone. "I need to get to the office to do the digging. That's where the equipment is. But you can come later to help me fill out a report."

"Ohhh, equipment?" Liv said, ignoring the report bit. "Can I come, too?"

Cervantes just waved her off, laughing. "I don't think so. It's police business."

After he left, Liv turned to the detective. "It's not just police business. This is too coincidental for me. Gracie got these messages and she vanished. So this is my business."

She pressed something in her phone and walked into the next room.

"I have to agree," Cora said. "We don't want Liv in any danger."

"Look," Brodsky said. "She's perfectly safe right where she is. Just like Paul over there. But tell her not to go out until you've heard from us."

"Can I get you some coffee? Banana bread?" Cora said.

"Certainly," he said. "Then we'll talk more."

Cora rushed into the kitchen to fix him the coffee and the bread.

"I don't like this, Dad," she heard Liv saying into her cell phone in the next room. "I'm kind of scared."

Poor thing. She sliced up some banana bread and poured the detective a cup of coffee. Then Cora walked back into the room where the others were.

Brodsky was circled in crafters who were laughing at some joke he'd just told them

"Okay," he said after Cora was situated. "What's been going on?"

She filled him in on their meeting with Chelsea, along with the fact that Liv connected Henry, Gracie, and the professor.

"And," Cora said, and took a breath, "the party the professor's soon-to-be ex-wife was having? They were all talking about him like he's a nutcase. Sounds like there might be something there for you to look into."

"Sounds like a typical divorced woman and her friends. Who hacked the files last night?" the detective asked. "The private campus files?"

"I didn't really hack them," Liv said, walking into the room. "I'm a student there. I couldn't get into any of the private medical records. Not yet, anyway," she said, and grinned.

"I'm going to ignore that," he said.

"Plus, Jane and I stopped by the Blue Note B and B, which is where Professor Rawlings is staying," Cora said. "He wouldn't see us. But we talked with Zora."

After a minute, Cora said, "So, what do you think?"

"I think we have quite a tangled web of things. It's going to take time to untangle all this. First, we have a disappearance and then a murder," he said, glancing at his watch. "I need to go. Take care, ladies," he said, turned, and looked at Liv again. "I mean it. You should stay inside and out of it from this point on." He glanced at Paul. "It would be a good idea for you to do the same. Just for a couple of days."

With a flourish of eating the last bit of banana bread, taking one more sip of coffee, the man exited the room and the house.

He left Cora feeling as if she'd just been on a roller coaster.

"That wasn't very smooth at all," Sheila said. She, along with Marianne and Donna, had been sitting there watching and listening.

"I'm sorry, Sheila, what do you mean?"

"I mean he's hiding something," she said.

"I thought the same thing," Liv said. "But I can be a bit paranoid, so I didn't want to say."

"I admit, I feel a little perplexed or something. They were in and out of here much too fast," Cora said.

"The only thing we've gotten out of the conversation is both of you should stay inside," Donna said.

"Yes, but he didn't tell the rest of us to stay inside, did he?" Cora said.

Of course, today was the last day of the retreat and she could not go gallivanting all over town asking questions. But she certainly could tomorrow. And she felt like she needed to corner the professor. Somehow.

Her phoned buzzed with a text message from Jane: Where the heck is everybody?

"Oops, look at the time!" Cora said. "Jane's class!"

The group gathered their belongings and high-tailed it to the carriage house.

Chapter 41

"Well, I'm kind of glad we missed that," Ruby said, after Cora told them why their little group was late getting to the charm class. The crafters were all gathered in Jane's small studio in the carriage house. Soft music played and glasses of juice along with plates of cheese and crackers were scattered about the studio. "Sounds like there's more going on than we know. I'll text Cashel and see what he knows."

"How would he know anything?" Jane asked.

"Small town," Ruby said. "Not many lawyers and cops, either. They all kind of hang out with one another. I'm sure they talk."

The women were positioned about the room working on finishing their necklaces and bracelets fashioned from the riverbank clay. The necklaces all were gorgeous in their own way. Cora was drawn to Liv's clay pendant as she dangled it.

"Powerful," Cora said.

Liv grinned. "It's the goddess, you know. It's one of the things I have in common with Jane and he work. We both like to use these feminine mythological designs." She sighed. "She's fantastic and so inspiring."

Cora agreed. "I love the spiral. You know we have a goddess at Kildare House."

Liv's head tilted. "Do you mean Brigid?"

"Yes, she's the Celtic goddess of poetry and crafting," Cora said, pleased with herself. She'd done a lot of research on the goddess when she moved in because she was so enamored with the stained-glass window in the staircase of the house.

"I've got some Brigid pieces," Liv said.

"Oh, I love Brigid," Marianne said, coming up beside them. "But that looks like Venus."

Liv grinned. "It is."

"Did everybody know about Brigid but me?" Cora said. "I didn't know anything about her until I moved here."

Marianne shrugged. "What were you doing before? Helping with abused women? You knew her. But you just didn't know it."

Cora blinked. That was something to think about. So many of the women she'd run into at craft retreats talked about goddesses as if they were real.

"Hey, look at the gorgeous purple on this!" Jane squealed, holding up a charm glazed with a sheen of purple.

Cora snapped a photo for her blog. The way the light shone on it made it glisten. She walked around and took more photos. Sheila and Donna, mother and daughter, laughing as they held up their bangles. Maddy and Ruby sitting back on the couch already donning their pendants, with glasses of wine in their hands. Rows of glass beads. Pretty crystals, sparkling. Strands of silk and rawhide.

This was going to make an eye-catching photo-blog post, Cora decided. Perhaps she'd have time to post between this class and the next.

Maddy let out a huge, drawn-out sigh. "Oh, I wish I could do this more often."

"You can," Ruby said. "I promise." Ruby's phone buzzed. "Oh, there's Cashel." Her brows knitted as she read over the text. "He's warning us to stay out of this case. Typical."

"Why is everybody worried about you butting into a police case?" Marianne asked.

"I don't know," Cora said, and shrugged. But she couldn't look at Jane. They both knew why. They had butted in before, hadn't they? But, all told, they had been helpful. Even so, the police looked askance at civilians taking over cases.

"He says from what he knows, this case is danger- ous. 'The police, of course, know more than they are saying. But it's for the protection of the public. So butt out, dear Mother. And you can tell Cora and Jane the same thing. I don't want to see them in the news or have to come and get them out of trouble as their lawyer again.'"

"Hey," Jane said. "I resent that remark!" she laughed.

"Men," Cora said.

"Sons. You birth 'em and then they act like the don't owe you a thing," Ruby said, and grinned.

"Well, since he didn't mention my name, I suppose I don't have to stay out of it," Liv said.

"Oh yes, you do," Sheila said with a warning note. "I've almost lost some good friends who were butting their noses in where it didn't belong. It affected us all a great deal. These criminal sorts are not playing games. I agree with your detective on this. You need to stay close by."

Liv, stunned by the older woman's obvious emotion, said, "Well, I have no choice, then." She shot a look at Donna and grinned.

"That's my mom," Donna said. "She's the coolest mom on the planet. But she does have an opinion or two."

Sheila chuckled, then became serious. "Oh, I know the dangers," she said, and gazed out the window into her own distance. "I know them too well—and how one moment can change everything."

The women sat for a few moments, considering.

"No point in rocking the boat, then," Maddy said.

"Besides," Marianne said, "we have one more class, then a party to go to. Why do we need to go anywhere else today?"

"Indeed," Jane said. "This will all resolve itself without our help. You are all here for a craft retreat, not a criminal investigation. Let's play nice."

Cora sat back and listened to Jane and wondered who she thought she was fooling.

Chapter 42

After the others left, Jane and Cora cleaned up the studio a bit before heading over to Kildare House. As Jane's sitter got settled in with London, Cora told her she hadn't believed a word of what she said earlier.

"I don't mean to lie," Jane said. "I really don't want the retreaters involved in all this. How about you?"

"I hear you," Cora said. "But poor Liv is now really involved because of the crazy game and her messages. She's really frightened. I heard her talking with her father."

"I bet," Jane said. "I'm afraid for her."

"Well, we will keep her as safe as we possibly can," Cora said. "She leaves tomorrow. Then I will really start to worry."

"I wonder, can the game and the messages really be at the heart of all this? I mean, at first I thought it was utter silliness, this gaming business. You know, when Henry and Paul came to see us?"

Cora nodded. "I know. I thought it was insane, too. I thought they should be out scouring the hillside instead of poking around on the computer."

"I read a little about the Darknet last night," Jane said. "You can almost do anything you want on there. You can hire prostitutes, get drugs, and there've been cases of people hiring killers. Crazy stuff."

Cora's heart jumped. "Hiring killers?" The first thought springing to her mind was that the professor, who seemed certifiable, could have hired a killer to off Henry. It was a gruesome possibility, sending a shiver up her spine. But why would he want to kill Henry? Just because they were under the same doctor's care didn't give him enough of a connection to care about Henry. Was a letter to the editor enough to want to kill someone? Had something else gone down among the three of them?

Cora and Jane walked from Jane's place to Kildare House and were almost to the back kitchen door when Jane stopped. "What are you thinking?" she asked Cora.

Cora shrugged. "I didn't know about the Darknet before any of this happened. It's scary. My first thought was maybe the professor hired someone to off Henry. He seems disturbed enough."

"I thought so, too," Jane said. "But why? I also imagined him hiring someone to nab Gracie. We should go and see Chelsea tomorrow and his soon-to-be ex-wife. What do you think?"

"Sounds like a plan. I'd really like to talk with him, though," Cora said, opening the door. "But first we have to get through the rest of the day and night."

A look of resolve came over Jane as they entered the house.

Commotion ensued toward the front of the house. The crafters were oohing and aahing over something.

As Jane and Cora approached, they saw it was a lovely bouquet of spring wildflowers.

"Did Uncle Jon send you flowers again?" Jane asked.

"I don't know! How thoughtful," Cora said. The scent of flowers filled the room as she read the card, feeling her face heat. "They're from Adrian."

The card read: *I can't wait to see you tonight. Warmly, Adrian.*

"Nice!" Jane said. "I knew you two were going to hit it off. New beau!" Jane said, looking at the gathered retreaters.

"Looks like a winner," Maddy said.

"Yes, he's a great guy," Jane replied.

He was. But Cora had forgotten about their date. In all the excitement of last night and this morning, he'd slipped her mind. As she thought about him, her mood lifted. But she didn't know if tonight was the best time for them to get together. She would probably be exhausted. Still, they hadn't seen each other in weeks. And the matter of the averted good-night kiss weighed on her mind from time to time.

"You forgot about it, didn't you?" Jane said.

"Yes," she admitted. "It's been a bit crazy, don't you think?"

Jane nodded. "But that doesn't bode well at all for the relationship. It's only your second date."

"Not much of a date really. We're just going to hang out at my place," she said. "I told him I'll probably be exhausted."

The other crafters were already scattered into the craft wing, where Marianne was set up with her finishing class. Baskets and tools lined the long wood table

The floor-to-ceiling windows provided them with great light at this time of day. She was prepped and ready to go. Cora snapped some photos as the women settled in. She needed to go back to her place and write up a blog post. In the meantime, she Tweeted some of the photos from earlier and from now. Even though most of her readers would probably never attend a retreat, she wanted them to feel as if they were here. She planned to experiment with some online retreats in the future. An odd concept to be sure, but she thought she could make it work.

"This has been a great experience for me as an artist and a teacher," Marianne said. "I hope you all have enjoyed this as much as I have. Now, let's get your baskets finished and you can take them home filled with charms and painted rocks and whatever else you've done this weekend. I can't believe how much I've done and how much fun I've had."

Cora noted teachers at these events were often pulled in too many directions to enjoy themselves. Artist–teachers were usually introverts, so these public appearances were intense and taxing. It was one of Cora's goals to make the retreats just as relaxing for the teacher as for the retreaters. Which worked with Marianne. Not so much Jane or Ruby this time around.

Gracie's disappearance affected Jane in difficult, thorny ways—much of it was because of London and her attachment to the young woman. As a mother, Jane was careful about who came into contact with London, and therefore whom she'd grow close to. Attachments and abandonment issues were everywhere in her little family—particularly since Neil had reared his ugly head, again, wanting to visit London.

"I want that," Jane had told Cora. "I don't want my child to grow up without a father. But is it better to grow up without one, or to grow up with one who is so damaged he comes in and out of your life at a whim? I just don't know. I don't want her heart to break again. But I can't protect her from everything. I'm sort of damned if I do, damned if I don't."

Chapter 43

After the basket finishing class, Cora excused herself to go and get some blogging done. Jane knew she'd probably catch a few winks while she was there—and hoped she would. She appeared frazzled and more pale than usual. Cora was a woman who needed her sleep. It helped with her anxiety issues. Her strong, fairy-warrior princess of a friend had been doing well since her last episode and Jane wanted it to hold.

She and Ruby puttered about the kitchen preparing for the caterers to come. They would be here any minute to ready for the chocolate reception tonight. Cora decided to make a closing chocolate reception a tradition of the retreat—with no argument from Jane or Ruby. You didn't have to be French to enjoy chocolate; though, as much as Jane loved chocolate, she did wonder if Cora loved anything else more. Maybe wine. Maybe.

"How do you think she's really doing?" Ruby asked, and leaned on the counter.

"Cora?" Jane asked.

"Yes," Ruby said. "She doesn't look good to me."

"What do you mean?"

"I mean she looks exhausted . . . agitated or something," Ruby said.

"She was up late last night," Jane said. "I'm sure she's just tired. She'll write up her blog post, get some shut-eye, and come down for the party completely refreshed and gorgeous." Jane wiped drops of water from the counter with a dish towel.

"This retreat has been awesome," Ruby said. For some reason the word *awesome* sounded strange coming out of Ruby's mouth. She'd been influenced by the younger crowd here this weekend. Jane tried not to grin.

"I think it's been great. And I'm looking forward to the Big Island Beach Retreat next month," she said.

"Me too. What are your plans for it?"

"Sand," she said. "I'm doing something with sand, sea glass, shells."

"I'm teaching a class on herbals near the beach," Ruby said. "So, will London be coming with us?"

"I'm not sure. She was going to stay with . . ."

"Gracie," Ruby finished for her. "How is she handling all this?"

"About as well as can be expected."

Ruby crossed her arms. "It's tough as a single mom, I know, in more than one way. You just don't know who to trust. But Gracie seemed so trustworthy."

"Yes, I still think she was an amazing sitter," Jane said.

"But maybe there's something we just don't know about her."

"I'm going to have a heart-to-heart with Chelsea tomorrow. She's the woman who hired Gracie as a nanny. Perhaps she knows something."

Ruby's eyebrows lifted. "I'm sure she does."

A tone in her voice prompted Jane to ask, "Do you know her?"

"Oh sure, not well, but she's a woman in the know. Very powerful family. Always has been. I'd think if there were any secrets to be known about a young woman working for her, she'd definitely know them."

"And she'd definitely tell other mothers, right?"

"You'd think," Ruby said. "Oh, there's the caterer." She walked off and opened the door for the crew.

Along with the crew came the scent of sugar, fat, and chocolate. Swoon-worthy. Plates, pan, and goodies were plopped down on the counters by the caterer, crisp and clean and dressed in their black and whites.

Jane thought Cora would be pleased—as the last event was catered by an annoying crew, especially its leader. But these folks were as pro as it could get. The kitchen was not a good kitchen for large events, and yet they managed beautifully.

Jane imagined each of these retreats would have a different set of challenges. Last time, well, it was the first one and there was a murder just down the street—plus the issue with the caterer. This time, unfortunately, murder and a disappearance of a young woman marred the retreat, but maybe only slightly. The retreaters seemed to still be retreating. Except maybe for Liv, who was in the corner of the dining room back on the phone with her father.

"No, Dad," she was saying. "I'll be fine. I'm here for

one more night. You don't need to come and get me tonight. Tomorrow's fine. I promise."

Liv was a joy to get to know—she was complex and standing at a crossroads in her life. Jane felt honored she could or would be able to guide her in any way. That she listed Jane as one of her artistic influences both amused and honored her. She mused about all of all the faces she had worn: Wife to a troubled actor who was an addict and abuser, daughter to a couple who adopted her, but then seemed to regret it, mother to the wonderful, but challenging London. And now, an inspiration to a young artist? Jane Starr, inspiration? Influence? Her heart filled with pride.

Chapter 44

As Cora walked through the garden to Kildare House, her phone buzzed. "Hello," she said.

"Cora," came the soft, lilting voice of her new acquaintance Zora. "If you want to speak with you-know-who, he's alone in the park, near the fountain. I just thought you might want to know."

"Thanks so much, Zora. I do think it would be helpful to talk with him," Cora responded, glancing at the time. "I better get moving."

"Yes," Zora said. "Time's a wasting."

Cora could be at the park in five minutes—if nobody saw her and tried to get her involved with a conversation. She decided to move quickly.

When Cora saw Professor Rawlings, she was surprised at how much younger he appeared in person than on his profile page from the university. Odd, usually it was just the opposite.

"Mind if I sit down?" she asked him.

He tilted his head up. "No, not at all." He smiled.

"I come here to feed the birds, when I can. I'm about done."

He was handsome, she supposed, in a kind of unassuming way: nice big brown eyes framed by dark lashes and a pleasant enough face. Certainly not an over-the-top handsome that she would expect from an older man having affairs with his students.

Birds flitted about them. Rawlings held a nearly empty bag of birdseed.

"I thought about becoming an ornithologist," he said. "I just love birds."

Birds? This professor who'd been painted an evil psychopath was sitting here feeding the birds?

The fountain gurgled behind them. Birds chirped and darted around them. It was a veritable Disney scene, Cora mused, half expecting Snow White to come dancing along in front of them.

"I like birds more the older I get," Cora said. "Or should I say I appreciate them more the older I get."

"You appreciate a lot more with age," he said, and scattered more seeds around. The birds flocked and landed, eating up the seed.

"I'm Cora, by the way. New in town," she said.

"Oh?" His eyebrow went up. "Nice to meet you. I'm Gerald. I've lived here for pretty much my whole life."

As he spoke, Cora was psychologically profiling him. He really didn't even want to be an English professor—he loved birds. He was aging—and was not happy about it. Plus, he'd lived here his whole life. Midlife crisis?

"How nice," Cora said. "You must know everybody here."

He grunted. "Yep."

"Tell me, do you know that poor Gracie who's missing?" Cora said after a minute.

His head snapped back around to look at her. His eyebrow gathered into a V.

"Say, you weren't just looking for me at the Blue Note, were you?" he asked.

"Yes, I was," she said. "We needed to know if Gracie was with you. The cops weren't telling us a thing."

He let out a whistle and puffed his cheeks out.

"Gracie was not with me, I can assure you," he said. "I knew her briefly. She's not from around here, but she was a student at the university where I teach English." He threw the last of the birdseeds, crumpled up the bag, rolled it into a ball in his hands, and kept rolling it back and forth.

"Not ornithology, then," she smiled, then laughed a little.

"No," he said, chuckling.

"You don't like your job?"

"It has its perks," he said, after a minute.

Perks, like young females? Cora wanted to say but didn't.

"I love the teaching part. I love being around young people, especially bright ones. It's fabulous. Inspiring. But I don't like the politics. The need to constantly be getting published. It gets tedious," he said.

"I guess you've got to take the good with the bad. In anything," Cora said, thinking of how she loved to craft, loved her crafters and her blog, but the organizing part not so much. How she used to love the women she helped at the Sunny Street Women's Shelter, but how she couldn't handle the flip side of it—when she couldn't help, no matter how hard she tried.

"True," he said. "What do you do, Cora?"

"I run a craft retreat," she said. She liked the sound of that, liked the feel of it. She was no longer a counselor at a women's shelter. It was taking time to get used to that. "We live over at Kildare House. Do you know it?"

He perked up. "Why yes, I do," he said. "I'd heard something about new owners. That's you, hey?"

"Yes, in fact, we have a retreat going on right now," she said. "I'm taking a bit of a break. Had to get out for a few minutes."

"I see," he said.

"Part of the reason we moved here is because it's so safe here, you know? The next thing you know there were the murders of the librarian and her ex-husband, and now that boy, what's his name, Henry, and then there's Gracie who's still missing," she said. "It doesn't seem so safe here anymore."

He bristled at the mention of Henry. "Henry was a brilliant young man." His voice cracked as his gaze fell off. "Gracie? She was a bright, hardworking woman. Good as gold, really."

"I hope they find her," Cora said.

He bit his lip. "Me too. It must be awful for her parents. I saw them on TV, pleading for her release. It broke my heart."

He was really torn up about this. He was not faking it. Cora was astute about knowing when someone was lying. She found herself feeling sorry for him, in a way. Yes, he was a lech when it came to young women. But sitting here on this bench, he seemed like a nice guy, maybe in the throes of a midlife crisis. He didn't seem crazy, as his soon-to-be ex-wife had portrayed him. She knew better than to leap to conclusions, but he didn't seem like a killer.

"But this is all very unusual for Indigo Gap," he went on. "Don't judge us quite yet. Stick around a while longer."

She had no choice. She was deep in debt for the mortgage. She and Jane had to make this work.

"Well," he said, standing. "It was nice chatting with you, Cora. Maybe we'll see you around sometime."

"Sure," she said. "Maybe you can come and do crafts with us."

"Crafts?" he said. "Nah, I'm a woodworker. I bet you don't give classes in that."

"You never know, Gerald. Don't judge us yet," Cora said, and grinned.

After he left, Cora sat, listening to the fountain and watching the birds. Gerald Rawlings surprised her. She was glad of it. A good reminder that you couldn't judge people based on what others said about them, what was online about them, and not even really, what they had done in their past.

Chapter 45

After she got back to Kildare House, Cora uploaded the photos to her Web site and wrote some captions to go along with them. Her Web site and blog were her pride and joy. Throughout the years of hard work, she'd learned a lot about blogging and technology and the intersections of it all with her own creativity. It felt more like work than passion sometimes, but most of the time, she loved what she was doing. But she'd rather be crafting, of course.

This week, after everybody left and her life settled back down a bit, she was giving herself an inspiration week. Several new craft projects called out to her for exploration and she was going to give herself time to do it. Several guest posts were scheduled for the week. One from a grief-stricken knitter she'd met during the last retreat. But her post on "Knitting a Life Without Your Partner" was beautiful and scheduled to publish on Wednesday. Another guest post was coming from a famous crochet artist in Paris, all about the new trends in crochet. In the meantime, crochet was one of the things Cora wanted to delve into. She planned to catch up on some upcycling projects. She recently found some pretty old cotton shirts at a yard sale and thought about turning them into aprons. She wasn't the world's best seamstress, but she liked sitting and stitching. She also thought she might make some bags from the shirts. She had purchased linen towels that begged to be bags or aprons or something. The shirts and linen towels were piling up in her bedroom.

She had collected more old silverware, one of her favorite items to craft with. She wanted to make standing frames with them. A box of silver with pretty flourished handles sat on her kitchen table. Oh, and they sat next to the whisks Cora wanted to turn into candleholders.

She drew in a breath as a wave of weariness over-took her. Soon, tomorrow, she and Jane would visit and make inquiries into the Gracie and Henry situa-tion—and then her time would be her own. A week. For her. And for the business.

She crawled on top of her quilted bed and pulled an afghan over her. Luna jumped on her stomach, kneaded the blanket with her claws, and curled in a purring ball on Cora's lap. Cora concentrated on the relaxed purring and drifted off into a dream of goddesses and light and cats and candleholders.

She awakened about an hour later, which was longer than she expected to sleep. She curled on her side and thought about her dreams. Yes, she thought, the next room would be a Brigid room. Kildare House now offered "Mémé's Boudoir," "Clothilde's

Tapestry Room," and now she planned a Brigid room. She knew the exact room, and as she thought it over, she realized it had been happening all along.

She rose from her bed. Luna meowed, letting her know it was time to eat. Cora fed her and then hopped into the shower to prepare for the big night.

She selected a black and orange polyester minidress, along with her platform boots. This would be a fun night, she told herself, willing away the skittering of nerves she felt when she thought of Adrian. Or when she allowed her thoughts to wander to Liv, or Henry, or most especially Gracie. Where was she? Was she dead or alive?

Did Detective Brodsky have any answers?

She hoped he did by now.

She slipped on her boots and smeared matching orange lipstick onto her lips. *Wild,* she thought. It really matched. She dug around for her huge gold hoops and the chain she wanted to wear, found them. Then she ran her fingers thought her red hair.

Ready or not, here I come.

As she walked down the steps, she thought of this moment. She wanted to capture it; it was every bit as special as the first retreat. Perhaps more so. Holding the first successful retreat was glorious, but doing two? A triumph!

The scent of chocolate welcomed her. The sound of the banjo quartet she hired was providing a festive atmosphere. All the crafters were gathering in the living and dining rooms and as Cora walked around they smiled at her with warmth. Ah yes.

The table in the dining room was stacked with chocolate-covered fruit, cake, bread, and oh yes, fondue.

Women were piling their plates high—as she soon would.

"Look who's here!" Jane came over, dragging Adrian alongside her.

"Why, hello!" Cora said, and hugged him politely. Well, he was looking fine, his jade-green eyes taking her in. "Glad you could make it," she said.

"Of course," he said. "You look stunning. And very groovy, I might add."

"Thank you," Cora said. "You look great, too." *Extremely great, as a matter of fact.*

She allowed herself to be whisked away momentarily for a bit of private conversation, knowing it could not last because she must socialize with the other guests.

"How are you?" she asked.

He glimpsed away for a second and then looked back at her. "I'm fine. Or, um, I'll be fine. It's been tough."

"I'm so sorry," Cora said. "Is there anything I can do?"

He cocked an eyebrow and grinned flirtatiously. "Perhaps we can talk about that later."

Brave words for a man who'd yet to even kiss her. Good Lord, the man made her tingle! She struggled to keep her composure.

Their conversation was interrupted by Cashel O'Malley, who was full of smiles and swagger, as usual. "Who's this, Cora? A crafter?" He gave a sarcastic tilt of his head and a crooked smirk.

Cora refrained from swatting him, but then made the introduction he so clearly wanted.

Cora sipped from her champagne glass and surveyed the room. Cashel and Adrian were chatting about something near the fireplace. She didn't know why that made her curious. What could the two of them possibly have in common?

Adrian was sweet and bookish. Cashel was brash and annoying. Yet, they stood smiling and chatting, as if they were best friends.

Maddy came up to her just then. "I just wanted to thank you, once again."

"For what?" Cora said.

"For the retreat," Maddy said. "My life is so crazy. You have no idea. This has been such a treat. I feel like I found a part of myself I've been missing. I hate to leave this place."

Cora blinked back a tear. "You can always come back," she said. "And please stay in touch." Her throat constricted the way it did when she was trying not to cry. This is one of the many reasons she wanted to hold these craft retreats. Today's women were often pulled in so many directions they rarely reflected, or paused for anything like crafting or reading. Or whatever.

She didn't hold the retreats just for the battered and damaged women—but also for the woman who just needed to learn to carve space for herself. It was a different kind of healing. If you were working on a craft project, it could help to carve inner space.

Cashel laughed loudly from the other side of the

room. Adrian laughed a charming, not too boisterous laugh.

"I hope to come back. But I saw in an ad you're doing the Big Island Beach Retreat soon. I've read a lot about that retreat. It's pretty famous," Maddy said.

"It's going to be fun," Cora said, but she wasn't certain. So far, the organizers had yet to firm up the plans and the retreat was only six weeks away. "I've read a lot about it as well. I think this is the fifteenth year."

"The resort looks fabulous," Maddy said, as Sheila and her daughter joined them.

Cora pictured it in her mind. Yes, it did look relaxing and fabulous.

"I taught there last year," Sheila said. "It worked out."

Something about the tone of her voice made Cora bristle. "That's good to know. We've not gotten an itinerary or anything yet."

Sheila laughed. "Sounds about right. They seem disorganized. But it always works out."

"We love it here. So inspiring," Donna said.

"I'm glad you enjoyed it, even with the problems," Cora said.

"Please let us know how that turns out," Donna said. "We're leaving tomorrow afternoon. We're going to hang out in town a bit before we go. Indigo Gap has so many wonderful shops to explore."

"Have you visited Patty's Paperie?" Cora asked. "They just opened. Fabulous paper products. Loads of scrapbooking supplies."

Cora saw Paul enter the room and he gravitated

toward Liv and the group of women she was sitting with. Then the two of them walked toward the table, where he started loading his plate with food. He probably really needed to eat.

"It's on our list," Sheila said. "But we also wanted to check out the basket shop."

"Marianne has really inspired us."

Just then Marianne's head turned toward them, letting them know she'd heard the comment, and she grinned.

Jane clinked on her glass and stood on the bottom stair. "Can I have your attention please?"

The room quieted.

"I'd like to make a toast to Cora," she said, then cleared her throat. "A few years back, she envisioned a craft retreat. A safe place for women to come and explore new crafts and get away from it all. Kildare House is her vision made real. Thank you, Cora, for allowing me to tag along."

"Hear, hear!" Ruby said, and whooped.

Marianne joined in the whooping. The crowd cheered and laughed, toasting Cora, who was grinning from ear to ear.

Later, after the cleanup, Cora and Adrian planned to get together, but both were so exhausted they said their good-byes on the front porch. His arms slipped around her and his lips found hers. Finally.

He tasted of chocolate and champagne and as he pressed his lips against hers, he drew her farther into him. This was not a man who lacked confidence.

His control, tinged in tenderness, left her breathless, her heart racing, and the world seemed to stop spinning. The night circled around them as she kissed him back and felt her insides quiver.

More was the only word forming in her mind, as she willed her knees to stop trembling.

Chapter 46

Monday morning found Cora waking up with a stretch and a smile. Life was good. Her second retreat was over. Her love life was taking a good turn. And she felt rested and refreshed.

As she readied to meet Jane to attend an early meeting with Chelsea, she thought about the missing Gracie, the murdered Henry, and the professor.

Most importantly, how were they all connected—if they even were? She and Jane hoped to find out. After all, Paul was staying with her. And Jane's London was heartbroken and frightened over Gracie's disappearance. They both had a vested, personal interest in this case.

Luna reached up her paw and gently touched Cora's mouth.

"Good morning to you, too," Cora said. Luna began to purr. "I suppose you want to eat."

She untangled herself from her quilts and rose to meet the day.

* * *

After Jane dropped London off at school, she drove Cora to the diner to meet with Chelsea, who was already there, perched at a corner table. After they ordered breakfast, they got down to it. She was not one to mince words—she didn't have time for pleasantries.

"I'd like to help, but I'm not sure what you want from me," she said, and lifted her cup of steaming coffee to her mouth. She blew on it, then gingerly took a sip.

"We're curious about a couple of things," Jane said. "Did you know about Gracie's depression?"

She nodded. "Yes, I knew. Of course. But she was on medication and she was seeing a doctor. I never had any qualms about leaving my kids with her. She had it under control."

Cora thought it was mighty generous of her. As was her turning over the keys to Gracie's apartment at her house. Gracie's apartment was situated over the family's attached garage. Cora and Jane were going to trace Gracie's day. And it began at her apartment. Of course, the police would have already been there. But it still might be helpful.

"I have to be honest," Jane said. "I'm not sure if I would have been quite so comfortable with her staying with London if I had known. Sometimes the medication just stops working. Sometimes, something happens to set a depressed person off. What would happen to London if she had an episode when she was under her care?"

Chelsea hesitated.

Cora was impressed with Jane's line of questioning.

"Depression doesn't exactly work like that," Chelsea

said. "At least it didn't with her. I kept in touch with her about it. We chatted about it often. She seemed fine."

She squirmed in her seat, as if she couldn't get comfortable. The server arrived with a huge tray full of their breakfast orders. She placed plates down in front of the three women.

Cora's stomach growled. The smell of her chocolate pancakes heightened her hunger.

"Why didn't you tell me about it?" Jane asked, before biting into her cheese omelet.

"Well, it wasn't a secret. I guess I figured you knew. Besides, she's such a capable young woman," she replied. "Even with her problems, she was the best." A group of gray-haired ladies walked by, laughing.

Was, Cora noted. Cora was not ready to use the term *was* when referring to Gracie.

"So, do you think she's dead?" Cora asked.

"Cora!" Jane said, and dropped her fork.

"As a mom, as a person, I have hope, I suppose," Chelsea said, "But as a lawyer and someone who has seen missing person cases . . . Well, with each passing day I have to say it would be a miracle if she turned up alive." Her voice cracked and she gazed off. Her carefully made-up eyes began to water. She dabbed her napkin at the corners.

"I'm sorry," Cora said. "I didn't mean to upset you."

She waved her off. "My kids are heartbroken. That's what hurts. I don't quite know how to handle it. And I need to hire another nanny soon. I don't know what to do about it. Right now, my mom is staying with the kids, but that's not an ideal situation. I may have to find another student. But that can be iffy."

She shoved food around on her plate—but nothing made its way in her mouth yet.

"What have you heard about Professor Rawlings?" Jane asked.

"What do you mean?" she asked.

"Is he still being questioned?"

"I can't comment on any of that," she said. "But I can tell you that the police are looking at him."

Cora was nearly swooning over her pancakes, which were fluffy cakes full of chocolate pancake goodness. She cut a piece and held it up to her mouth, lifting her eyes, feeling like someone was watching her. Her eyes met those of a man at the cash register, who quickly shifted his gaze. Who was he? He looked so familiar.

"Why don't you call Brodsky for an update?" Jane asked. "He seems to like you."

Chelsea laughed. "If he likes you, you're one of the few."

Cora swallowed her bite of pancake. "I'll give him a call later. But he won't tell me anything he's not supposed to tell me. Believe me."

She glanced back up where the man had been standing. He had his back to her. But now she remembered him—she'd seen him in here once before and had thought he might be a tourist. And he was the young man who came to her door peddling computer repair services. Today, his long, stringy hair was pulled into a ponytail.

"But you helped him with the last case. It seems like he might come to rely on you," Jane said.

Now Cora laughed. "The only reason I was involved with it is because I had to be."

"Kind of like this case," Jane said.

"There's actually two cases here," Cora said, her attention now back squarely on Chelsea and Jane. "Have they made any headway with Henry's murder?"

Chelsea nodded. "We are expecting more DNA results this morning." She glanced at her watch.

"DNA? So quickly?" Cora asked.

"There was a rush placed on it," she said. "And there was an opening at the lab, which helped."

"What kind of DNA did they get from him?" Jane asked.

"I know there was some hair and skin. He put up a good fight evidently," Chelsea said, and finally took a bite of her scrambled egg.

Cora's stomach twisted into a hard ball. Put up a good fight. Poor Henry. So young. She said a silent prayer to the universe that justice would be done for Henry.

"So many times DNA evidence leads nowhere. I've seen it so often. It could be his girlfriend's hair he still had on him, for example. I know he didn't have a girlfriend, but you know what I mean."

"But of course they have to try," Jane said.

"Of course," she replied. The conversation halted as the women ate their breakfast. Cora mentally sorted through what she learned here this morning. *Not much.* But they did know the professor and his girlfriend were still being held. And they also knew the DNA results on Henry's murder were rushed and would be in this morning. Cora knew enough about these matters to know the rushing of DNA tests meant someone was taking quite an interest in his case. These things were not taken lightly. Shoving aside other tests in order to do his. Perhaps it meant they were close to finding the killer.

"I wonder if Henry's death has anything to do with Gracie's disappearance. I hate to keep harping on this, but it seems too coincidental these events both occurred to such good friends. Friends who were both linked to the professor and were in this group therapy thing at the school," Cora said.

Chelsea shrugged and she bit into a piece of whole wheat toast.

"We know the professor is an egotistical ass," Jane said.

Chelsea laughed and coughed.

"Are you okay?" Cora said.

She nodded, her face red from coughing and choking a bit on her toast.

"I love hearing him described that way. So spot-on," she said.

"But I think the question is, does being an egotistical ass mean you're a killer or an abductor?" Cora said. She didn't think so. The image she held in her mind was of him sitting on the park bench feeding the birds. Sure, he could be both an egotistical ass and a bird lover. But a killer?

Chelsea lifted her eyebrows in surprise. Jane didn't.

"I wish things were that simple," Chelsea said.

Chapter 47

Before Jane and Cora began on their journey
retracing Gracie's activities on the day she disappeared, they headed back to Kildare House to check
on things there. It was still early in the day, around
9 AM. They knew some of the retreaters were still
around. Sheila and Donna were staying until the
next day. Liv planned to leave today. They were still
concerned about Liv's safety and wanted to check in
with her before the day got away from them.

"She's not up yet," Donna told them. Donna and
Sheila were sitting at the kitchen table, planning their
day of touring the local craft shops.

"She does like to sleep in a bit," Jane said.

"She was up late," Sheila replied. "I heard her in
her room around two, I think."

"Two?"

"What was she doing up at two?"

"I thought she went to bed when we all went to
bed," Cora said.

"I think she couldn't sleep. I heard her digging around in the kitchen," Donna said.

"Well, I'll leave her a note to call me when she gets up," Cora said. She scribbled the note and placed it in front of the coffeemaker.

"Hope you two have fun," Cora said. "We'll catch you later. If you need anything, call me. Okay?"

"Sure thing," Donna said.

By the time Cora and Jane arrived at Gracie's apartment in Chelsea's home, they sorted over all the possible scenarios of Henry's murder, Gracie's disappearance, and how it could be connected or not. But nothing they imagined prepared them for walking into Gracie's apartment.

Cora reached over on a wall and flipped on the light switch. There was only one window in the place and it was dark, almost dungeon-like. The light helped. But even the décor was dark. One wall was painted black. No posters, no pictures, nothing.

"I'd never imagined Gracie would have a black empty wall," Jane said.

"Maybe she didn't do the decorating. This really isn't her place, you know? She lived here for free for taking care of the children," Cora said.

Jane sighed, deep and heavy. "Okay," she said. "Her day. It would start in her bedroom, of course," she said.

They walked passed the black wall and Cora told herself it was just a wall, why did it unsettle her so much?

The bed was made—a burgundy chenille bedspread. Cora almost yelped with relief that her bedspread offered a little color. On either side of her bed were matching nightstands, both filled with photos. Most of them were her with Paul. There they were at a wedding, sitting at a table, his arm around her, she was holding a drink, smiling. There they were at a park, riding a carousel, laughing. Or at least she was. He was gazing at her.

"Wow, they took a lot of photos together," Cora said.

"Paul loved to take her picture. I remember her mentioning something about that," Jane said. "So she woke up and made her bed."

"Probably went into the bathroom," Cora said as she walked into the tiny room. It was full of beauty products: makeup, lotions, and a blow-dryer still plugged in. She walked back out into the bedroom.

"She would have gotten dressed here," Jane said. She stood next to her dresser, which held a small jewelry box and a book. Jane picked up the book. "Oh, here's her calendar," she said.

"That's odd, you'd think the police would have taken it," Cora replied.

Jane flipped through it. "There are only a few things in it. Maybe that's why they left it. It looks like she didn't keep up with it."

"She probably used her phone more," Cora said. "I know I do. I'd be lost without mine."

"Oh, this is interesting. It slipped out from between the pages," Jane said, holding up an old postcard with ruby red shoes on it and the quote, "There's no place like home." She turned it over. "From some guy named Ted. *'Saw this in an old shop, thought of you. Love, Ted.'"*

"Ted? I wonder who that is?" Cora said.

"No last name," Jane replied.

Cora shrugged. "She does appear to be over the top about *The Wizard of Oz*," Cora said. "Look at that." She pointed to a print of Dorothy and all the main characters on the far wall.

"She was reading the book when she was at our place earlier," Jane said.

"Have you ever read it?" Cora asked.

Jane shrugged. "No, I've seen the movie countless times. Never wanted to read the book. Have you?"

"I may have," she said. "I remember having the book. I just can't remember if I read it."

The two of them walked out of the bedroom and back into the living room, where there was another print of a *Wizard of Oz* scene.

"She probably went into the kitchen for coffee next," Jane said. The two of them walked into the kitchen. Coffee was still in the pot.

"It's odd she would have left any coffee. She was quite the coffee drinker," Jane said.

"Maybe she was running late. Or got distracted," Cora said.

Jane opened the refrigerator. "Milk, beer, butter. All the usual stuff."

A rinsed-out bowl was in the sink. A cereal package sat on the counter.

"So she had time for a bowl of cereal, but not to finish her coffee?" Jane said.

"It could be her second pot?"

"I don't know. I don't see any coffee cups around."

"Maybe she took it with her. Yes, she always had a take-along coffee mug in her hand," Jane said.

"Then leftover coffee in the pot is even more odd," Cora said.

Jane nodded.

"So she eats her cereal, rinses out her bowl, and leaves in a hurry, leaves some coffee behind and heads to your place?"

"No, she had an appointment that morning," Jane said. She pulled out her phone and reviewed her notes. "She had a hair appointment, but she never showed. She wasn't scheduled to be at my place until later."

They walked back into the living room. The garage apartment was small and efficient, but it did have more room than Cora thought. Other than the black wall in the living room, it was decorated pretty much the way she would have imagined a law student's room—except, of course, for all *The Wizard of Oz* stuff. Bookcases filled the living room and there was even one in the bedroom—mostly legal books and textbooks.

"I'm not sure this exercise has yielded any results," Jane said.

"It's told us a lot," Cora said. "She was a very serious student, looking forward to law school."

"I guess you're right. But I could have told you that."

"She had a thing for *The Wizard of Oz*," Cora said.

"We already knew that," Jane said.

"But we didn't know how much. I mean, really, it's the only kind of decoration she has."

"True."

"Law and *The Wizard of Oz*," Cora said.

Jane sat down on the couch and crossed her arms.

"And we know she was either in a hurry or distracted enough to not finish the coffee she made."

Cora sat next to Jane. She had a feeling they shouldn't be here. Or like they were invading Gracie's privacy. But they really hadn't dug through drawers or cabinets or anything. Cora's stomach fluttered at the very thought of it.

"Should we look around more?" Jane asked.

"I don't know," Cora said. "What would we find in her drawers and closets that would lead us into knowing where she's disappeared to? The point of this is to see how she went through her day, trace her footsteps to see if anything is out of order. I have a weird sense of invading her personal space."

Jane nodded. "Me too. I feel sad here."

The room, with its black wall and *Wizard of Oz* prints, a couple of mismatched chairs and worn sofa, was not warm in the least. The two of them sat there, taking it in, when Cora's phone rang.

She glanced at her screen. "It's Brodsky," she said.

Jane pulled a face. "Don't tell him where we are."

"Hello," Cora said.

"Hey, it's Brodsky," he said. "We need to talk. Can you come to the station?"

"When?" she asked.

"Now," he said.

"What? Why? This sounds urgent."

"It is," he said.

"I'll be right there," Cora said, clicked off the phone, and turned to Jane. "He wants to see me at the station. It's urgent. Do you want to come along?"

"Just try to stop me," Jane said. "After all, it is the prettiest police station on the planet."

Chapter 48

Indigo Gap was a historic town on steroids, as was evidenced by its police department, housed on the main street, low-key, but classically designed. Eggplant façade and window boxes graced the outside and its waiting area was beautifully appointed. But, as you walked back through the snaking hallways to offices of the detectives, it felt more like the police stations back in Pittsburgh.

The secretary showed them the way, even though both Jane and Cora had been there before. They walked past the cubical where Officer Glass sat—Cora was glad he wasn't around, but she also noticed a good bit of activity in the open room. She'd never witnessed it here.

Detective Brodsky was standing behind his desk looking out a window when Jane and Cora entered the room.

"Please sit down, ladies," he said. He wasn't wearing his suit jacket, as was the usual. His shirt sleeves were rolled up and his tie was loosened and crooked.

Cora and Jane glanced at one another and sat down.

"I have a bit of a problem," he said.

"How can we help you?" Cora said.

"I'm not sure you can," he said, folding his arms. "But since Paul is in your house . . . you know him as well as I do."

"Paul? He's not in trouble, is he?" Jane said.

"He might be. We do have a killer on the loose."

"What? Why Paul?"

"No, you don't mean he's a suspect, do you?" Cora said.

He sat down with a grunt. "None of this makes any sense. But the DNA evidence is clear."

Cora felt as if her stomach were in her mouth. She breathed deeply. What was going on? Was she housing a murderer? Had she placed her guests in danger? She took in more air.

"We know who killed Henry and it wasn't Paul," Brodsky said.

Cora exhaled.

Jane's grip released on the chair arm.

"It was Gracie."

The room was silent for a few beats. Cora blinked and peered at Jane.

"Excuse me?" Cora managed to say.

"Gracie killed Henry."

"That's absurd!" Jane said. "Gracie is not a killer. She's a gentle soul. You should have seen her with my London."

"Besides," Cora said. "She went missing before Henry was killed."

"Exactly," Brodsky said, and pointed to Cora. "Which

makes me wonder if she was really missing or just was lying in wait for the opportunity to kill Henry."

"Ridiculous!" Jane said, and pounded her fist on the chair handle.

"Calm down," Cora told her, and reached for her hand, which was tense and hard. Cora rubbed her hand. But chills came over her as she considered what Brodsky just said.

"Now, DNA evidence is hard to trump," he said. "It isn't always one hundred percent accurate. But this was absolutely clear. She killed him."

"How could she kill him? I mean, physically, she was much smaller than Henry. Did she have a gun? Some kind of weapon?" Cora asked.

"A blade," he replied. He gazed in another direction. "It was a gruesome scene. In fact, some of my officers wondered if it was an animal attack, until they found the blade."

Jane sobbed. Her face crumpled. "No, I just can't believe it."

Cora's arm went around her friend.

She tried to sort through what she knew of Gracie, what she knew of Henry, and the professor.

"What would her motive be?" she asked. "It doesn't make sense that she'd kill Henry. They were friends," Cora said.

"I know. I've been trying to piece it together. I've found nothing. I've asked myself . . . were they having an affair? No evidence of that."

"Even if they were having one, what would he have done for her to want him dead. It doesn't fit with her personality. She was a nanny. A law student," Cora said.

Jane sobbed. The detective handed her a box of tissues.

Cora suddenly remembered the woman she grew up with who'd had a complete nervous collapse one day and killed her entire family. "You know, Gracie was seeing a therapist and was on antidepressants," Cora said.

"Pshaw," Jane said. "A depressed person isn't a psychotic person!"

"I know that, sweetie," Cora said with a gentle inflection in her voice. "But remember our neighbor when we were kids?"

Jane nodded.

"Sometimes, there are no answers as to why murder happens. Why a person sort of breaks and freaks out."

"True, but those cases are extremely rare," Brodsky said. "If that's what happened, it's more imperative than ever to find her before she harms someone else or herself."

"But you've searched everywhere," Jane said.

"It's frustrating," he said under his breath. "I've got my best guys on this. I've called the state and FBI for help. I'm still waiting to hear back on both counts."

"Wait. What about the professor? What does he know about where she is? It seems like he'd know something," Jane said through her sobs.

"He's not talking," he said.

"Of course," Cora said. Her arm was still around Jane. "I spoke with him yesterday. He seems more concerned about Gracie than anything else."

"Why were you talking with him?" Brodsky said. "Never mind. I just don't want to know."

Jane's phone beeped, alerting her to a text message. She glanced at it. "It's Ruby, wondering we are. London's awake. I need to go."

"Wait," Brodsky said. "I need your word you won't tell anybody about this."

"Sure," Jane said. "Who'd believe it, anyway?"

"I need you both to keep your eyes and ears open in regard to Paul," he said.

"What do you mean? Do you think he's in danger?"

"I don't know. But, as I've said before, I think he knows more than he thinks he knows," he said. "Do you follow?"

"I think so," Cora said.

"Just let us know if there's anything suspicious about his behavior, or if he disappears for any long amount of time. You know, things like that."

"Do you think she'd come for him?" Cora asked, her heartbeat quickening.

"We have no way of knowing what kind of shape she's in, or even if she's still alive," he said. "But if she is, and she needs help, I'm betting Paul would be the first person she contacts."

Chapter 49

"We should just go home, right?" Jane said as they climbed into the car.

"I reckon," Cora said. "I suppose it's more important we're at Kildare House today than scouting around about Gracie. So much for playing detective."

"Yeah, we should probably be keeping an eye on Liv, too," Jane said, after a few moments. She sniffed.

"This is truly bizarre," Cora said as she put the car into gear and started to drive toward home.

"Yeah," Jane said, and blew her nose. "I just don't know what to think. I don't think I can believe Gracie killed Henry."

"It's beginning to feel like *Alice in Wonderland* to me," Cora said. "Curiouser and curiouser."

"Not *The Wizard of Oz*?" Jane said, and laughed, halfheartedly, then sniffed again.

"No," Cora said. "*The Wizard of Oz* was about finding home, right? 'There's no place like home' and all that."

"Well, on one level, yes. But it was also about knowing your strengths and weaknesses, and realizing you had all this power all the time," Jane said. "Strength and magic you didn't know were yours."

Cora stopped at the only red light in town. She glanced at Jane. "Are we really talking about *The Wizard of Oz* now?"

"It would appear so," Jane said with drollness.

Cora noted her hands were still shaking on the steering wheel. "We are so in over our heads."

The light turned green and Cora crept along in the car, making certain she did not go over the twenty-five miles per hour speed limit.

"Yep, I've almost given up."

"Almost?"

"Well, there is Paul."

"Staying at Kildare House."

"Yep, and now we have this mission to watch him. How are we going to do that? He's a grown man and comes and goes as he pleases."

Cora grunted. "He sticks around the house mostly. He's kind of a homebody."

"But what if Gracie is still alive and shows up at Kildare House, half-crazed?" Jane asked, eyes wide.

"What if?" Cora said, pulling into the driveway. "What can we do about that? If she's alive, she's been hiding and she's been clever about it. The search teams have not found a trace. There's not been a trace of anything until today."

"I think I should send London to stay with someone for a few days, just until this blows over," she said.

"That might be a good idea," Cora said.

When the two of them entered the front door of

Kildare House, they saw Liv sitting on the couch with her laptop.

"Hey," she said. "My dad will be here soon and I'll be out of your way."

"You can stay as long as you like," Cora said.

"Have you seen Paul?" Cora asked, trying to sound nonchalant. From Jane's slanted glimpse in her direction, she hadn't been quite successful.

"He went to lunch with his parents," she said. "I think they were going to check out apartments as well."

Cora's heart began to thunder as she sucked in air. Calm down, she told herself, he was with his parents. He wasn't alone. Still, she felt the need to sit down. She found her chair and her basket of embroidery next to it. She needed to focus on something else or she was going to have a panic attack in front of Liv. Why did he have to go out today?

"Have you been getting any more notifications from the game?" Jane asked as she was texting someone herself. Cora assumed it was Ruby, who'd been staying with London.

"All morning long," Liv said. "I finally shut my phone off."

"I think that's good news," Jane said.

"Why?" Cora asked as she threaded her needle with red embroidery thread.

"Well, they must not know the police are watching. It means their technology is not as good as they think," Jane said, slipping her phone back into her bag.

Cora started to sew. The gentle motion of thread weaving into fabric always soothed her. She was hoping it would work its magic on her racing heart and fluttering stomach.

"Not necessarily," Liv said, snapping her laptop shut. "They may know and don't want the cops to know they know and so they are continuing to harass me, but going deeper underground."

Cora's stitches were not exactly even, but she wasn't going to care about perfection when she was trying to breathe. "Tell us about that. You know, that Darknet thing."

Liv sighed. "A lot of people won't even go on it for fear of viruses. But I have kickass security software."

"So people play games on it and what else do they do?" Jane asked.

"Buy drugs, prostitutes, commit all sorts of crime," she replied.

"What? How do they get away with that?"

"Sometimes they're busted. Like this guy who was running something called the Silk Road. What was his name? Let me think. Ross Ulbricht. His Silk Road was a black market with bitcoin as currency. He was busted on seven counts, including narcotics trafficking, and sentenced for life," she said.

"Why does it even exist? Isn't it illegal to even have it?" Jane asked.

"No, it's not illegal, but some of the activities are. And I have to tell you it's not all bad. It's been useful for journalists, dissidents, and whistleblowers, you know, that kind of thing," she said. "You need special software to access it. It was started by the government years ago as a way to safely share sensitive information online. Of course, others found out about it."

"So is this something students use a lot?" Cora asked.

"Some do," Liv said. "Some people just aren't interested. The school frowns on it, of course. There was a group of students a few years ago who got busted buying pot from the Darknet. But there was a mastermind behind all of that. He was on campus. What was his name? Ted. Yeah, Ted Brice. He was the same guy who wrote that letter, I guess."

"Interesting guy," Cora said.

"That's one way of putting it," Liv replied.

London and Ruby came through the front door. "Mommy!" London said, running to Jane and jumping on her lap.

Cora watched as Jane snuggled her daughter. The two of them sometimes nearly broke her heart.

Chapter 50

"What's on your mind?" Ruby said, as she plunked down on the couch next to Cora.

"Nothing," Cora said, watching as Jane and London left the room to find something to eat in the kitchen.

"You're sewing," Ruby pointed out. "You usually sew when something is on your mind."

"It helps me to think and to calm down, I grant you," Cora said, and kept her eyes focused on the design and her work. "But nothing in particular is worrying me. Just life in general."

Ruby grunted. "Any news on Henry's murder case? Or on Gracie? I know you two met with Chelsea this morning."

Liv's head tilted in interest.

"Not really," Cora said, and sighed. She was such a bad liar. "She knew all along Gracie had problems and didn't take issue with it."

"Mighty big of her," Ruby said.

"That's what I thought, but I'm not too sure about

Jane. She probably wouldn't have hired her if she knew."

"That's a tough call," Ruby said after a minute. "It's your kid, you know?"

Cora nodded, keeping her eyes focused on the red coffee cup she was sewing into the fabric. She was thinking about so many things—Gracie's depression and maybe other mental problems were the least of them. She was also thinking about the coffeepot this morning; in fact, images of Gracie's apartment tugged at her. *Wizard of Oz. Darknet. Gracie killing Henry.* Too much to think about. Her heart was calmer now, now that her thoughts were elsewhere. She wasn't going to dwell on Paul being out and about with his parents. No, if indeed Gracie was still alive and roaming the streets of Indigo Gap, Cora was certain she would not approach Paul with his parents around.

"You know, I've been thinking about this game," Liv said.

"What game?" Ruby asked.

"*The Wizard of Oz* game," Liv said. "The one I've been playing. The one Gracie had been playing."

"Oh," Ruby replied.

Cora kept sewing, weaving her red thread in and out of the fabric.

"I really didn't have any concerns about playing it, but maybe these messages are part of a virus. Or something like a virus," she said. "I mean, I have kick-ass security software, but maybe this is different."

"Humph," Ruby said. "I don't know nothing about computer viruses or software. But I do know about people. Just sounds like some lunatic has crossed wires and enjoys making everybody jump through his hoops."

"Gamers can be like that," Liv said, after a minute of what appeared to be deep thinking on her part.

"What if it's not a game?" Ruby said. "What if people only think it's a game?"

"I don't follow," Cora said, looking up from her embroidery.

"What if it's a front for some kind of other thing. I don't know what. And you all have just stumbled into it?" Ruby said.

Liv's dark eyebrows lifted, and violet eyes sparkled with excitement.

"Sounds like something out of a sci-fi novel," Cora said.

"But it's possible," Liv said. "On one level it makes a lot of sense."

"Wouldn't the police know about something like this?" Cora said. "They don't pay attention at all when anybody brings up this game. Henry and Paul were adamant about it and they wouldn't listen."

"That leaves us with three possible explanations. One possibility is the police are right. There's no reason to check into the game. It's just a game. Period. Or they know something is fishy and are clamming up. Or, the last possibility is they don't know anything and are complete fools," Liv said. "You know your local cops, which is it?"

Ruby harrumphed. She crossed her arms. "It could be any of those things."

"In any case, what can we do about it?" Cora said. "If the game is a front—highly unlikely—what's it a front for? And what do they want with you, Liv? Why you?"

She shrugged. "Gracie and I were the only two women in the country who got to the Gates of Oz in the game. This is the only thing we have in common. The game. She was a law student. I'm an art student."

"You both went to the same school," Ruby said.

"The same school where Rawlings teaches as well," Cora said. "Could someone at the school be behind all this?"

"Do you mean someone besides the creepy professor? My money's on him," Ruby said.

Liv laughed. "Sorry, ladies, I don't think he's smart enough to pull something like this off. I'm not sure anybody I know is."

"But still," Cora said. "The school does seem to be the one thing all the players have in common."

"There has to be someone at the school who is smart enough to do something like this," Ruby said.

"I'm not convinced the game is anything more than a game," Liv said, glancing at her watch. "My dad should be here by now."

"Maybe you should check your phone," Ruby said.

"I shut it off because of all the notifications from the game, which I can't stop," she said, reaching for her phone, which was on the coffee table next to her. She flipped it on. "Yep," she said. "Dad is having car trouble. Looks like I'll be here another day." She eyed Cora with a sheepish look. "Is that okay?"

"It's more than okay, Liv. You are welcome to stay," she said, but thinking her planned week of exploration and relaxation was turning into something else. She wasn't quite sure what.

She finished embroidering her red coffee cup. It turned out well. Um, well, at least it resembled a cup. She wasn't quite ready to stop stitching. Next, she'd work on the saucer. Maybe by the time she finished it, she'd feel a little less unsettled. No matter how hard she tried, it was hard not to think about Gracie killing Henry.

Cora, Jane, and Ruby had previously scheduled time together for an "after the event" meeting where they could discuss what went well and what didn't for that afternoon. This felt a little odd to Jane, since they still had three guests staying at Kildare House, plus Paul, who had yet to find a new apartment.

After Jane dropped London off at a friend's house for a few days, she made her way back to Kildare House.

The three of them sat in the fiber-arts room, which hadn't seen much action, really. But it was gorgeous with its shelves of yarn, felts, and fabric. A modern geometric quilt hung high on the wall, and underneath was a shelf with spools of thread and an assortment of needles.

"Well, I think it was a smash," said Ruby, opening up the meeting.

"I think it could only have gone better if things out of our control hadn't happened," Cora said.

"True, but how could we possibly plan for a person disappearing and a murder and—" Jane stopped. She had almost said and *now they think Gracie killed Henry*. But she didn't.

"True," Cora said. Her fingers tapped on her notepad. "Was there anything else we could have done to make it better?"

"We did the best we could with the circumstances we were given," Jane said. "But maybe next time you don't invite someone else to stay here during a retreat."

Cora shot her a glare. Then seemed to relax. "Okay. Fair enough. Maybe I shouldn't have invited him to stay."

"But I mean, come on, what else could you do?" Ruby said. "You thought he was in danger."

Cora glanced at Jane. *She still thinks he is,* Jane thought. *And he might be.*

Cora bit her lip. Jane saw. It was getting difficult not to bring Ruby into the fold. Not to tell her the police think Gracie killed Henry. Those words rolled around in Jane's head and she wondered at the strangeness of them. This woman, Gracie Wyke, who tucked London into bed, fed her, bathed her. This gentle, smart, young woman killed a man? She could not make sense of it. Her stomach fluttered and she felt a chill travel up the length of her spine. She shivered. What if Gracie had harmed London? She would never forgive herself. Jane trusted her!

"Okay, besides all the other stuff going on," Cora said. Jane's head was still swimming. She was trying to concentrate on what Cora said. "What about the crafts? Did we stay in budget? Did people like them?"

The women all agreed that the crafts and catering went well. They may have even turned a bit of a profit during this retreat. They needed to firm up plans for the next retreat. But before then, all three of them were guest teaching at another retreat.

"Speaking of next time, the Big Island Beach Retreat is coming right up," Ruby said.

Jane hadn't even thought about it. She had been too busy thinking about this charm class and the disappearance of her babysitter. *Gracie, where are you? What have you done?*

She was trying to tamp down the feeling she placed her daughter in grave jeopardy by allowing Gracie to babysit her.

Cora poked her. "Jane?"

"Oh, I'm sorry," she said. "What?"

"What are you going to do at the Big Island Beach Retreat? They want our class synopsis next week," Cora said.

"I've been giving that some thought. But I'll let you know when I make up my mind," Jane said.

Cora sighed. "Okay. The deadline is next week, ladies. Get it together."

"Oh, there you are," Paul said as he entered the room.

Jane turned toward him. He was trailed by his mother and father, who examined the room in awe of the floor-to-ceiling fabrics and yarns.

"Hi, Paul," Cora said, then nodded to his parents. "What's up?"

Jane's heart started to race. There was something about this man she didn't quite like. She couldn't put her finger on it. And it was kind of absurd of her. He seemed so in love with Gracie. Refused to believe she ran off with the professor. Turned out he was right. Why didn't she quite like him?

"I think I found a place," he said, "but I won't be able to move in for a few weeks."

Weeks? Jane wanted to say. This man would be around Kildare House for weeks? That was it. That was one reason she didn't like him. Couldn't he see what an imposition he was? Couldn't he see the danger he was bringing to Cora and everybody who lived on the property?

But she knew Cora. And she knew she couldn't help but want to help people. It was in her genes. The disease to please. That's why she became a counselor. It was not something she could shake.

"Do you mind if I stay on until then? I promise I won't be a bother," Paul said. His puppy-dog eyes blinked. Jane knew what Cora's answer would be— she didn't have to wait.

Chapter 51

Cora mentally checked off the people who were still staying in Kildare House even though the retreat was over. Sheila and Donna would be leaving early in the morning—as would Liv. That left just her and Paul. For two weeks. Jane was glaring at her from across the table and she knew what she was thinking. Why didn't Jane trust him? Well, Jane didn't trust anybody—especially men—and with good reason.

"Of course, you can stay here. I wouldn't have it any other way," she told him.

Jane looked away.

Ruby sat back and crossed her arms.

Cora saw her week of exploration and relaxation being chipped away. Tomorrow, after everybody (except Paul) was gone, she'd etch out some time for herself to start a new project. Which one first? She wanted to try to crochet a rug. Maybe she should start there. She'd also been collecting old lightbulbs to experiment with—she'd seen them used as planters. But then, there was a spoon project she wanted to try. Spoons made into jewelry—necklaces using old jewelry pieces and spoons. Hmmm.

"How are you doing?" Cora asked as Paul came into her view.

He shrugged. "I'm on edge. I don't know what to think. I knew my Gracie wouldn't run off with that creep. But at the same time, at least I'd have known she was alive. Now—" His voice cracked. "I just don't know what to think."

"Have they released Henry's body yet?" Ruby asked.

"Nope," he said.

Jane glanced at Cora, then glanced away. Of course it was necessary to keep the body for evidence. But only the two of them knew what the evidence yielded. Cora's stomach clenched. Suddenly, she wished she hadn't been told about any of it. Paul was still in the dark. What would his reaction be when he learned the evidence pointed to his missing girlfriend killing his best friend? It was too much. Cora's heart lurched. Poor Paul.

"I keep thinking I'll get a text from her any minute. Or a call," he said, sitting down at the table. He was holding his phone. "But nothing."

"Something is bound to happen soon," Ruby said with a soothing voice Cora had not heard from her before. "The cops are working on it. Cashel has told me to stay out of things. He said they are close to cracking the case."

"Which case?" Jane said.

"I assumed he meant Henry's murder," she said.

Paul tapped his fingers on the table. "I miss her," he said. "I don't know what I'll do if she never turns up. Or if they never find her or whatever."

"That reminds me," Ruby said. "How did your day go? You were going to trace Gracie's footsteps. What happened?"

Paul sat up straighter. "You what?"

"Yes," Cora said. "We thought maybe we could figure out what happened if we traced her footsteps the day she disappeared."

"But we didn't get very far. We were sidetracked," Jane said.

"How far did you get?" Ruby persisted.

"Well, we did get a chance to search her apartment a bit this morning," Cora said.

"You did?" Paul said.

"Did you notice anything out of place?" Ruby asked.

"Well, we wouldn't know if something were out of place, but for the most part it just resembled a typical law student's apartment," Jane said.

"There were a couple of odd things. The black wall—"

"Yeah, we just painted it. It's chalkboard paint. She wanted a floor-to-ceiling chalkboard," Paul said.

"Oh, I didn't realize that's what it was," Cora said.

"You know, we did notice something odd. Knowing Gracie was such a coffee freak, I found it strange about the leftover coffee in the pot," Jane said.

Paul's dark head tilted. "That is odd."

"I mean, she always carried the big cup with her, right?" Jane said. "It's not like her to leave any coffee behind."

"She must have been in a hurry," Ruby said, shuffling some papers around on the table.

"No," Paul responded after a beat. "Not like her at all."

"Did she drink coffee all day long?" Cora asked.

"She used to. But she stopped. She had a few cups in the morning. And a few around three. She said if she drank more after three, she'd have a hard time sleeping."

"So what time did the cops say she probably disappeared?" Cora asked.

"I think it was between two and four," Jane said.

"So, she had made her afternoon pot of coffee, and maybe had one cup?" Cora said.

"I didn't notice the sink. Were there cups?"

Paul shook his head. "No, nothing in the sink. Well, just the cereal bowl."

"She's a very tidy person," Jane said.

"And very caffeinated," Ruby said.

Paul laughed. "It was her one weakness, she used to say. She didn't drink or do drugs or anything like that. But she did love her coffee."

Cora didn't know why her brain was stuck on the image of the half-full tiny coffeepot. But maybe what they had just come up with—a sort of timeline—was significant. She'd give Brodsky a call later to see what he thought—but that meant she'd have to tell him they were in Gracie's apartment. She knew he'd be unhappy.

Chapter 52

Before Cora settled in for the night, she checked her text messages.

There was a text from Adrian: **How about lunch tomorrow? —A.**

Okay, she texted back.

His response came right away: **My place? I make a mean Greek salad.**

His place? Hmm. It gave her pause. But as she thought about it, she didn't know why. He had taken his good old time kissing her. She was certain he was a good guy.

"Okay," she responded.

Then she checked over her other messages. There was one from Brodsky. She called him. After saying hello, he explained that he just wanted to check in with her about Paul.

"He's fine. But I just wanted to tell you about something. Please don't be angry," she said. And then she explained about being over at Gracie's place with Jane and about the coffee. "Anyway," she said. "I don't know why, but I thought the detail about the coffee might be important."

There was silence on the other end of the phone. "Brodsky?"

"Just a minute. I'm checking my notes," he said.

Cora heard the shuffling of paper. "Yeah," he said. "There was no coffee in the pot when we were there. Someone has been in the place. But since Chelsea is letting everybody and their brother in, it could be anybody. Even her."

"She said it was okay," Cora said.

"It's not a crime scene," he said. "But I specifically told her to stay out of there."

"Clearly, she's not thinking straight. Can you blame her? So, who else could have been in her place?" Cora asked.

"Probably Chelsea. But I'll get a tech crew over there right away. Maybe they can get some prints," he said. "I'd appreciate it if you'd stop your sleuthing."

"Well, we did. When you called, it interrupted our plans," she said, and laughed nervously. "We planned to trace her footsteps the day she disappeared, but then you called and stopped it," she said.

"Why are you so interested?" he asked.

"Well, you know Gracie babysat for Jane. London is taking this hard. She's having bad dreams and so on," Cora replied. She was sprawled out on her quilt-covered bed and getting sleepy. She suppressed a yawn. "And then there's Paul, who's staying here. So, of course I'm interested. I want to help."

"I think the best way for you to help is to let the

police do their jobs. Believe me, we are on it," Brodsky replied.

"You know, I don't mean to be a bother," Cora said. "We're staying out of your way. We're not doing anything illegal or dangerous. We didn't find anything, really."

"True," he said. "And you've been very helpful." There was a tone of exasperation in his voice.

Had she overstepped her bounds?

"I'm sorry, Brodsky," she said.

"It's okay," he said after a minute. "Just don't make it a habit."

"Now, I've still got some guests here, so I'm not quite free to move on."

"Who's still there?"

"One of my teachers and her daughter and Liv."

"I thought her father was picking her up today," he said.

"Car trouble," she said. "He thinks he'll be here tomorrow."

"She hasn't gone out, has she?"

"No, she's frightened," Cora said. "She keeps getting messages. She shut her phone off at one point."

"I'll pass it on to the cybercrimes unit and see what they say," he said.

"They probably already know," Cora said. "They're monitoring her phone and computer, right?"

"Hell, I don't know. If you say so. I don't understand any of that. I can barely send an e-mail," he said, and laughed.

Cora knew that was true. But he did seem to use his cell phone to send texts just fine.

He sighed. "It never used to be a part of my job."

"I hear you," she said, twisting a strand of her red hair. "What I can't believe is these gamers. So many of the young people are into these games. And this Dark-net stuff is scary."

"The game is on the Darknet, right? I was just read-ing about it."

"Yes, it is. Ruby thinks it's a front for something else. You know, the game is a front for some kind of criminal activity." She laughed. "That Ruby. We told her it sounds like something out of a sci-fi movie."

But Brodsky wasn't laughing.

Later, after Cora was actually in bed with Luna tucked between her shoulder and her neck, she grinned when she thought about her old crew at the women's shelter and what they would think about Brodsky. He was a good cop. She knew there were all kinds. They knew some bad ones, but mostly they were decent people just trying to do their jobs.

She tried not to think about it. She tried to fill her mind with pleasant images. Once everybody was gone and all this was over, she could have her explore and relax week, couldn't she?

But the events of the past five days nagged at her. Gracie disappearing. The craft retreat's success. Henry's murder. Paul staying with her. You just never knew what was going to happen. Life was funny.

But she remembered nobody offered her a plausi-ble explanation as to why she had received that weird text about a kidnapping. Was it because she was listein Jane's phone as an emergency contact? That's what someone said. But nobody knew for sure. Evidently the brilliant cybercrimes unit wasn't so brilliant after all.

Cora closed her eyes and concentrated on Luna's purring until she drifted off to sleep.

Chapter 53

A loud knocking woke Cora up. She squinted to see the clock: 3:18? The knock came again.

"Cora!" a male voice said. "Open up. You won't believe this."

She untangled herself from her blankets and quilts.

"Who is it?" she managed to say.

"It's Paul."

Paul? What was he doing here at this time?

She searched for her robe. "Just a minute," she said. "I'm coming."

"This better be good," she mumbled under her breath.

She opened the door to a wild-eyed Paul holding up his cell phone.

"I've gotten a text message from her!"

"Her? Who?" Cora managed to say as he walked through her door.

"From Gracie! Who else? I knew she wasn't dead. knew it," he said.

Gracie? Detective Brodsky was right! She was aliv and she had reached out to Paul. He told her to watch

Paul, but he didn't tell her what to do if Gracie actually contacted him! Cora stood there, her brain slowly waking up, her heart pounding. Air, she needed air.

"Cora?" he said.

"Yes? I mean, please sit down, Paul," she said.

"Sit down? She wants to meet me," he replied.

"Let me make some coffee. Let's talk about this, okay?"

"What's wrong? Why are you not excited and happy about this?"

Cora made her way to the coffeepot. "You woke me up out of a sound sleep. Give me a minute, okay?"

"She's alive!" he said, and started pacing. "I need to get to her. She needs my help. I'm not sitting around waiting for you to make coffee."

He started for the door.

"Wait!" she said. "Wait! You can't go until . . . until I tell you something important."

"About Gracie? How important can it be? She's alive and that's all I need to know," he said.

Cora filled up the coffeemaker with water, then hit the button.

"Yesterday, Detective Brodsky called me into to his office," she said. The coffee was starting to brew.

"And?"

"He told me some unbelievable news," she said, eyeing him up and wondering how he was going to take this. "Please stop pacing and sit down."

He stopped and finally sat down at her kitchen table.

"We were told not to tell you, but to watch you, in case . . . in case she contacted you."

"Gracie? You knew she was alive and you didn't tell me?"

"Wait!" she said. "There's more."

He popped up out of the chair and started for the door.

He stopped and turned around to glare at her. "How could you keep this from me?" How to tell him? How to find the words? Sometimes it was just best to be blunt. "The DNA evidence on Henry's murder indicates Gracie killed him."

Paul's jaw dropped. His face reddened with what—rage? Fear? He crunched into himself. Was he going to pass out?

She placed a hand on his shoulder.

When his head rose, his shoulders began to shake. He was laughing. Laughing.

"Paul?" she said.

She'd seen this reaction before.

"There's no way she killed him," he said. "They think Gracie killed Henry?"

"They are certain," she said, leading him back to the kitchen table. The coffee smell was filling the room now.

He sat down, still laughing, slightly hysterical.

"You like your coffee black, right?" she said, turning to her cupboards.

"Gracie is not a killer," he said, as Cora poured the coffee.

"And yet the evidence suggests she is," Cora said, and sat the coffee down in front of him. She sat down. He finally stopped laughing.

"Someone is trying to frame her," he said after a moment.

"That could be," Cora said. "But the person would have access to her DNA and have gone to a lot of trouble to frame her. Why?"

Paul's face fell into his hands as he sobbed.

Cora touched his shoulder. "If she reached out to you for help, you need to go to her. But first, try to drink your coffee and get it together. I'll call Brodsky."

She tried to ignore the immediate crushing sensation in her chest. But she knew she couldn't ignore it much longer. The last time she took one of her pills was at the last retreat. She didn't want to take another one.

"Don't be so hard on yourself. If you need one, take it," she heard her therapist's voice ringing in her head.

"I'll be right back," she said.

She went into the bathroom and took one of her pills. She didn't even peek at herself in the bathroom mirror. She felt sick about keeping this from him. The cops didn't want her to tell him, but it would have been the decent thing to do.

She came out of the bathroom intending to apologize to him—but he was gone.

Chapter 54

Cora tore out of her apartment, almost running into Liv, who was picking herself up off the floor.

"I heard all this commotion and it woke me up. Paul knocked me over," she said. "What's going on?"

"He heard from Gracie," Cora managed to say, but she kept moving. Where was he going? Did he say where Gracie said she'd meet him? She had to stop him! What if Gracie killed him, too?

"What?" Liv said, following her down the stairs.

Cora ignored her, trying to run through the house and get to the door. Stop him. She must stop him. She opened the door just in time to see his car pull away.

"No!" she said.

Liv was right behind her. She grabbed her by the shoulders. "What's going on, Cora?"

"He's running off to meet her," she said.

"So?"

"She may be dangerous," Cora said. She walked to the table where she kept an extra set of car keys. "I'r following him. Can you please call Detective Brodsky and tell him what's happening?"

"What? Wait. You need to stay here," Liv said.

"I agree," came a voice from the stairs. It was Sheila.

But Cora headed for the door. "You don't understand. This is my fault. If I had told him. If only I had told him." She was running on adrenaline. She felt it course through her system.

"No matter," Sheila said forcefully. "It will do you no good to place yourself in danger."

"The cops can track him if he has his cell phone," Liv said. She handed Cora the phone. "Call Brodsky yourself."

Maybe they were right. Maybe she shouldn't try to follow him. Maybe she should call Brodsky first.

He answered, sounding groggy, then said he'd be right over.

"Try not to worry, okay?" he said. He knew about her anxiety condition. "We can trace him through his phone. It will be okay. She probably won't hurt him."

But as they hung up, the word *probably* hung in the air and poked at her.

"Liv, can you trace Paul's phone? You know, work your hacking magic?"

"I don't know."

"It doesn't matter," Sheila said. "You need to leave it all to the police."

Cora felt a sense of calm starting to take over. Her pill was taking effect. She knew what Sheila said was true. But a part of her felt responsible for this.

"If anything happens to him, I'll never forgive myself," she said.

"He's a grown man," Sheila said. "He can take care of himself."

"Henry couldn't," Cora said, after a moment. "The police think she killed Henry."

"What?" Liv said.

Sheila gasped.

"So Paul thinks he's off to meet the love of his life and she might be luring him in for the kill," Liv said.

Cora and the others stood for a few moments, letting it sink in.

"Let me see if I can trace him. I have this app on my laptop I've been wanting to try," Liv said, and she headed back to her room to fetch the computer.

"Where is Brodsky?" Cora wondered out loud.

"I'll make some coffee," Sheila said, and scurried into the kitchen.

Cora followed, and soon Liv came back downstairs. They sat at the kitchen table. Liv placed her computer on the table and opened it. Her fingers clicked over the keyboard. The blue light from the screen shone on her face.

Sheila pressed the button of the coffeemaker. The room was quickly filled with the scent of coffee and the sound of nothing but Liv's fingers moving across the keyboard.

"Where is Brodsky?" Cora wondered again.

Sheila sat a cup of coffee down in front of Cora and one next to Liv's laptop.

"He's probably not coming here," Liv said. "Looks like there is a car chase heading across the mountains."

"They are chasing Paul?" Cora asked. Her stomach churned.

"How do you know?" Sheila said.

"It's this app. It's kind of like a police scanner and a tracer."

"Why would you have something like that?" Sheila asked.

"My dad bought it for me last year," she said. "He used to be a cop. He said this might come in handy."

"It seems illegal for you to have something like that," Sheila said.

"It doesn't seem like Brodsky is coming," Cora said, and sipped from her coffee mug. "He should have been here by now."

"Maybe he's going after Paul?" Liv said.

"Where could they be going? Where would Gracie want to meet him?" Cora said. She was trying to imagine what there was on the mountain. A rest area? A restaurant? She hadn't been over that way very often. Only once, as a matter of fact. And she thought there wasn't much over there.

"Can you pull up a map of the road?" Cora asked.

"Of course," Liv said, and pulled one up quickly.

"It appears to just be wilderness," Sheila said.

"Yes," Liv said. "But if you look here, farther down the road—there's Oz World."

Cora's heart skipped around in her chest. Could they be meeting at the very place Henry was found dead?

"You don't think?" Liv said, her eyes wide.

"What?" Sheila asked.

"Henry was found there," Cora said. Was she dreaming? Would someone please pinch her and wake her up from this nightmare? Was Paul really heading toward the abandoned theme park where Henry's body was found? To top it off, it was a *Wizard of Oz* theme park, just like the game.

"This is kind of creepy," Liv said, and shuddered.

Cora felt a chill. Creepy, indeed.

Chapter 55

Jane's phone rang, rudely interrupting the sexiest dream she had had in a long time. She was with Harry Connick, Jr., and he was whispering a sweet song into her ear. It had to be Cora.

"I didn't want you to worry when you get up and don't find me at home," Cora said once Jane had answered. "I know we were supposed to go and talk with the professor's wife again today, but I'm on my way to the Oz World."

"What? Back up. What's going on?" Jane said, sitting up in bed. "Why are you going over there?"

"Because we think that's where Paul is meeting Gracie."

"Gracie? Whoa, girl. You need to start from the beginning. I'm lost," she said.

"I'll try. But the phone may go out. We're heading for the mountains," she said. And then she told Jane what happened.

Jane sat dumbfounded. Why would a group of seemingly intelligent women head up to the park, knowing there may be a half-crazed woman there?

Jane adored Gracie, but even she questioned the wisdom in this decision.

"You better just come back," Jane said. "I don't know what you think you're doing. What do you think you are going to accomplish by getting in the way of the cops? Girl, you need to look at this."

Jane didn't know how much Cora heard before the phone went dead. Reception while traveling across those hills was sporadic.

She glanced at the clock. It was 4:30 AM. *Really, Cora?*

She loved Cora, but she could be so daft. Her need to please, to help, often overcame her good sense. What did she think she was doing? If the cops were following him, why did Cora think she needed to be there? No good could come of this!

Jane willed away images of a half-crazed Gracie wielding weapons and attacking her friend. That is not who she is, Jane reminded herself. Still, Gracie did kill Henry. Maybe. She wasn't herself. Not at all. What had happened to her?

She lay back down on her pillow. No matter the outcome, she would have the answers to her questions soon. Her best friend in the world was heading into a potentially volatile situation.

Jane wanted to think that she'd go back to sleep—but she knew herself better than that. London was still at her friend's house, so she decided to get up and get the day started. How to get her mind off the fact that Cora and Liv and Sheila were heading up to Oz World?

She made coffee and took the pot into the studio.

Jane fired up her wheel, placed a lump of clay on it, and put her hands to the clay.

Her hands connected with the clay as the gentle noise of the whirring wheel filled the room. She closed her eyes, whispered a prayer to the universe, and lost herself in her clay.

As her vase was beginning to form in her hands, her doorbell rang. Who could it be at this time of the day? This could not be good news.

The doorbell rang again. "Jane?" A voice rang out as she wiped her hands on a towel. "It's Detective Brodsky. I saw your light on."

Pulses of fear shot through her. If he was here, who was Cora following to Oz World?

She opened the door. "Cora is gone," she blurted out. "She's following Paul and a car she thinks is being driven by you or some other cops up to Oz World."

"Okay," he said quickly. "Let me call for help."

"Please come in," she said.

After he made several phone calls, he turned around to Jane, shaking his head. "What is wrong with Cora? Why would she endanger herself?"

"She was afraid Paul was being lured into a bad situation. She feels guilty because she didn't tell him you think Gracie killed Henry. She thinks she should have warned him."

He started to pace. "There's no 'thinking' about it. Gracie did kill Henry. She's a dangerous young woman. We think she's gotten involved with an ex-tremely dangerous young man."

"What man? That's the first I've heard of it," Jane said.

"Never mind. You don't know him. He used to go

to school with Henry and Gracie. Suffice it to say, Gracie is very dangerous."

How could that be? Sweet, dependable, smart Gracie? "I gotta tell you, Detective, that's not the Gracie I know."

He shrugged. "I can't tell you how many times I've heard that."

Chapter 56

By the time Cora and her crew arrived at the abandoned theme park, there were already two empty cars in the parking lot. One was Paul's and the other, Cora guessed, was an unmarked police car.

"We need to be quiet and careful," Sheila whispered. "I don't think this is a good idea."

"Stop," Liv said. "If you didn't think it was a good idea, why are you here?"

"To protect you both from yourselves," Sheila said.

"Oh, please," Liv said.

"Please stop arguing," Cora said, and opened her car door. The other two got out of the car as well.

The three of them stood in the parking lot, looking around, wondering which way to go.

"Maybe we should split up. There's a lot of ground to cover here," Liv said.

"Absolutely not," Sheila said.

"I agree with Sheila," Cora said. "Until we see what's really happening here, we need to stay together."

"Which way should we go?" Liv said, placing her hands on her hips.

"Well, the park is abandoned, so it should not be hard to get in," Cora said.

Sure enough, the gate didn't prove much of a deterrent, as the women easily walked around it and entered the park.

Cora's heart lurched when she saw that a yellow brick path stretched out before them. God, why? Why the Yellow Brick Road?

"Okay, this is creeping me out," Liv said.

"Why?" Sheila asked. "It's just an old park."

"But the game," Liv said. "Now this. It's too strange to be coincidental."

"I agree," Cora said. "There's more going on here than we know. Let's be extra cautious."

The three of them stood on the Yellow Brick Road and took in their surroundings. Cora thought she heard a voice.

"Over there," Liv whispered, and pointed to an area marked with a faded sign that read: ENCHANTED FOREST.

They walked toward the cluster of fake trees interspersed with real. Etched onto one of the artificial trees there was a smiling face. Another had lips that formed an O. A chill traveled up Cora's spine. She'd never been a fan of *The Wizard of Oz*. It was a scary movie to her as a child, especially the flying monkeys. And these anthropomorphic trees weren't any better.

But she was an adult now and knew this was all make-believe. Yet, she couldn't shake the feeling that someone else was having trouble telling the difference between reality and make-believe. Could that person be Gracie? If so, what had happened to her? Did she have a mental collapse? Was she on drugs?

"Be careful," she said to the others, but it was a reminder to herself as well. Something was off. Someone was deeply disturbed. And the three of them might have just walked into a trap.

"I think we should go back," she whispered. "I don't think we should be here."

"What? We came all this way," Liv said.

"She's right," Sheila said in a whisper. "We shouldn't be here."

They heard voices once again in the distance, but this time they sounded closer.

"Let's just see who they are," Liv said.

"Okay," Cora said. "But then we need to sneak away. Fast."

She'd feel better if she could see that Paul was okay, if he and Gracie had reunited, and were walking hand and hand down the Yellow Brick Road. Happily ever after.

The three women crouched down and Liv pulled some leaves on the branch away so they could spy upon whoever was approaching.

There stood Paul. A couple of men were next to him. The police?

"Look, I'm just here for my girl," he said.

Wait, thought Cora, those guys weren't just standing next to him. They were holding him in place. One even had a gun. Why would the police have a gun pointed at Paul?

What was going on here?

"Your girl?" one of the guys sneered.

Cora eyed Liv, whose eyes were wide with fear. Sheila tapped her gently and mouthed, "Let's go!"

They slowly started to back away.

"Not so fast," a voice said. "Just what the hell are you doing here?"

The three women turned around to see a man with a gun pointed at them. Cora's heart pounded. He was the same man with long, stringy hair and glasses that she'd been seeing all over town—and even at her front door. What was his name?

All three women automatically put their hands up, despite not being asked to.

"Answer me! What are you doing here?" the stranger demanded.

"Ah . . ." Liv said. "We were going for a walk?"

He smacked her across the face with his free hand, which sent her to the ground.

So he wasn't a cop, then, Cora thought with a surge of fear.

Cora's brain shifted into high gear. She and Sheila were still standing. They outnumbered the man, but he had a gun. *A gun.* But it wasn't as if she had no experience with guns, was it?

Cora jumped forward and stepped down hard on his foot. He yelped and, as he bent forward slightly, she jabbed her knee into his stomach. Yes! The move had never failed her in the past. At that same moment, Sheila jumped on his back. The gun slipped from his hand.

"Jesus," he grunted, as all three of them fell to the ground.

Sheila managed to grab the gun and pointed it at him. This time his hands went up. "Now," she said.

"We just came for Paul and Gracie. That's all we want."

Cora helped Liv stand up. She was still a bit woozy and was going to have a shiner where she had been struck.

"Pat him down, Cora," Sheila said. "He probably has other weapons."

Cora's hand searched the man's flabby body. She found a blade tucked into his boot.

"Good call," Cora said, holding up the blade.

She held it to the man's side and Sheila lifted the gun to his other side. Slowly they guided him into the clearing where Paul stood, Liv trailing behind him.

"Let him go," Sheila said, forcefully, as the group of men turned to look at them.

Cora was in awe of the way Sheila took control of the situation. Her own heart was racing, even though she had swallowed a pill just a few hours ago. Was it wearing off? Or was this just a normal reaction?

"Let him go or we blow his head off," Sheila said.

Whoa! This little woman of a scrapbooker is one quick-thinking, tough cookie of a woman, thought Cora.

"Please," one of the men holding Paul said, sneering. "Do you really expect us to believe that?"

"Cora!" Paul said. "What are you doing here?" As pale as the cottony-white clouds in the morning sky, Paul appeared as if he were going collapse any minute.

"Later," she said.

"There will be no later for any of you," a female voice said from behind them.

Cora turned to find a woman almost completely naked. Burlap and leaves covered her breasts, and a burlap skirt covered her behind. Her flesh was covered in something—what was it? Red needle marks. Scabs. Everywhere. She was holding a semi-automatic rifle in her hands. Cora's throat caught. Could this possibly be Gracie? She resembled Grace, but at the same time she looked like some wild goddess-like creature of the forest.

"Gracie?" Paul said. "Gracie! I found you!"

Chapter 57

They all stood, as if time were standing still. They were in the center of a fake forest, but surrounded by the beauty of the real forest. The two men held Paul, and Sheila and Cora held another man by the arms. Liv stood behind him. And Gracie stood surveying them all.

She was higher than anybody Cora had ever seen in her life. And that was saying something. She was full of drugs. But what kind? How much of Gracie was left inside the husk of her needle-marked body?

"Gracie," Cora said slowly, calmly. She didn't want to startle her. "I'm a friend of Jane and London. Do you remember London?" She was trying to stall for time, trying to reach Gracie, and perhaps shift her awareness to something other than this bizarre, frightful situation. Cora didn't want to see anybody get hurt.

Cora thought she glimpsed a twitch bordering on a smile on the woman's face.

"Jesus," one of the men said. "Gracie, put the gun down. You're going to hurt someone."

"Shut up!" she said, moving toward him. "Let Paul go or I'll let you have it. I'm telling you!"

"Fine," he said, and moved away from Paul. The other man followed his lead.

"Now," she said, flinging the gun around as if it were a stick and not a powerful weapon. "Get in your car and leave. You got no business here anymore," she said.

"Gracie, c'mon. You know we can't do that," the same man said.

"I mean it!" she screamed, and fired a shot at his feet. The two men didn't need further convincing; at the sound of the shot they slowly backed into the woods. Cora hoped they really did leave. But she had a feeling they wouldn't.

Who were they? Criminals or cops?

The car they had seen in the parking lot screamed "undercover police" to Cora, but they could have been counting on that. She couldn't trust them.

Cora gripped the arm of their hostage even tighter. She didn't want to stab him, but she held the blade so it poked into his side.

She wondered about Detective Brodsky. So much for Liv's app, which claimed Paul was being followed by the cops. Unless the two men who had just left really were the cops?

Then who was the guy she was holding? Cop? Criminal?

A cop wouldn't have smacked Liv, she told herself. Would he?

Paul stood watching Gracie, who was now standing just a few feet in front of him. His face held a mix of emotions. Relief. Love. Confusion. Fear.

"Gracie?" he said, opening his arms.

She dropped her gun on the ground and fell into him.

The couple stood on the Yellow Brick Road, with the fake trees surrounding them, and seemed to melt into one image as the sun beamed from behind them.

Cora shivered. Just what exactly was going on?

Did she want to know?

"You can let him go now," came a voice from behind them.

Brodsky. Finally.

"You've got a lot of explaining to do," he muttered to Cora.

"So do you," Cora said back to him, as she noticed the two men with him. They were the same men who had held Paul.

"This is our guy," one of them said. "I don't know who you ladies are, but great work."

"Don't tell them that," Brodsky said tersely. "It only encourages them."

The men cuffed the guy and read him his rights as Liv and Sheila both edged closer to Cora. They watched Paul and Gracie, who stood still, their arms wrapped around one another.

"Look at them," Liv said. "Now that's true love."

Paul never gave up hope. Had always believed in his and Gracie's love. He also had always believed she was alive.

Cora remembered the determined look on his face as he said he knew she was still alive. "I'd feel it if she were gone."

But as she took in the scene and considered Gracie, she wondered if the young woman could ever be the same. Cora didn't know what exactly had happened to her. But she was certain whatever it was, was devastating. A traumatic event could affect your whole life. She'd seen it time and again. Gracie would carry the scars—both physical and emotional—for years to come.

"Can they overcome this?" Sheila asked.

"If anybody can . . ." Liv said.

Cora chose to believe that.

"We're going to need a statement from you all," Brodsky said. "So, how about following us to the station?"

"Whatever you say," Cora replied.

"If only," he said, and turned away from her.

Paul and Gracie slowly followed the police as well. She was now wearing Paul's jacket over her burlap and leaf outfit. Her eyes never left him. But she was still as high as could be and was babbling incoherently.

Gracie's confused babbling matched Cora's own confused thoughts. None of this made any sense to her yet. She couldn't wait for the story to unfold.

Chapter 58

When Cora, Sheila, and Liv returned to Kildare House, they were met by some worried and angry people.

Donna ran to her mother and almost knocked Sheila over. "Mom, what were you thinking? I could shake you!" But instead she hugged her.

"Cora!" Jane said with her arms crossed. "You have a lot of explaining to do!"

"I imagine," Cora said.

"Why don't we all sit down and we can fill you in," Cora said.

"It's pretty convoluted and mind-blowing, I have to warn you," Sheila said as they followed Cora into the living room. Obviously this is where the three of them had camped out while they were gone. A pot of coffee, donuts, cell phones, and computers were scattered around the room.

They all took seats as Jane said, "Where's Paul?"

"He's with Gracie," Cora answered.

"Or what's left of Gracie," Liv said gloomily.

"What?" Jane asked.

"She's been drugged," Cora said. "A lot. The police and doctors have no idea what is flowing through her system, but maybe crack, among other things."

"So she was abducted and drugged?" Jane asked.

Cora nodded.

"How did this happen?" Donna said.

"Well, as far as they police have been able to tell, the man who took her was enamored with her because of the way she played the system. He knew her from school and was impressed with how she played the game they were all obsessed with."

"The game?" Jane said. "How can you have a relationship with a game?"

"Oh boy, Jane. We need to talk," Liv said, and grinned. "It's not a real relationship for most players, but some of these guys have nothing or nobody else. It's sad."

"To complicate matters, the police have been watching this game for a while now because they suspected it was really a front for a drug operation," Sheila said.

"I don't get it," Donna said. "The game was on the Darknet. It's supposed to be anonymous. That's the whole point of the Darknet."

"True," Cora said. "But the cops went in undercover as players."

"Turns out the game was not a front for anything, as far as they could tell," Liv said. "But this business with Gracie? They thought it was all linked."

"It turned out they thought Gracie was involved with the drug operation. But there was no operation. It was just this one crazy, but brilliant guy who hacked into the system and had everybody chasing their tails," Cora said.

"Including you," Jane said. "He's the one who sent the text message on your phone about the kidnapping, right?"

Cora nodded.

"In any case," Cora said. "This guy was getting off on confusing everybody, including the cops. He thinks he's a wizard. He thinks Gracie is Dorothy."

"Warped," Donna said.

"Indeed," Cora said, nodding her head.

"But what about Henry?" Jane asked.

Cora took a deep breath.

"We still don't know what happened there. Gracie is confused about Henry. But she is completely and utterly stoned out of her mind. Even if she confessed to killing him right now, it wouldn't be admissible in court," she said. "But, it turns out that the man who abducted Gracie also despised Henry, hated him enough to lure him to the park. Brodsky mentioned that he'd not be surprised if he set Gracie up for the murder. She can't really piece it together for us, yet."

"Is she that bad?" Jane said with her voice wavering.

Cora nodded, feeling a wave of weariness overcome her. She couldn't get Gracie's haunted eyes and the expression on her face out of her mind.

"I had been seeing the guy who had Gracie, Ted Brice. He also probably killed Henry. His name was linked to theirs. We just overlooked it. He was the poet who wrote a letter to the editor. It was right in front of our faces the whole time."

"Are you okay?" Jane asked.

"I'll be fine. I just need some rest," Cora replied.

"It's been quite a morning," Sheila said. "Why don't you take a nap?"

"I'll fix lunch," Jane said. "You go and lie down."

Lunch! Cora just remembered she was supposed to be at Adrian's house for lunch. She glanced at the clock. She was already late.

"I was supposed to meet Adrian," she groaned.

"I'll call him," Jane said. "Now, off to bed with you. In fact, I think you could all use some rest."

Jane made her way to the kitchen and invaded the cupboards and refrigerator, searching for lunch.

Soon, Adrian came to the back door, with flowers in his hands. "Is she okay?" he asked.

"She'll be fine. She just needed some rest and food will do her good," Jane said. Adrian sat the flowers down on the table.

"Can I help?" he asked.

"Why don't you slice the loaf of bread over there?" Jane said.

Adrian set the flowers on the table and started to work.

"Hey there," Ruby said as she entered the back door. "I've seen a good bit of commotion over here and thought I'd come and see what's going on."

Jane filled her in and Ruby just stood and shook her head. "Yes, Cora needs some food. Good move."

Just then the doorbell rang.

"That must be Cashel," Ruby said. "I bet he's looking for me," she said as she went to answer the door.

Cashel? Oh, that's just what they needed now, thought

Jane. She peeled the shells off of two more hardboiled eggs. If there was food involved, Cashel would stick around. Jane was mixing the egg salad when Cashel walked into the kitchen.

"Where's Cora? I want the scoop."

"You can get the scoop from me," Jane said, lifting the bowl of egg salad and taking it into the dining room.

"Is that soup I smell?" he said as he followed her into the dining room.

"Yes," she replied. "Veggie soup is on the stove."

"So what happened today?" he said with his voice lowered.

She told him everything. He stood with his mouth agape.

"They could have been killed," he said. "What were they thinking?"

"You have to understand," Jane said. "Cora felt responsible for Paul. And she thought he was heading for danger."

"So she wasn't thinking," Cashel said. "She was feeling."

"I guess you could say that," Jane said.

"I don't think I've ever known anybody like her," he said, looking off.

Jane thought she detected a note of longing in his voice. She felt a little uncomfortable.

"Um, I can guarantee you've never known anybody like her—and you probably never will."

"What do you know about this Adrian character?" he said in a lowered voice, as Adrian was around the corner in the kitchen.

"Nice guy," she said, and shrugged. "Cora likes him, which is all I need to know."

She left the dining room and entered the kitchen. "What does everybody want to drink?"

"I've got drinks covered," Adrian said. "Maybe you better go check on Cora."

She climbed the stairs to Cora's place and knocked on the door. No answer.

"Cora?" she said.

"Jane, is that you?"

"Yep," she said.

"Come on in," she replied.

Jane was astounded when she entered the apartment.

"What are you doing? I thought you were resting."

"I am," she said.

Jane sat down next to Cora, sitting in the middle of the living room floor, preening over her charms.

"A friend sent me this polymer clay and I've been working with it," she said. "So much fun. You see, it came with stamps. I've gotten a ton done and just pulled out a batch from the oven. This clay is done in like fifteen minutes."

"Why didn't you catch some sleep?" Jane asked.

"Every time I close my eyes, I see Gracie," Cora said. She set down a charm she worked into a cross-like design. "This is Brigid's cross," she said. "I've been thinking about Brigid. And you see it's different than a regular cross. It's even. Each one of the arms is the same size."

"I like this one," Jane said. She held it up and saw the word LOVE sketched into it.

"She had needle marks all over her."

"Gracie?" Jane said.

"Yes, the guy who abducted her drugged her as well."

"Creepy," Jane said.

They sat in silence a minute or two.

"Lunch is ready," Jane said gently.

Cora fidgeted with her charm. "This is my favorite I think. It's the Tree of Life."

"Adrian is downstairs, you know," Jane said.

"He is?" Cora brightened.

"Yeah, when I called he took it all in stride, then asked if he could come for lunch."

"Nice," Cora said, then sighed. "I suppose I should put some lipstick on. Or something."

"You should. You're looking a little wasted, friend," Jane said, and smiled.

"I bet," Cora said. She took a deep breath. "I guess life goes on."

Chapter 59

When Cora and Jane entered the light-filled dining room, Cora was taken aback by all the people there—Sheila, Donna, Ruby, Cashel, Liv, and Adrian.

"Quite a party going on, I see," Cora said.

Adrian stood and kissed her cheek. "Good to see you," he said quietly.

She felt a blush creeping onto her face. She sat next to him.

Cora spooned steaming veggie soup into her bowl. It might be just what she needed. She glanced across the table at Cashel and caught him looking at her. What was his deal? She turned back to Adrian. "I'm sorry I couldn't make our lunch date."

"I understand," he said. "Don't worry about it."

"Where did you learn your moves, Cora?" Sheila asked after a few minutes.

"Moves?" Cora asked.

"Yeah, the way you took down that guy," Sheila said.

Cora laughed. "Oh yes. I learned self-defense at my last job."

"I couldn't believe it," Liv said.

"The Krav Maga does you well again," Jane said.

"I think I surprised him," Cora said, grinning.

"You always do," Jane replied. "Nobody expects a pixie like you to kick ass."

The people around the table laughed.

"That's my secret weapon," Cora said, laughing. Then she turned to Sheila. "But you're no slouch, lady."

Sheila's face reddened. "I don't know what came over me. I've never done anything like that in my life."

Donna appeared confused. "What?"

"When I knocked the guy down, your mother jumped on him and grabbed his gun."

"Jesus, mom!" Donna said. "What were you thinking?"

Cora slurped her soup and tried not to laugh. They chatted, ate, and laughed. Cora was beginning to feel better. A part of her felt like the events of the day weren't real, like she'd been having a nightmare, or stepped into another realm. But eating, drinking, and chatting with friends, along with making the charms, seemed to be undoing whatever spell she was under. Intellectually, she knew it was probably a form of shock, but it would take some time to sort through it emotionally.

"What's in the little bag?" Adrian asked.

"Charms," she said. "I just made them this afternoon. I wanted everybody to have one." She held up the bag. "I have one for each of you. This one is for you." She handed one to Sheila.

"This is lovely," Sheila said. "I've always loved the Tree of Life."

"Yes, I like it, too," Cora said. "It's affirming, isn't it? And you are such a tough cookie, but I can see how important your family is and what a good mother you are. It's so heartwarming. I thought of you immediately."

Sheila looked up at her with a hint of a tear in her eyes. "Thank you."

They had shared a horrible moment together at the abandoned theme park. Cora thought they would always be friends now.

"Now, let's see," Cora said, and dug farther into the bag. "Here, this one is for you, Donna."

"What is it? It's lovely," Donna said.

"That's a Brigid's Cross. It's for protection and strength," Cora said. "Not that you need it, with your mom on your side. But we can all use a little extra protection."

Donna beamed.

Cora handed Liv a charm shaped like a goddess with spirals etched into her.

"She is gorgeous! Thank you," Liv said, her eyes wet with tears.

"This one's for you, Ruby." Cora handed her a charm with an impression of rosemary leaves.

"Rosemary for remembrance," Ruby said with a winsome note.

Cora wondered if she was also thinking about her long-lost sister, Rosemary. Though at first she had been unsure of Ruby, with each day she'd gotten to know her better, she was more and more grateful for her presence on the property—and her life.

"I even made you two a couple of charms," Cora

said to Cashel and Adrian. "They're bookmarks, see?" She handed Cashel and Adrian her charmed bookmarks. She'd fashioned each of the charms into little books. Both of them loved to read.

"Those are so cool!" Jane said.

"Yeah, thanks so much!" Adrian said.

"Yes, Cora, thanks," Cashel said.

"What about me?" Jane said. "Don't I get one?"

Patience was not Jane's virtue.

"Of course," Cora said, and lifted the charm from the bag.

Jane's hands went to her face and she gasped.

"What?" Ruby said. "Let us see!"

Jane held up a tiny pair of ruby-red slippers. "So adorable," she managed to say.

"'There's no place like home,' you know, and I think we've found one. Don't you?" Cora said.

Jane nodded. "Yes. Yes, I do."

Cora glanced around the table. "I wish Paul were here."

"Where is he?" Adrian asked.

"He's at the hospital with Gracie," Cora said.

"To Paul." Ruby held her glass of iced tea up and everybody toasted.

"To Cora, Jane, and Ruby," Liv said. "What a fabulous retreat! I could have done without the side attractions, but, well, you know, it was so worth it!"

"Thank you, Liv," Cora said. She breathed a sigh of relief. It had been quite a retreat, even if they were sidetracked a bit. Their second retreat was hampered by Gracie's disappearance and Henry's death, but somehow the women kept crafting and even helped.

As she gazed out over the table, she felt her strength returning. This gathering of crafters and others, eating, chatting, and toasting one another, was what it was all about. It was what she wanted—fellowship and healing.

"Thank you, everybody," she said. "For hanging in there with me. Let's hope the next retreat is not quite as adventurous."

Epilogue

So many changes happened within two weeks after the retreat. But there they stood in Kildare House—Paul, Cora, and Jane. Paul was getting ready to leave Kildare House—and the friends he had made there.

Paul blinked. Was he holding back tears?

"I owe both of you so much," he said to Cora and Jane.

"Are you sure you have to go all the way to England?" Jane asked.

Cora couldn't speak because of the lump in her throat. She was certain if she spoke, she'd make a fool of herself, blubbering all over him.

"Her parents and I found a great place for her here. The best doctors for her. The best situation," he said. "It's all about Gracie. It's all about getting her back."

Last week, Cora and Jane had gone to visit Gracie in the hospital and Jane was shocked by her appearance. She'd had to step out of the room.

"That's not Gracie," she said to Cora in the waiting room at the hospital.

"What?"

"I mean, it is her, but something is gone," she replied.

The young woman had been drugged and accused of murdering one of her friends. But that's not exactly what happened. Gracie saw her captor attacking Henry and tried to help. But her hands were tied and all she could do was kick.

Her captor and classmate, Ted Brice, had finally confessed to killing Henry, after he tried to frame Gracie for killing Henry, using her DNA—strands of her hair and fingernails. He was astute in his evil brilliance. He even had the pros fooled. The police were ready to convict Gracie up until he confessed. Cora felt much more secure knowing that he'd be in prison for a very long time.

She tried not to dwell on the image of Henry standing on the Yellow Brick Road trying to make sense of what had become of his friend, trying to defend himself. Cora hoped Henry knew in his last moments that Gracie was trying to save him.

Cora had seen some difficult and harsh situations in her life, but this had to be the worst. But every time she thought about it, she tried to replace the image with the one of Gracie finally escaping and stealing the rifle from Brice. Gracie had waited until he was asleep and then made her move, grabbing the gun and her phone and taking off, hiding in the forest. That image made Cora want to scream joyously from the rooftops.

"I'm hopeful," Paul said. "I know she's going to be okay. I can feel it."

"You know, you said that about her when she disappeared, you said you'd know if she were dead. You were right," Cora said.

"Such a romantic," Jane said.

Paul grinned. "Guilty," he replied.

Cora's heart fluttered. Two years ago her heart was broken, and she'd seen countless broken hearts in her work. To see a young man so in love, so dedicated to his woman, gave her hope. This was a huge step for her. She might be able to trust and love again. Maybe Adrian had come along at the right time after all.

Adrian had seized on to the cybercrimes aspect of what had happened. He'd taken his sharp research librarian skills and found out about new apps Cora could use in order to protect herself from getting any more text messages. If a person wasn't listed in her directory, their call or text would be blocked—it didn't matter what software or Web site the other person used. There were countless Web sites and apps that promised users could send anonymous texts.

The game, however, was another matter. The FBI shut it down, and the owners of the game were now working with the FBI and Paul to create a more secure version. They had even hired Paul as a creative consultant.

"When did you say you're coming back again?" Cora asked.

"Gracie needs to be back in September for a legal evaluation of her mental condition," he said as a horn sounded from the street outside. "That must be my parents."

"Stop by when you're back," Cora said. "Please."

He nodded. "Will do." He hugged Jane, then hugged Cora, picked up his suitcase, and headed out the door.

The foyer felt so empty. Paul Eugene Garrett had wormed his way into their home—and their hearts. Cora and Jane stood for a few minutes in silence.

"I need a drink," Jane said after Paul had driven off with his folks.

"Wine?" Cora said as they walked into the kitchen, willing away the worry she felt about Paul.

Jane nodded. "What a great guy. And to think I didn't like him at all at first."

"Proving once again you have lousy taste in men," Cora said, and laughed. She pulled out two wineglasses from the cupboard and poured the wine.

"I can't argue with that," Jane replied. "But I do have great taste in friends."

The two women clinked glasses.

"To us," Cora said. "To our friendship and to what we've crafted together."

Pressing Flowers

There's so many fabulous things you can make from pressed flowers—bookmarks, frame mats, ornaments, sun catchers, jewelry, and so on. Here's how to start right, by pressing the flowers.

Press flowers when they've been freshly picked. I recommend pressing the same day you take them home.

If you don't have blotting paper, you can also use wax paper. Paper towels may leave an impression on your flowers (if textured), and newspapers tend to shed ink.

Depending on how you plan to use your dried flowers, you may want to snip your stems. This step is completely optional and will vary depending on the type of flower you're working with.

Place flowers between two sheets of blotter (or wax) paper, making sure the petals do not touch one another.

Position your paper at the back of a heavy book and close. You'll want to leave your flowers alone for about four to six weeks. The longer the press time, the longer they'll be able to retain their coloring when exposed to the sun again.

Making Pressed Flower Bookmarks

In the story, Ruby leads a class on crafting wildflower bookmarks using a laminator, but if you don't have a laminator, you can use an iron for a different effect.

<u>Supply List</u>

Wax paper

Iron

Paper

Flowers of different colors, shapes, and sizes

<u>Directions</u>

Fold a piece of wax paper in half and place flowers along the fold.

Fold the wax paper back over the flowers.

Turn your iron on to a medium warm setting.

Fold a sheet of paper around the wax paper and lay a sheet down to protect your ironing board.

Slowly and firmly iron the paper until the impressions of the flowers and wax begin to show through.

Look inside and your flowers will be sealed in the wax paper.

Take scissors and trim.

Use as a bookmark, make a greeting card, a scrapbook embellishment, or whatever else your imagination desires!

Making Pom-Poms

You can make pom-poms from yarn, ribbon, twine, or tinsel. The really fun part comes in play when you decide what to do with them. Cora has a rug made of big, fluffy pom-poms. But you can make animals, decorate gifts, or craft mobiles with them. Here are simple instructions on how to make them out of yarn.

Take your yarn or ribbon and wrap it around something hard, such as a small piece of cardboard, a book, or a stack of Post-its. You can also use the best tool—your hand. For larger pom-poms, four fingers is a good width; for smaller pom-poms, use a two-finger width.

Wind the yarn around and around and around. The more you wrap, the fuller the pom-pom will be.

When you've wound to your desired "poof," slide the yarn off of the surface and tie a piece of yarn around the center in a knot.

Take a pair of scissors and cut through the loops on both sides of the pom-pom.

Pull the yarn strands up and give your pom-pom a trim. This step is a must. Just keep cutting until it looks full.

Coffee-Filter Paper Flowers

The paper flowers in the basket for the guests at Cora's Craft Retreat were made from coffee filters.

Supply List

Six basket-style coffee filters (any/all sizes) per flower

Floral stem wire (or anything else you want to use for a stem)

Floral tape or masking tape

Scissors

Stapler

Directions

Flatten up to six coffee filters and stack them one on top of the other in a neat pile.

Fold the stack in half.

Trim around the edge of the folded quarter. Cut any shape you like, from scallop to fringed.

Staple the bottom corner together.

Scrunch the paper around at the staple so it's not quite as flat, as above.

Put a small hook in the top of your stem and run it through the flower from the inside of the middle, out through the bottom. The hook should keep the stem from slipping all the way through the bottom of the flower.

Wrap the floral tape around the bottom of the flower (covering the staple) down the wire stem about an inch and back up over the bottom of the flower. Pinch and secure in place.

Gently begin to unfold the layers of the flower starting with the outer layer and working your way in toward the center of the flower.

Painting Rocks

<u>Directions</u>

Collect smooth rocks found at the beach or riverside. Even if your stones look clean, you should scrub them with a little soapy water and a brush before you paint on them. There is always a little residue of dust and dirt on them. This would result in smudges or paint that chips off once it dries. Use acrylic craft paints to paint the whole rock or use permanent waterproof markers.

Draw the outline of your design using a very fine Sharpie.

Paint in the design using a very fine brush using the acrylic paints. The nicer your brush, the better your painting.

Use the Sharpie to trace the lines.

Coat with clear nail polish when they are all dry if you want more gloss.

Creating
Flower Impressions on Clay

<u>Directions</u>

To create flower impressions on clay, you need a drop cloth or plastic sheet to protect your work area, soft terra-cotta clay, a rolling pin, natural or artificial flowers, and a clay knife. Drape the drop cloth or plastic over your table or work area.

Prepare the clay: Knead the terra-cotta clay for 10 minutes to remove any air bubbles. Leaving air trapped inside the clay could cause it to crack or burst once you fire it in a kiln. Roll out the clay into a 1/2-inch-thick slab.

Press the flowers: Select the flowers you want to press into the clay slab. You can use either fresh flowers from your garden or from a bouquet or artificial flowers. Place the flowers on top of the clay slab without actually pressing them into the clay, until you feel satisfied with the arrangement. Once you're happy with the flower positions, use the rolling pin to roll over the clay slab, gently pressing down to create an impression of the flowers on the clay. The flowers will stick into the clay. Use the very tip of a clay knife to lift up the flowers and remove them. You can now paint the clay with ceramic paint and fire it in a kiln.

Tips and warnings: Avoid pressing the flowers too deeply into the clay or you could have trouble removing them.

Making Polymer Clay Charms

At the end of *No Charm Intended,* Cora gifts her guests and friends charms she's made from polymer clay, a fun, easy-to-use clay.

Supply List

Clay: Sculpey is the least expensive of the clay brands and it works just as well as the others.

Stamps: Cora uses stamps to make some of the designs in her charms. If you have stamps from card-making and scrapbooking use, they will work just fine with clay. You can also use other kinds of impressions here, like doilies, plants, and so on.

Cutters: You can use shape cutters and get a perfect shape. But you can sculpt clay shapes freehand. And, yes, you can use cookie cutters and other things.

Please note: Sculpey is non-toxic; however, if you use a kitchen item on it, don't put it back in your kitchen to use on food. The clay leaves a slight residue on things, so if you use a cookie cutter on your clay, dedicate it as a clay-only cutter from then on.

Stylus: You will want something like this to help you with your design and also to add the word to your pendant. If you don't have one, don't worry, just use a tooth pick.

Other things you will need: wax paper, small paint brush, paint, Mod Podge, and string/hemp for necklace.

Directions

Lay out a piece of wax paper for your work space. Clay is non-toxic, but you want to keep it away from any food areas. It leaves a little residue and the wax paper helps keep things clean.

Pick your clay color and break off a piece. Clay needs to be "conditioned," so knead it for a few minutes to soften. Once it is soft, roll it into a ball and press it out flat. Keep it all a consistent thickness.

Use your stamp (or plant or some other texture) and make an impression in the clay. You don't want to press so hard that you see the edges of the stamp base, but you do need a good, deep impression.

Cut your clay into the shape you want and then carefully remove the excess clay. Tip: It might be better to stamp the design before cutting. It makes for easier cutter-design alignment. Plus, if you stamp after the shape is cut, you risk flattening the edge and your pendant will be lopsided.

Add any details—designs, words, and so on. Make certain you leave a hole for string or chains.

Preheat oven to 275 degrees and bake your clay for fifteen minutes. (Different clay brands have different cooking instructions, so read the label on your package.) Also, use either a disposable pan or a dedicated cookie sheet for clay projects—remember, you don't want your clay to touch surfaces that also touch food.

Once they are done cooking, let them cool completely! Now that it is cooked, you could just string it on a necklace and be done. But you can add a little paint for more creativity.

Craft paint works great. Add paint into the stamped impression. Then with a damp paper towel or rag, quickly wipe most of the paint away. ***Do this step quickly or else the paint will start to stain your clay***. If you wipe off too much paint the first time, just repeat the process until it looks like you want it to. I like mine to have just enough paint to show the depth of the design.

Next add a protective coat, such as Mod Podge.

We're almost done. Now you just need to put the necklace/bracelet/whatever together.

If you enjoyed *No Charmed Intended,*
be sure not to miss the first book
in Mollie Cox Bryan's Cora Crafts Mystery series

DEATH AMONG THE DOILIES

For thirty-something blogger Cora Chevalier,
small-town Indigo Gap, North Carolina,
seems like the perfect place to reinvent her life.
Shedding a stressful past as a counselor
for a women's shelter, Cora is pouring all her
talents—and most of her savings—into a craft
retreat business, with help from close pal and
resident potter Jane Starr. Between transforming
her Victorian estate into a crafter's paradise and
babysitting Jane's daughter, the new entrepreneur
has no time for distractions. Especially rumors
about the murder of a local school librarian . . .

But when Jane's fingerprints match those found at
the grisly crime scene, Cora not only worries about
her friend, but her own reputation. With angry
townsfolk eager for justice, and both Jane's
innocence and the retreat at risk, she must rely on
her creative chops to unlace the truth behind
the beloved librarian's disturbing demise.
Because if the killer's patterns aren't pinned,
Cora's handiwork could end up in stitches . . .

Keep reading for a special excerpt.

A Kensington mass market paperback
and e-book on sale now!

Chapter 1

Did Jane just say "police station?"

"What did you say?" Cora Chevalier said, then typed on her laptop: *Every detail—from the mundane cleaning of the chestnut floors and ordering of broom straw and beeswax, to crafting centerpieces and designing class curriculums—has been attended to.*

No wait—attended to? Was that right?

"Cora!" Jane said, bringing her attention back to the voice on the phone.

"I'm sorry, Jane," Cora said, turning away from her computer. "Writing about our first craft retreat takes more focus than blogging about crafting paper lanterns or making bird feeders out of old teacups and saucers. I'm in the zone. But you have my full attention now. Did you say you're at the police station?"

"Yes. Please pick up London from school. We'll talk about this later," Jane said, with exasperation in her voice. Cora's best friend throughout childhood, and now her partner in a new business, Jane and her daughter lived in the carriage house on the property.

"But wait—" Cora said, but Jane was already gone. Cora pictured her sophisticated-looking, long-legged friend sitting at the police station, surrounded by Barney Fife types. A totally unfounded image, of course; she'd never even seen a police officer in her new hometown. They now lived in North Carolina, which was also where the fictional Mayberry was located, but Indigo Gap was no Mayberry.

Why was Jane at the police station? What was going on? It was odd that she couldn't get away to pick up her daughter from school. Why wouldn't the police allow her to pick up London?

Cora pressed SAVE on her blog post, glanced at the clock on her computer, and realized she'd need to hurry if she was going to fetch London. She dreaded going inside the school. Because she wasn't an actual parent, she wasn't allowed to collect her from the car. For being in such a small town, the school was extremely concerned about security. Maybe it had something to do with the recent suspicious death of the school librarian.

Cora left her attic apartment, which also housed her makeshift office, and walked down the narrow half flight of stairs to the third story. The door opened to a wide hallway. Four bedrooms, already prepared for the guests, were located here. The lemon scent of polish tickled Cora's nose as she took in the gleaming chestnut floors before descending the next flight to the second floor, also shiny and smelling clean and fresh. She moseyed down the half flight to the landing before the main story, where she always paused to take in the stained-glass window, its colors vibrant or soft depending on the time of day. Crimson, gold, and shades of blue glass pieces formed an image of Brigid, goddess or saint.

After moving into her new home, Cora had done some research on both the history of the house and St. Brigid and discovered that Brigid was a goddess in ancient Ireland. She was the goddess of poetry, fire, the hearth, and crafts, an appropriate deity for a craft retreat. Through the centuries in Ireland, the myth later became tangled with stories of the abbess and much later, the saint. These stories became so enmeshed that it was difficult to tell the Brigids apart.

Cora loved to muse about Brigid and thought of her as her patron goddess. The original owners of the house must also have had a strong connection to Brigid, as they had immigrated from Kildare, Ireland, where St. Brigid's Cathedral still sat.

Cora ambled down the rest of the stairs to face a mess in the foyer. She was knee-deep in a shipment of broom straw, which she navigated her way around. Their first guest teacher, Jude Sawyer, an award-winning broom maker, hand selected and ordered the straw for the upcoming weekend retreat.

Now, where had she left her purse? Cora worked her way around the boxes and moved toward the kitchen, which was in the back of the house and where she usually left her purse.

Ah-ha! She spotted it on the kitchen counter. She

grabbed her crocheted bag and turned to leave, running smack into Ruby, the woman who came with the house. Literally. She was grandfathered into the mortgage. She'd lived in the gardener's cottage for years and wanted to stay. Luckily for Cora and Jane, she was a gifted herbalist and fit right in with their plans for the old place.

"Oops!" Cora said, dropping her purse and bending over to get it.

"Where are you off to in such a hurry?" Ruby said, sounding accusatory.

"I'm off to pick up London. Something's come up with Jane." Cora was again thinking of Jane at the police station—she wanted to laugh the image off, but ominous feelings tugged at her.

What the heck was Jane doing there? Where was the police station, anyway? Cora had witnessed much of Jane's troubled past and hoped this incident was not a harbinger of more trouble heading her way.

"Okay. I need to talk with you," Ruby said, following Cora to the door.

"Sure," Cora said. "But can it wait until I get back?"

"I suppose. It's about the beeswax shipment. They sent me the wrong stuff."

"Great." Cora sighed as she slid in her car. "Just what we need. We'll take care of it later."

Ruby stood with hands on her hips, shaking her head as she watched Cora drive off.

"Take a deep breath, girl," Cora told herself. She'd smooth things over with Ruby after she picked up London. Ruby, a slightly stooped white-haired woman of a certain age, used specific suppliers for her herbal crafts. But if Cora was going to pay for them, she thought she should get a say in it. Simply one of the little hiccups in establishing a new business, Cora told herself. There had been plenty—and she expected more.

Getting the place in shape and up to code had been a challenge, but things were finally coming together. The paper-craft room was almost finished. The fiber-arts room still needed a lot more work. And her first three-day retreat was scheduled to start Thursday night with a welcome reception. Classes were to be led by Cora herself, a guest teacher, and Ruby. Nine women registered to stay, plus three locals signed up for the classes. Cora couldn't have been more pleased with the number. Oh sure, they could take more crafters, but for their first retreat, nine was manageable.

Cora parked the car in the school lot, and noted the snaking line of cars full of harried parents. She was impressed with herself, as she'd reached the school a few minutes early. Cora had been to the school before and knew the earlier she arrived, the better. She walked into the office and was met by a well-coiffed receptionist. "Can I help you?" the woman asked.

"I'm here to pick up London Starr."

"Are you on her approved list?" She gazed at Cora over the top of her glasses.

"I think so," Cora said. Something about the woman's tone made her self-conscious. Her perfectly made-up face and hot-pink nails tapping impatiently on the desk didn't help matters.

Cora tried to remember if she'd even brushed her hair today. At least she had gotten dressed earlier than usual because of the expected deliveries. She wore her favorite 1970s vintage blue baby-doll dress with leggings and red tennis shoes. Nothing wrong with what she was wearing, yet this woman spewed bad vibes. Was it Cora's unruly red hair? She ran her fingers through her bangs and tucked a few strands behind her ear.

"Name?" said the receptionist.

"Cora Chevalier."

"Yes, Ms. Chevalier. You are on the list," the receptionist said, after checking her computer files.

Cora stood a little straighter, now that she'd met with official approval.

"Ms. Teal?" the receptionist said into the phone. "Please send London Starr to the front office. She'll be right down," she said to Cora and went back to her work on the computer.

Cora shifted her weight, looked at the clock, and folded her hands together in front of her. The office behind the receptionist buzzed with end-of-school-day activity. Phones were blaring, backpacks were handed over, and weary office workers glanced at the clock.

Soon the door flung open and there stood London, holding Ms. Teal's hand. When she spotted Cora, the girl ran toward her.

"Cora!" she said and hugged her, but then immediately asked, "Where's Mommy?"

Cora was just about to blurt out the news when she realized that everybody in the little school office was within hearing range. Best not to say, *Your mom's at the police station.*

She reached for London's hand. "Let's go, sweetie. We'll talk in the car."